"Are you saying...that you believe she's my daughter?"

Alex sat back abruptly. "I'm not saying anything of the kind."

"Then why am I here?" Naomi asked in frustration.

He drew a breath as his gaze met hers. "I asked you to dinner because I have a proposal for you."

Naomi frowned. "What kind of proposal?"

"A marriage proposal."

The world as Naomi knew it stopped. The murmur of voices in the restaurant faded, drowned out by the roaring in her head. She was hearing things. "I beg your pardon," she whispered.

"I want you to marry me."

Dear Harlequin Intrigue Reader,

What's bigger than Texas…? Montana! This month, Harlequin Intrigue takes you deep undercover to the offices of MONTANA CONFIDENTIAL. You loved the series when it first premiered in the Lone Star State, so we've created a brand-new set of sexy cowboy agents for you farther north in Big Sky country. Patricia Rosemoor gets things started in *Someone To Protect Her*. Three more installments follow—and I can assure you, you won't want to miss one!

Amanda Stevens concludes her dramatic EDEN'S CHILDREN miniseries with *The Forgiven*. All comes full circle in this redemptive story that reunites mother and child.

What would you do if your "wife" came back from the dead? Look for *In His Wife's Name* for the answer. In a very compelling scenario, Joyce Sullivan explores the consequences of a hidden identity and a desperate search for the truth.

Rounding out the month is the companion story to Harper Allen's miniseries THE AVENGERS. *Sullivan's Last Stand*, like its counterpart *Guarding Jane Doe*, is a deeply emotional story about a soldier of fortune and his dedication to duty. Be sure to pick up both titles by this exceptional new author.

Cowboys, cops—action, drama…it's just another month of terrific romantic suspense from Harlequin Intrigue.

Happy reading!

Sincerely,

Denise O'Sullivan
Associate Senior Editor
Harlequin Intrigue

P.S. Be sure to watch for the next title in Rebecca York's 43 LIGHT STREET trilogy, MINE TO KEEP, available in October.

THE FORGIVEN
AMANDA STEVENS

TORONTO • NEW YORK • LONDON
AMSTERDAM • PARIS • SYDNEY • HAMBURG
STOCKHOLM • ATHENS • TOKYO • MILAN • MADRID
PRAGUE • WARSAW • BUDAPEST • AUCKLAND

ISBN 0-373-22630-6

THE FORGIVEN

This edition published by arrangement with Harlequin Books S.A.

® and TM are trademarks of the publisher. Trademarks indicated with ® are registered in the United States Patent and Trademark Office, the Canadian Trade Marks Office and in other countries.

Visit us at www.eHarlequin.com

Printed in U.S.A.

ABOUT THE AUTHOR

Born and raised in a small Southern town, Amanda Stevens frequently draws on memories of her birthplace to create atmospheric settings and casts of eccentric characters. She is the author of over twenty-five novels, the recipient of a Career Achievement award for Romantic/Mystery, and a 1999 RITA Award finalist in the Romantic Suspense category. She now resides in Texas with her husband, teenage twins and her cat, Jesse, who also makes frequent appearances in her books.

Books by Amanda Stevens

HARLEQUIN INTRIGUE

Don't miss any of our special offers. Write to us at the following address for information on our newest releases.

Harlequin Reader Service
U.S.: 3010 Walden Ave., P.O. Box 1325, Buffalo, NY 14269
Canadian: P.O. Box 609, Fort Erie, Ont. L2A 5X3

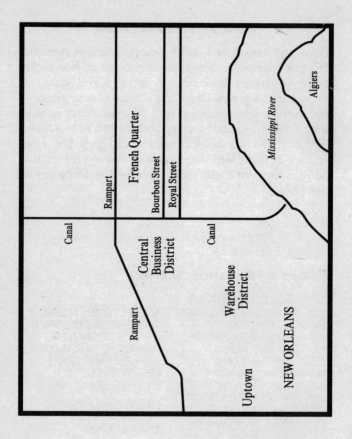

CAST OF CHARACTERS

Naomi Cross—Her daughter disappeared ten years ago, and Naomi has been searching for her ever since.

Alex DeWitt—He is attracted to Naomi Cross the moment he first sets eyes on her. But he also knows that she has the power to destroy his life.

Aubree DeWitt—She took terrible secrets to the grave with her ten years ago.

Taryn DeWitt—She's determined to uncover her suppressed memories from the night her mother was murdered, but is the identity of a killer hidden in her subconscious?

Joseph Bellamy—He will do anything to avenge his daughter Aubree's death.

Foley Boudreaux—Did Alex's best friend and attorney have a thing for Aubree?

James Robicheaux—The good lieutenant has vowed to bring Aubree's murderer to justice. Except, has his zeal been bought and paid for?

Gwen Bellamy—She and her stepdaughter were not exactly close.

Ray Beauchamp—A stalker with murder on his mind.

Sadie Cross—She disappeared ten years ago without a trace.

Prologue

"...National Weather Service has issued a tornado warning for the northeastern portion of Jefferson County. A funnel cloud was reported on the ground near Eden at approximately 8:37 this evening. If you are in the designated area, you are urged to take cover immediately. Repeat. A tornado warning has been issued—"

Eighteen-year-old Naomi Cross strained to hear the weather advisory over the static on her car radio. A shudder of fear ripped through her as a siren blasted a warning in the distance. But she kept on driving. Storm or no storm, she had to get to the hospital.

As she cast an uneasy glance toward the sky, she felt a tightening in her abdomen and braced herself, trying to will away the intense pain she knew would follow. She was still a good twenty minutes from the hospital, and the contractions were hitting her hard and fast. Too fast. The twins were coming early. The doctor had said that might happen. But tonight of all nights!

Her mother and sister had driven down to Jackson for a basketball tournament and wouldn't be back until after midnight. Naomi had been home alone as she'd listened to the increasingly severe weather reports on the news. Then the wind had started to blow, and the power went out. By the time the first contraction hit, the phone lines were down. Naomi, trying desperately not to panic, had surveyed her options—try to wait out the storm, or drive herself to the hospital.

Not much of a choice, considering Dr. Simms had warned her that multiple births were often a tricky business. Naomi didn't dare risk her babies' health by going through labor all alone, but now, as she plunged head-long into the storm, she had to wonder if she'd made the right decision. She could feel the gusts of wind tugging at her car, and it was all she could do to keep the vehicle on the road.

Gripping the steering wheel, she peered straight ahead. A wicker rocking chair, swept from someone's front porch, tumbled along the shoulder of the road, and moments later, parts of the front porch landed with a thud on the highway directly in front of her.

Heart in her throat, she braked and swerved, then sat for a moment, her path blocked by the debris. Shoving the gearshift into Park, she got out of the car. The wind tore at her hair and clothing, almost knocking her off her feet. Battling against the gale force, she fought her way to the front of the car, then lifted the heavy two-by-fours and dragged them from the road. As she turned back to the car, a contraction bent her double.

Leaning heavily against the front fender of the car, Naomi struggled to control the pain. Somewhere off to her right, she heard the loud *crack* of an uprooting tree, and as she turned toward the sound, her breath caught in her throat.

For what seemed like an eternity, she stared, paralyzed, at the funnel cloud moving toward her. She'd never seen anything like it! The size. The sheer force. The deafening roar as the twister whirled across a field, claiming everything in its path.

The roof of an old barn peeled away as cleanly as the lid on a tin can, and the walls crumpled. Fence posts were sucked from the ground and tossed like giant lawn darts fifty yards away. And still the storm came.

Get back in the car! a voice screamed inside Naomi. *Move!*

The wind almost whipped the car door from its hinges as she climbed back inside. Using both hands, she finally managed to slam the door, and then, with one last glance at the tornado, moving with frightening speed across the open ground, she put the car in gear and floored the accelerator. The car shot forward, almost slamming into a sheet of tin roofing that spun crazily in the wind. At the last moment, the metal lifted, just missing the top of Naomi's car, and swirled away.

On the radio, the announcer's excited voice, intermixed with the static, drew icy fingers of dread down Naomi's back.

"If you are…path of…storm…seek shelter immediately! Repeat…shelter immediately—"

Naomi glanced around frantically. She was in the middle of nowhere. Still miles from town. No houses in sight. No overpasses. On the flat highway, she was helpless.

She glanced at the field to her right. *Oh, God. Oh, dear God.*

The storm was so close she could feel the pressure building inside the car…could feel the automobile being pulled off the road…

She clutched the steering wheel as she pressed the

accelerator to the floor. Faster, she urged the car. Come on!

Please. Oh, please.

Never, ever try to outrun a tornado, she'd always been told. Now she knew why. Her car was no match for such power. She was going to be swept off the road, swirled up into the vortex of the storm.

My babies...

Faster. *Come on.* Faster. *Please. Please...*

Her knuckles ached from gripping the wheel. She felt the familiar tightening in her stomach that signaled another contraction. *No. Oh, no...*

She gasped out loud from the pain, but somehow she managed to hold on. Somehow she managed to keep control of the car.

She glanced out the window. The twister was right there. Right on her. *Oh, God, oh, God, oh, God!*

Something hit the back window, and the glass shattered into a million pieces. The din from the storm was thunderous, the suction incredible. Naomi clung to the steering wheel for dear life. The car swayed in the wind. Debris whirled thick outside her windows.

Glancing in her rearview mirror, she saw the funnel pass across the highway behind her. But for a moment, as the sound dissipated and the pressure inside the car lessened, Naomi still couldn't breathe. She still couldn't comprehend that she had outrun a tornado, that she might yet make it to the hospital to have her babies.

Then, sobbing in relief, she said a silent prayer as she raced toward Eden.

By the time she reached town, the streets resembled a war zone, but she didn't stop to assess the damage. The contractions were getting closer with each passing moment, and she knew she wouldn't be able to hang on much longer.

As she pulled into the emergency area of the tiny hospital, she all but tumbled from the car. Clutching her stomach, she lurched inside, seeking help, but the emergency room was in chaos. Bodies lay everywhere, some moving, some not. And the wails—of terror, of grief, of disbelief—were the sounds of a nightmare come to life.

"Please," Naomi said to one of the harried nurses. "Help me."

The woman turned, as if to brush Naomi aside, but then her gaze dropped and her eyes widened. "Get a gurney over her, stat!" she shouted.

It was only then that Naomi looked down to see blood pooling at her feet.

She was dimly aware of being lifted, of being rushed down a long corridor with the echo of screams in her ears. One of the nurses said in a hushed tone, "We've got another mother prepped, but we still haven't heard from Dr. Simms."

"How's she doing?" someone else asked worriedly.

"Not good. We're having trouble finding the baby's heartbeat—"

Naomi tried to lift her head. "My babies—"

"Shush," the first nurse soothed. "Not you. You're doing fine. Just try to relax."

And then another voice, from a distance, shouted, "Oh, my God, there's a second one!"

Yes, Naomi thought in a haze of pain. *I'm having twins.*

"Another tornado!" the voice screamed.

And then the walls began to tremble.

Chapter One

Present day...

Naomi Cross was no stranger to tragedy. Fifteen years ago, she'd regained consciousness two days after giving birth to twin daughters only to be told that one of her babies had died just hours after delivery.

Naomi had been devastated, but even in the throes of deep despair, a part of her had realized that she was luckier than some. Whole families had been wiped out in the two killer tornadoes that ripped through Eden, Mississippi, on that fateful night, and countless homes were destroyed. At least Naomi still had a beautiful, healthy baby girl she named Sadie, and a mother and sister who loved her unconditionally, who were there to help her through those first traumatic days when her grief had seemed boundless.

Then, five years later, when little Sadie had vanished from the playground at Fairhaven Academy, the second loss had all but destroyed Naomi. She'd sunk into a deep depression, but somehow she'd fought her way out of the darkness. In time, she'd founded the Children's Rescue Network—where she remained director—in Sadie's memory. For almost a decade, she'd worked tirelessly on behalf of other missing children and their families.

Over the years, Naomi had come to realize that her tragedies were not without meaning. As a result of her struggles, she'd grown strong and independent, oftentimes fearless when the cause was worthy. But even she felt overwhelmed by the events that had unfolded in the past several days.

The remains of a child had been unearthed down in Grover County, near the Louisiana border, and the bones were being studied by a forensics anthropologist at Louisiana State University. If tests proved that the remains were Sadie's, then Naomi's ten-year quest would finally be over. She would finally be able to bring her daughter back home.

But as one search ended, another was just beginning.

"I wish I could be of more help," Tess Campbell fretted as she sat across her kitchen table from Naomi. Tess was a lovely young woman with a pale, fragile complexion and luminous hazel eyes. She tucked an errant curl behind her ear as she sighed. "But I've already told you everything I remember."

Naomi nodded. "I know. But Mr. Donnelly has a few questions, if you don't mind." She gestured toward the middle-aged man seated at her left. Michael Donnelly was an investigator from Jackson who Naomi had hired after Tess's devastating revelation. He had the reputation of being one of the sharpest private detectives in Mississippi, specializing in missing persons, but he hardly looked the part. Naomi supposed the best word to describe him was ordinary. Gray eyes behind wire-rimmed glasses, slightly crooked nose, a receding hairline he didn't bother trying to disguise. He wore a wed-

ding ring which, for some reason, had surprised Naomi
when she'd first met him

"I'll answer any questions I can," Tess said ear-
nestly. "It's the least I can do considering everything
you've done for me."

Naomi waved off her friend's gratitude. Just over a
month ago, she and Tess Campbell had been hardly
more than acquaintances, although they'd both lived in
Eden for most of their lives. But after Tess's daughter,
Emily, had been abducted from the same school playground ten years to the day that Sadie had disappeared,
the two of them had grown close, drawn to each other
through their mutual pain, grief and fear.

Thankfully, Tess's daughter had been found unharmed, but in rescuing Emily, Tess had uncovered a
bizarre story that had the power to change Naomi's life
forever.

The nerves in her stomach tightened as she leaned
forward slightly. "Why don't you start by telling him
exactly what you told me?" she urged Tess.

Tess's hands trembled as she laced her fingers together on the table. "I still have a hard time talking
about Emily's abduction. I still dream about it. Sometimes I still think about what could have happened."
She turned away, her eyes filling with tears.

The man standing behind her put his hand on her
shoulder, as if to reassure her. Tall, handsome, with an
elegant and self-confident bearing that money and good
breeding seemed to engender, Jared Spencer had remained silent during the interview, but his presence was
undeniable, as was his devotion to Tess.

Naomi reached across the table and placed her hand
over Tess's. "Believe me, I understand how you feel. I
wouldn't ask you to do this if it wasn't so important."

Tess nodded. "I know that. I just hope—" She broke off, biting her lip, but Naomi knew what she was thinking. *I just hope you aren't getting your hopes up for nothing.*

So do I, Naomi thought with a little quiver of fear. She was stronger now. She'd fought her demons and won. But to battle back from yet another crushing disappointment...

She shuddered at the prospect.

Beside her, Michael Donnelly cut through the sentiment. "Mrs. Campbell, can you tell me again what Willa Banks told you the night you found out she'd taken your daughter?"

Although she was familiar with the story by now, Naomi still could hardly believe what had happened. Willa Banks, the school nurse at Fairhaven Academy, had been the mastermind behind little Emily's disappearance. She'd kept the child hidden away from the outside world for over a month, had witnessed Tess's pain day in and day out, and said nothing.

Who would have thought that such a nice, seemingly uncomplicated woman could have harbored such a twisted mind? But her intent hadn't been evil, Naomi reminded herself. Willa Banks had just been horribly confused. Guilt could do that.

"When I got to her house, I saw a little girl standing at an upstairs window. I knew it was Emily, but when I went inside, Willa insisted I must have seen Sadie." Tess's gaze darted to Naomi.

"She said that?" Naomi asked softly. "She said the child was Sadie?"

Tess nodded. "I knew it was impossible. Sadie has been missing for ten years. Wherever she is, she's fifteen years old."

Present tense, Naomi thought gratefully. So many people referred to missing children in the past tense without even realizing it. But Tess, like Naomi, knew better. She knew how much it hurt those left behind.

Naomi thought of the remains that had been found in Grover County, and she closed her eyes as a fresh wave of pain washed over her. Sadie. My poor little Sadie…

"Go on," Michael Donnelly said to Tess.

"When I started up the stairs to find Emily, Willa said, 'I was at the hospital the night Naomi's other baby got taken. I can't let you take Sadie from her.' Those were her exact words," Tess said with a shudder. "I'll never forget them."

The night Naomi's other baby got taken. For a moment, Naomi was transported back to that night. Back to the terror and confusion inside the hospital. Back to the blood pooling at her feet. She remembered little after that until she'd awakened two days later in another hospital. Her mother and sister had been standing at her bedside, and she'd known, just from looking at their faces, that something was wrong. Her mother had told her about the baby, and then she'd drawn Naomi into her arms, holding her tight.

"I know how you must feel, Naomi. But you can't let yourself fall to pieces. You still have another baby who needs you, and considering what you went through to bring her into this world, her birth is a miracle. She's strong and healthy and so beautiful. Just wait until you see her."

But it had been almost a week before Naomi could bring herself to hold Sadie in her arms. It wasn't that she didn't love her. She did, with all her heart. But she ached for her other baby, little Sela, named for an aunt Naomi had adored. She wouldn't let herself hold Sadie, wouldn't let herself fall in love with her sweet baby girl, because she was so terrified something would happen to her, too.

It was only after the guilt finally subsided that Naomi had come to understand her reticence. In keeping her daughter at arm's length those first few days, in denying herself that all-too-fleeting bonding time, Naomi had been punishing herself. But she'd also deprived Sadie of something precious, and that memory, along with the guilt, had come back to haunt her in the days and nights following Sadie's abduction.

Tess said gently, "Naomi? Are you okay?"

Naomi snapped her attention back to the present. "Yes, of course. Please, go on."

"There's not a lot more to tell, I'm afraid. Willa said she'd never forgiven herself for her part in taking your baby."

"Did Willa Banks give you any indication who helped her take the baby? And why?" Donnelly asked.

Tess shook her head. "I asked her, but she wouldn't say. I know now that I should have pressed her for a name, but at the time…I was just so desperate to find Emily. And now Willa is dead, and she can't tell us." Willa Banks had died of a heart attack the night Tess had rescued her daughter. She'd very nearly gone to her grave guarding her fifteen-year-old secret.

"Evidently, the other woman's baby died the night the tornadoes hit," Tess said. "And there you were, Naomi. Young and unmarried, with two healthy baby girls. How could you care for one baby, let alone two? That's how she rationalized it, I guess."

Naomi said nothing, but anger flared inside her. Young or not, she would have found a way to take care of her babies. She would have loved them and sheltered them, and if necessary, she would have given her life for them. *She* was their mother, not some stranger. Not some woman Willa Banks had deemed more fit.

As if sensing Naomi's turmoil, Tess said carefully, "Willa watched you from afar for years knowing all the while what she'd done to you. When she heard about Sadie's disappearance, something snapped. The guilt must have finally consumed her. She couldn't accept that both your children had been taken from you. I think over the years she became more and more confused, and that's why she took Emily ten years later, on the anniversary of Sadie's abduction. In her mind, it was Sadie, not Emily, she saw on the playground that day. She thought she'd finally found a way to atone for her sins. She couldn't give you back the baby that she helped take from you, but she could bring Sadie home to you."

"That one woman could do so much damage," Jared Spencer muttered darkly.

Tess took Jared's hand, drawing it to her cheek. The tenderness that passed between them made Naomi painfully aware of the emptiness inside her own heart. *There you were, Naomi. Young and unmarried.*

The fact that Clay Willis had decided to leave town on graduation night and join the army instead of marrying her had probably been a blessing in disguise, Naomi had long ago decided. And when she'd heard a few years later that he'd been killed in a helicopter crash overseas, she'd grieved for her daughters' father, not for her first love. Anything she'd felt for Clay Willis had died on the night he'd left town.

But there had been moments when she had to admit that having someone in her life, someone to lean on, might have helped her through the hard times, might have kept her from hitting rock bottom when Sadie had gone missing.

She was thirty-three years old and she'd lost two children. *Two.* Sometimes even now her despair threatened to overwhelm her. But Naomi had found the strength to go on because she'd had a purpose.

For ten years, her search for Sadie had been her whole life, the faint hope that she would someday find her daughter and bring her back home her only salvation. With the discovery of the remains in Grover County, that hope had been diminished.

But now Naomi had learned that her other child had been alive all this time, that she was out there somewhere.

And if it took her another ten years, Naomi knew that she would find her.

"CAN YOU HELP ME find her?" In the light from the dash, Naomi saw a frown flicker across Michael Donnelly's brow as she spoke. He'd driven her home after they'd left Tess's house, and as he pulled to the curb, she said anxiously, "Well, can you?"

He cut the engine and turned to face her, resting his arm across the back of the seat. "I told you last week I could help you, but let me remind you again that we're operating on the secondhand confession of a dead woman. I don't have to spell out the legal ramifications of such hearsay."

"I don't care about the legalities," Naomi blurted. "I just want to find my daughter."

Donnelly's frown deepened. "If I'm going to help you, I want you to be fully aware of all the pitfalls. If Willa Banks *was* out of her mind toward the end, it's possible she made all this up. It's also possible she was a very shrewd woman. She could have concocted this whole elaborate story in order to save her own hide. An insanity plea would have kept her out of federal prison for kidnapping.''

''I don't think you believe that any more than I do,'' Naomi said impatiently. ''The fact that the story is so elaborate is what makes it so believable. Nobody could make up something like this.''

''You might be surprised,'' Donnelly muttered.

Naomi shoved back her short, dark hair. ''Look, you wanted to hear Tess Campbell's story for yourself, and you did. She repeated exactly what I told you when I first came to see you last week. Willa Banks helped steal my baby, and she kept it a secret for fifteen years. The guilt ate away at her until she finally went off the deep end. So much so that ten years after my other daughter was kidnapped, Willa tried to repent by taking little Emily Campbell to replace her. It's complicated, yes. Crazy, yes. But in some twisted way, it all makes sense.''

''Maybe because you want it to,'' Donnelly suggested. ''You lost two children. A baby fifteen years ago, another child ten years ago. No one would blame you for grasping at straws here.''

Heat flashed through Naomi as her gaze on him narrowed. ''I'm not paying you to psychoanalyze my motives, Mr. Donnelly. I'm paying you to find my daughter. That's what you do, isn't it? Locate missing persons?''

''And supposing I do find her for you, Miss Cross? Have you given any thought to the consequences?''

''I don't know what you mean.'' Naomi turned to stare out the window. She knew exactly what he was getting at.

"Assuming everything Willa Banks said was true. Assuming your baby was stolen from you fifteen years ago. She won't know you now," Donnelly warned in a low voice. "You'll be nothing more than a stranger to her. I've seen this kind of thing before. The kid won't appreciate having her whole world ripped apart, and it's a good bet, she'll blame you for doing it."

Pain welled inside Naomi's heart. "I don't want to hurt her. I wouldn't hurt her for anything in the world. But I have to find her. I have to make sure she's all right."

"No matter the cost? Because any way you handle this, someone is going to get hurt," Donnelly predicted grimly. "Someone always gets hurt in cases like this."

Naomi balled her hands into fists. "She's my baby! I gave birth to her, and then someone stole her from me. I have a right to find her. I have a right to make sure she's okay, that she's being taken care of. Can't you understand that?"

Donnelly's gaze met hers in the darkened car. "Yeah," he said softly. "I can understand it. I have three daughters of my own."

"Then you'll help me?"

He reached over the back of the seat and clicked open the latches on his briefcase. "I already have."

Naomi's anger faded. She stared at him in shock. "You mean...oh, my God." Her hand flew to her mouth. "You've found her, haven't you?"

When he nodded, Naomi suddenly felt at a complete loss. She'd searched for Sadie for ten years. Ten exhaustive years. Now, after only a matter of days, she was about to learn the whereabouts of another daughter she'd thought dead for fifteen years.

She drew in a long breath, trying to slow the adrenaline pounding through her bloodstream.

Donnelly pulled a folder from his briefcase and switched on the reading light in the car. "Piecing together what happened that night hasn't been easy," he said. "As you can imagine, the hospital records are a mess."

Naomi nodded. "I'm sure they are. The hospital suffered extensive damage from the second tornado. All the patients were evacuated as quickly as possible that night and moved to the county hospital. But the staff at both facilities were overwhelmed by the sheer number of casualties." How easy it must have been, in the pandemonium and hysteria, to switch two babies—one alive and one dead—and no one ever the wiser. Until now.

"You and another woman who'd also given birth at Eden Memorial were admitted to County hospital sometime just before midnight," Donnelly said. "I tracked down one of the nurses on duty at County that night, and she remembers that you were both rushed into ICU. The other woman suffered from a head injury she'd sustained during the storm, and you'd lost a lot of blood during delivery."

"And the babies?" Naomi asked in a near whisper.

"Baby Cross arrived at County sometime after you did, but the other baby, listed as Baby Doe at Eden Memorial, was taken to the neonatal unit at St. Mary's in Memphis."

"Baby *Doe?*" Naomi hadn't realized how fast her heart was racing, but suddenly she was short of breath. She could hardly speak. She wondered fleetingly if this was all a dream, if she would wake up shortly to find that both her daughters were still lost to her forever.

"They didn't yet know the mother's name." Donnelly glanced down at the open folder he'd placed on the seat between them. "Evidently she showed up during the storm in hard labor and was rushed to delivery without being processed. She suffered a concussion when part of the roof collapsed, and it was only later, after she'd been moved to County, that someone gave the admittance desk her name, Aubree DeWitt, and a New Orleans address for her. The next day, in the midst of all the confusion, arrangements were made to have her and the baby transported to a New Orleans hospital."

"You couldn't find out who'd given her name to the admittance desk?"

"No one remembered, but it's not surprising, considering everything they had to deal with in the aftermath of the storms."

"You said she was unconscious when she was moved to County. Is it possible she didn't know her baby had died that night?"

Donnelly shrugged. "It's possible she never knew. But it's irrelevant now because she's dead."

Naomi glanced up. "Dead? When...how?"

"She was murdered ten years ago."

Naomi gasped in shock. "What about the child?"

"She wasn't harmed. I don't have a lot of the details, but I spoke with a cop I know in New Orleans. He remembered the case vaguely, but he seemed to recall that Aubree and her husband were estranged at the time of the murder. DeWitt worked for a big oil company, and his job took him out of the country quite a lot. After Aubree's death, her parents tried to get custody of the child, but apparently, DeWitt was able to pull some strings, and after the funeral, he took the little girl back to London with him.''

"You mean they don't even live in this country?" Naomi asked in alarm.

"No, you're in luck there," Donnelly said. "A few months ago, DeWitt was transferred back to New Orleans."

They were in New Orleans, Naomi thought. In a matter of hours, she could see her daughter.

Sela...

She turned to Donnelly anxiously. "What did they name her?"

"The child? Taryn. Taryn Josephine DeWitt. Would you like to see a picture of her?"

"A picture..." If possible, Naomi's heart pounded even harder. She watched, speechless, as he took a photograph from the folder and handed it to her.

The picture had been shot from a distance with a telephoto lens that gave it a slightly grainy quality. And to make matters worse, the girl's face was partially obscured by a curtain of long, dark hair as she hurried through the gates of what looked to be a private school somewhere in New Orleans. A nun had been captured in the background, and her disapproving gaze in the girl's direction seemed to portend a boatload of trouble. Naomi immediately understood why. Taryn DeWitt was a knockout.

Tall and slender, with a lithe body already hinting at the womanly curves that would come all too soon, she'd tried to hurry the maturing process by using heavy makeup—eyes rimmed with black liner, lips thickly glossed. She'd rolled the plaid skirt of her school uniform to a shocking length, displaying long, coltish legs that would turn the heads of not just boys, but men twice her age. No wonder the nun in the background looked so worried.

Naomi felt an unsettling somewhere deep inside her. As she studied the photograph, she experienced not so much as a quiver of recognition. Was this the right girl? Surely, even under all that heavy makeup, there would be some resemblance, no matter how slight, to Sadie.

Ten years was a long time, Naomi reminded herself. Sadie had disappeared when she was five, and Naomi had always remembered her just the way she'd looked on that fateful day when she'd gone off happily to school. Naomi had expected—wanted—to see that same child, that same innocence in the face of Taryn DeWitt.

But Taryn was no longer a child, and any resemblance to her twin sister, Sadie, had been obliterated by the years. And perhaps by her environment. She'd lost her mother at a very early age, and that alone would have changed her.

And her father? What kind of man was Alex DeWitt? What kind of home had he provided for his daughter?

For *my* daughter, Naomi thought with uncharacteristic bitterness. Had *he* known? Was he the one who had coerced Willa Banks into stealing Naomi's baby?

She started to pass the picture back to Donnelly, but stopped, her hand trembling. She'd seen something…

There!

Naomi sucked in a sharp breath. The girl had a tiny dimple at the right corner of her mouth. Barely visible in the photo, but unmistakable. The same dimple that had charmed Naomi in Clay Willis. The same dimple that she'd kissed each night before Sadie went to sleep.

"It *is* her," Naomi said in breathless wonder. "She is my daughter. Sadie's sister."

"You sound pretty certain of that."

"I am. Oh, I am." Flattening the picture against her heart, Naomi closed her eyes. "I don't think I really believed she could still be alive until this very moment."

"Miss Cross—"

She ignored the warning tone in Donnelly's voice, and leaned over to briefly put her hand on his. "I don't know how I can ever thank you."

"Your gratitude may be premature," he said in that same deliberate voice. "However you decide to handle this, I urge you to proceed with caution."

Naomi frowned. "What do you mean?"

His gaze on her darkened. "I can tell by the look on your face that your first instinct is to rush to New Orleans and demand to have your daughter returned to you. I advise against such action. For one thing, proving what I've just told you in a court of law is going to be extremely difficult. The hospital records from that night are so chaotic they might not even be allowed as evidence. I've had to rely mainly on witnesses' memories to piece together what little information we've amassed so far, and given the traumatic circumstances of that evening, their testimony could easily be discounted. Unless you can somehow persuade Alex DeWitt to allow his daughter to undergo a DNA test, odds are you won't have a legal leg to stand on."

"Then what do you suggest I do?" Naomi asked with an edge of desperation.

"You could let the police handle it."

She shook her head. "I have a sister in law enforcement, Mr. Donnelly. I know how long these things can take, even if Abby was still here to pull strings for me. I've already missed out on fifteen years of my daughter's life. I'm not going to wait for a police investigation that could drag on for months, or even years. I'd rather take my chances with Alex DeWitt.''

"Then there's something else you should know.''

"What is it?''

"Aubree DeWitt's murder was never solved, and according to my source, there are some people in New Orleans who still point the finger at her husband. Evidently, Alex DeWitt became a very wealthy man upon his wife's death. Not to mention the fact that he gained sole custody of their daughter.''

A cold finger of fear traced up Naomi's spine. "What are you saying, Mr. Donnelly?''

"I don't know if Alex DeWitt was involved in his wife's murder or not. No one does. But I can tell you this. A man who kills once, even in passion, usually finds it much easier to kill a second time if he feels threatened.''

Chapter Two

"Mr. DeWitt?"

The man seated behind the wide desk glanced up as his secretary called out his name, and Naomi, standing just behind the woman, felt the impact of his gaze all the way across the vast room. Her breath lodged in her throat, and it took her a moment to gather her wobbly poise.

Then, before she lost her nerve, she brushed passed the secretary and strode into Alex DeWitt's office, trying not to let the sumptuous surroundings intimidate her. She barely let herself notice the thickness of the gray carpeting that muted her footsteps, the mammoth granite desk piled high with folders and stacks of computer printouts, the floor-to-ceiling windows on two walls that offered an impressive view of the city.

What she did notice, what she couldn't help noticing, was the man who sat behind that cold, imposing desk. Slowly he rose to his feet.

"I'm sorry for the...intrusion." She faltered, her gaze slipping unexpectedly over the elegant lines of his suit, the rigid bearing with which he held himself. "But...I have to speak to you at once. It's a matter of—"

His eyebrows rose before she could finish her urgent pronouncement, and Naomi had the immediate impression that here was a man who wouldn't respond favorably to melodrama. She would have to present her case in a measured and straightforward manner. She would have to use all her self-control to get him to see reason.

And if he didn't, if he refused to grant the DNA test she'd come to ask for, then Naomi was fully prepared to take more drastic measures. What those measure were, exactly, she didn't yet know. But she was willing to bet that Alex DeWitt, in all his years of wheeling and dealing in the oil industry, had yet to encounter the kind of ferocity a mother could call forth when battling for her child.

Then again, maybe he had. Maybe that was why Aubree DeWitt had died ten years ago. *"Evidently, Alex DeWitt became a very wealthy man upon his wife's death. Not to mention the fact that he gained sole custody of his daughter."*

Apprehension prickled the back of Naomi's neck. Maybe Michael Donnelly had been right. Maybe she should have left the matter to the police.

But what, legally, could they do? There was no evidence a crime had been committed, no proof, other than a dead woman's confession, that Naomi's baby had been stolen fifteen years ago. The local authorities would take their own sweet time investigating. They might eventually be able to enlist the aid of the FBI. Naomi's sister, Abby, who would be enrolling in the FBI Academy in a matter of weeks, and the man she was in love with, an ex-FBI profiler named Sam Burke, could perhaps pull a few strings, grease a few wheels, but at the end of the day, all any of them might succeed in doing was scaring Alex DeWitt—and Taryn—back to London. Naomi couldn't sit around and wait for that to happen.

Still she had to admit that throwing herself on the mercy of a man who may or may not have murdered his wife no longer seemed like a great idea. There was no warmth, no charity in the depths of Alex DeWitt's sage-green eyes. Just a cold, keen intelligence.

"I'm sorry, Mr. DeWitt," the secretary said behind Naomi. "I don't know how she got past the receptionist. I told her you were busy, but she insisted on seeing you. Should I call security?" she asked a bit hopefully.

Naomi lifted her chin defiantly as her gaze met Alex DeWitt's. *Go ahead,* she silently challenged him. *But they won't get here before I have my say.*

Something flickered in his eyes. Annoyance. Amusement. Attraction? Naomi thought with a flutter of nerves in her stomach.

She was accustomed to admiring glances. Even crossing the marble-and-brass lobby of the Ventura Oil Building earlier, she'd attracted the stares of more men than she cared to acknowledge, but Naomi neither reveled in nor repelled their attention. Nor did she hide behind false modesty. She knew she was beautiful, but she took no particular pride or satisfaction in the knowledge, because it wasn't her doing. The genes had come from her parents, and her mother had taught her a long time ago that true beauty came from within, and that courage, perseverance and a good heart wouldn't fade as the years passed by.

Naomi tried to call on that courage now as she waited for Alex DeWitt to speak. He was a handsome man, she thought fleetingly. Tall and broad shouldered with dark hair and those extraordinary eyes. She was willing to bet he turned a few heads himself.

His gaze moved momentarily past her to his well-groomed secretary. The woman still lurked in the doorway, and every now and then, Naomi caught a whiff of her perfume, something rich and exotic. A fragrance designed to attract the opposite sex. *Poison,* Naomi thought fleetingly.

"It's all right, Margaret," Alex DeWitt said in a deep, cultured voice. He'd lost his drawl while in London, but it would have been a stretch to say he'd acquired an English accent. The inflections were more subtle than that, and much more interesting. "I'll handle this." His gaze swept over Naomi, leaving her with a fluttery feeling in the pit of her stomach.

"What about the helicopter?" the secretary inquired crisply. "Shall I schedule a trip for the end of the week?"

"I'll let you know. Might not be a bad idea to let them cool their jets out there on the rig for a few days," he muttered. "I hear a storm's blowing in. A little bout with seasickness might smooth over the negotiations."

"Whatever you say, Mr. DeWitt."

He nodded briefly, as if barely aware of the woman's departure. He gestured toward a thick, tufted chair in steel-gray leather, and after Naomi was seated, he said with ill-disguised curiosity, "How *did* you get by the receptionist? She has something of a reputation around here."

Naomi shrugged nervously. "I rode up from the lobby in the elevator with one of your colleagues. We got to talking. I told him I was on my way to see you, and he insisted on showing me to your office."

"I'll just bet he did," Alex muttered, his gaze moving over her legs.

Naomi resisted the urge to tug at the hem of her beige

linen skirt. "He led me right past the receptionist. She didn't say a word."

"Very resourceful, Mrs.—"

"It's Miss. Naomi Cross."

"The question is, Miss Cross," he said smoothly, "why did you go to so much trouble to see me? Unless I'm very much mistaken, our paths have never crossed. Have they?"

Lying awake last night, Naomi had crafted any number of scenarios she could use to persuade Alex DeWitt that Taryn was her daughter. Rather than just blurting out the truth, she would let the story unfold gradually. She would somehow get him to confess that his wife had given birth at Eden Memorial, and then, when Naomi had him hooked, she would tell him why she was here. What she wanted.

But facing Alex DeWitt across the breadth of his desk, equivocating no longer seemed an option. Those green eyes were far too shrewd.

"Actually, our paths have crossed, Mr. DeWitt."

His dark eyebrows rose, but he waited for her to explain.

"Are you familiar with a town in Mississippi called Eden?" she asked tentatively.

He lifted a careful gaze to hers. "Why do you ask?"

The moment of truth. Naomi grasped the arms of her chair as she drew a long breath. "Fifteen years ago, your wife gave birth in Eden Memorial Hospital on a night when two tornadoes all but destroyed the town."

His gaze went very dark. "My wife was driving from New Orleans to Memphis when she went into labor. She drove into Eden, trying to find a hospital, and she got caught in the storm. But I don't see how any of this is your concern, Miss Cross."

"I was in Eden Memorial Hospital that same night," Naomi said as calmly as she could. "I gave birth to twin daughters. I was told that one of them died shortly after her birth."

"I'm sorry," Alex DeWitt said. "But I still don't understand what that has to do with me."

"I believe I gave birth to two healthy babies that night. I believe your wife was the one whose baby died. I believe that—"

Alex DeWitt stood so abruptly his chair rammed the credenza behind him and turned over. His fist slammed against the surface of the desk as he leaned toward Naomi, his eyes, not blazing with anger, but cold and deadly. "What the hell is this?"

"I'm trying to explain what happened—"

"He put you up to this, didn't he?"

The question, spoken with such deadly contempt, took Naomi aback. Her hand fluttered unconsciously to her heart. *"Aubree DeWitt's murder was never solved, and there are some people in New Orleans who still point the finger at her husband."*

Yes, Naomi thought almost breathlessly. She could see the way it might have happened that night. Alex DeWitt's suppressed passion and rage exploding in an act of violence. His hands, large and strong, closing around a delicate throat—

Except Michael Donnelly said that Aubree DeWitt had been bludgeoned to death.

Even worse, Naomi thought, her hand creeping to her chest.

When Alex DeWitt strode around the desk suddenly, it was all she could do not to scream for help. But she doubted that the dour-faced Margaret would come rushing to her aid.

"Why?" he demanded, staring down at her. "Why are you doing this? How much did he pay you to come up with this garbage?"

Naomi finally found her voice, and she rose on shaky legs to face him. "I don't know what you're talking about. No one paid me to come here. I came because I want to find my daughter—"

His gaze on her hardened. "If you dare to come within ten feet of my daughter, if you try to contact her in any way, I swear I'll—"

"What?" Naomi shot back, her own anger finally overriding her shock. "What will you do to me if I try to see my daughter?"

"*Your* daughter? God, woman. Are you crazy or just morally corrupt?"

"I'm neither," she said angrily. "I'm a mother whose baby was stolen from her fifteen years ago. And you can make all the threats you want, Mr. DeWitt, but nothing you can do, just short of murdering me, will ever make me give up on finding my daughter."

This time, it was he who looked taken aback. He lifted a hand, and for a moment, Naomi thought he was either going to grab her or strike her, and she braced herself, although her pride wouldn't allow her to flinch.

But what he did, instead, was drag his fingers through his dark hair, and for the first time, Naomi noticed the sprinkle of silver at his temples. He was older than she'd first thought, probably somewhere in his late thirties or early forties. He had experience and connections and a past fraught with secrets. But he also had Naomi's daughter, and that alone gave her the courage to stand up to him.

"It's true," she insisted. "I know it must come as a shock, and I don't blame you for your reaction. But I assure you, I'm acting on my own here. No one paid me to come and see you. I'm from Eden, Mississippi, and…recent events there uncovered the truth about the night your wife and I both gave birth.''

''And I'm expected to just take your word for that?''

Naomi lifted her shoulders helplessly. ''You can have me checked out if you want. You can call the sheriff in Jefferson County. His name is Mooney. Or my sister. Until recently, she was a detective with the sheriff's office, but she's attending the FBI Academy—''

''Wait a minute,'' he cut in coldly. ''If the police are involved, why aren't they here instead of you?'' When Naomi hesitated, his expression hardened. ''Because they think you're a crackpot, too, don't they? It's true, isn't it? You've concocted this bizarre story for God only knows what reason, but I'm willing to bet the local authorities, let alone the FBI, wouldn't give you the time of day. Because the simple fact is, you have no proof. Am I right, Miss Cross?''

YEARS OF DELICATE NEGOTIATIONS in the volatile international petroleum markets had taught Alex when to hold back and when to pull out all the stops. He saw defeat flicker in Naomi Cross's gorgeous brown eyes, and without hesitation he moved in for the kill.

''I don't know who you are or why you've decided to come forward with this outrageous claim. Instinct tells me it has something to do with money. It almost always does. But I can promise you this, Miss Cross. If you try to harm my daughter in any way, I'll make your life a living hell.''

Naomi glared at him. ''And I promise you this, Mr. DeWitt. I'm going to prove Taryn is my daughter. With or without your cooperation. And when I do, I won't lose her again.''

She turned then, pulling herself up to her full, impressive height and strode from the room, leaving in her wake the light, subtle fragrance of her perfume and something potentially much darker. Something that Alex feared had the power to destroy his whole world.

What lingered in the air was the ring of truth in her words. The absolute conviction in her voice sent a chill up his spine. Naomi Cross believed every word she'd spoken, and that made her a very dangerous woman.

Looking at her, no one would believe that dementia lurked behind such an appealing facade. She was quite possibly the most beautiful woman Alex had ever laid eyes on, and that, too, made her dangerous. He was not a man given to impulses, not since his hasty marriage to Aubree had proved so costly, but Naomi Cross was a woman few men could resist. She was the kind of woman who made intelligent men do stupid things.

She was tall and lithe, with glossy dark hair—nearly black—and large, soulful eyes. Eyes that could weaken a man's knees as well as his resolve.

He'd been tempted before, by women far more experienced and sophisticated than Naomi Cross. But the stakes had never been this high, and that alone readied Alex for battle. He would do anything to protect his daughter. She was going through a difficult time right now, and the last thing she needed was for some stranger to show up on their doorstep, claiming to be her long-lost mother.

It was the last thing Alex needed, too.

He walked back over to his desk and picked up a framed photograph of Taryn, studying her features for a moment as he tried to dispel his lingering disquiet.

He'd snapped the picture in the garden of their London town home just months before they'd returned to New Orleans, and he still couldn't get used to how much she'd changed in such a short time. He hardly knew her anymore.

Gone was the shy smile, the sweet disposition, the beguiling child who'd been so anxious to please it sometimes broke Alex's heart. In her place was a sullen, moody teenager, a complicated, unpleasant stranger who barely had two civil words for him these days.

He supposed it served him right. It was hard to believe now, but there'd been a time when he hadn't wanted a child, when he'd been adamant about not bringing a baby into the world for the sole purpose of trying to resuscitate an already dying marriage.

When Aubree had told Alex she was pregnant, after first admitting she'd thrown away her birth control pills, he'd been furious with her and too proud and stubborn to turn down the position Ventura Oil had offered him in their London office.

Instead, he'd tried to convince Aubree to go with him, even though by then he'd known the marriage was in trouble. But out of the country, far away from her father's meddling, it was possible the two of them could still make a go of it, if only for the baby's sake.

But Aubree had remained just as stubborn, storming out of their modest home in Metairie to ensconce herself in a lavish house a block off St. Charles Avenue, bought and paid for by her father. And Alex had left for London alone. He'd returned as often as he could, but because of the miles and the growing estrangement between him and Aubree, he'd seen little of Taryn during those first few years of her life, and for that, he would never forgive himself.

This was his punishment, he decided. There'd been a time when he'd had no room in his life for a child, and now there was no room in Taryn's life for him. What goes around comes around, as his mother used to say.

But putting it all into perspective didn't make his recent difficulties with his daughter any less painful. Nor did the animosity between him and his former father-in-law ease the tension. Joseph Bellamy was an old Louisiana aristocrat who had never accepted his daughter's marriage to a penniless nobody who'd grown up in Gentilly, who'd attended New Orleans Community College for two years before he'd gotten a scholarship to Tulane.

From the beginning, Joseph Bellamy had insinuated himself into his daughter's marriage, undermining any kind of bond Alex and Aubree might have forged. He'd discouraged her from joining Alex in London, and once Taryn was born, he'd tried to turn both his wife and daughter against him.

And Alex had been only too willing to supply the necessary ammunition. He could have given up his job at Ventura Oil, could have come back to New Orleans and fought for what was rightfully his, but he'd been young and ambitious. He hadn't wanted to turn down what he'd viewed then as the opportunity of a lifetime.

If he'd only known...

He'd made a lot of wrong choices back then, Alex thought grimly, staring down at his daughter's picture. Choices he wouldn't repeat if he had it to do over again. Nothing would keep him from his daughter now, and no one was going to take her away from him, either.

He returned Taryn's picture to the corner of his desk

as a cold, dark anger spread like a cancer through his soul.

Ever since they'd returned to New Orleans, Joseph Bellamy had been trying to undermine Alex's relationship with Taryn by feeding her lies about the past, by making her become almost obsessed with a mother she barely remembered. A mother who had fallen far short of the sainthood Joseph had anointed her with after death.

When Alex had found out he was being transferred back to New Orleans, he'd hoped that age would have mellowed the old man, but at seventy-six, Joseph was still just as shrewd, still just as ruthless, still just as consumed by hatred as he'd ever been. And he still blamed Alex for Aubree's death.

In those terrible first days after Aubree's body had been found in the house off St. Charles, he'd lashed out at Alex, had railed against him to anyone who would listen. He'd even convinced the police, for a while at least, that Alex might have somehow slipped into the country aboard a Ventura jet, done Aubree in for her money and then returned to London before anyone was the wiser.

When the investigation cleared Alex, Joseph hadn't been satisfied. In his mind, justice would never be served until Alex got what was coming to him. And so he'd tried to take Taryn from him.

And now it seemed that he'd picked up right where he'd left off on the night he'd vowed vengeance for his daughter's murder. The price, he'd said, would be Alex's own daughter.

Alex didn't know how or why, but he was certain Joseph was behind Naomi Cross's visit here today.

Grabbing up the phone, he punched in his ex-father-in-law's number. The Bellamys resided in one of the restored mansions along River Road, but Joseph, a former federal judge, maintained an office and a senior partnership at his old law firm, one of the most prestigious in the city.

When Alex heard the old man's voice, he dispensed with the formalities and got right to the point. "I don't know what the hell you're trying to pull this time, but it's not going to work, do you hear me? I'm not going to let you drive a wedge between my daughter and me."

"Taryn is *Aubree's* daughter."

Amazing, Alex thought, how much venom could drip from just four words. His grip tightened on the phone. "She's *my* daughter, and nothing you can say or do will ever change that. I know you sent Naomi Cross to my office with that cockamamie story about her being Taryn's real mother—"

Joseph's breath sucked in sharply. *"What?"*

"You heard me. Naomi Cross just left here. I don't know where you dug her up, but I have to give you credit. She was pretty darn convincing. Almost had me believing there for a minute that she and Aubree had given birth in the same hospital in that podunk town in Mississippi, and that one of her babies had been swapped for Aubree's and mine."

There was dead silence on Joseph's end. Then, his voice quivering with rage, he said, "Now you listen to me. I don't know who this woman is. I never heard of her. But if she repeats this nonsense to anyone else—if *you* repeat it—I will make you both very, very sorry. Taryn is Aubree's child. She's all that I have left of my daughter. God help anyone, including you, who tries to take that away from me."

Chapter Three

Naomi had been to New Orleans a few times before, and she'd fallen in love with the city each and every time she'd come. Her father had been born and raised in the Crescent City, and Naomi always figured that eventually he would have come back here after leaving his wife and two small daughters behind years ago in Mississippi.

"N'awlins is in my blood," she'd heard him once say to her mother. "Once she starts calling you home, there's nothing you can do but go on back to her."

They'd never heard from him after he left, not one phone call or postcard, much less a child-support check. But in all the years of her struggle to raise her children alone, Naomi's mother had never said a bad word against him, although there were plenty, Naomi included, who would have thought her justified. She'd been that kind of woman. The kind Naomi, as an adult, had tried to emulate. Strong, independent. A woman who lived for the present instead of wallowing in the mistakes of her past.

But Naomi had learned the hard way that the past was always with you. It never died. It was like a dream you wake from abruptly, all fuzzy and indistinct around the edges but haunting nonetheless. And binding. It was like New Orleans, she thought. Once it had you, it never let you go.

Before Sadie had disappeared, Naomi and her sister, Abby, had come down here together a few times. Abby had still been a teenager, Naomi in her early twenties. By silent agreement, they'd come not so much to search for their father, but to find something that had been missing inside themselves. Something that was as elusive as it was fragile.

They'd walked the streets of the French Quarter, blending with the tourists, window-shopping the antique stores along Royal Street, touring the voodoo shop on St. Peter, and all the while their eyes had carefully studied the faces of passing strangers, the weathered visages of street corner musicians and the artisans who gathered in Jackson Square. Was *he* among them? Would they recognize their own father if they met him face-to-face? Would he have the same eyes that stared back at them from a mirror? The same mouth? The same color of hair?

After Sadie had gone missing, Naomi had come back here by herself once. She wasn't sure why. Something had called to her, she supposed. Or maybe it was just loneliness. Desperation. Perhaps it had been nothing more than her fascination for a city she found both mystical and exciting.

Whatever her reason, she'd walked the same streets she'd walked with her sister, searched the same crowds, only this time she found herself looking for her daughter's face as she did everywhere she went. And the same thought tormented her always. As the years passed, would she recognize her own daughter if she saw her on the street? Would Sadie recognize her?

It seemed to Naomi that she'd been searching for someone all her life. Her father. Sadie. And now for a child she'd been told fifteen years ago had died at birth. A young girl who had no idea Naomi was her real mother. Those times when she had come to New Orleans—Taryn had been here. *So close.* Naomi wondered now if it had been the bond with her daughter, and not her search for her father, that had drawn her back to this city time and again.

But was the bond just as strong for Taryn? When she learned the truth, would something that had been missing inside her finally click into place?

Or would it be as Michael Connelly had predicted? Would she turn against Naomi for tearing her world apart?

Shivering, Naomi noticed that the room had grown quite dark while she'd sat contemplating her situation. She glanced around the living room of her hotel suite, thinking that the gloomy atmosphere had been caused by her thoughts, but then she realized that as the day melted into late afternoon, storm clouds had gathered over the city.

From where she sat at the small cherry-wood desk near the windows, Naomi could see the dark clouds rolling in from the Gulf of Mexico, and she watched them for a moment, remembering that it had rained every time she'd come to New Orleans. Should she take that as a sign? she wondered.

She reached over and switched on a white alabaster lamp that sat at the corner of the desk, but the warm glow of light did little to cast off the storm's pall.

The Spencer Hotel, located on Royal Street in the heart of the Vieux Carré, was a beautiful hotel, oozing with Old World charm and Southern hospitality. Normally Naomi wouldn't have been able to afford such luxury. She drew only a small salary as one of the directors of the Children's Rescue Network. But Jared Spencer, the president of the Spencer Hotels Corporation, had insisted on making all the arrangements for her when he learned she was coming to New Orleans.

Under ordinary circumstances, Naomi would have refused. She liked to pay her own way, but Tess Campbell had made Naomi understand that it was something Jared wanted to do. Having been reunited with his own long-lost daughter, he was compelled to do everything he could to help Naomi find hers.

"You're lucky you and Jared have each other again," Naomi had told Tess.

Tess had merely smiled, but it was the luminous smile of a woman in love. A smile that had made Naomi all too aware of the emptiness in her own life. The next day, she'd left for New Orleans.

And here she was, alone and searching for her daughter. Always searching. Always alone.

But Naomi had learned a long time ago that feeling sorry for yourself got you nowhere. Far better to put her efforts into something positive—like leaving no stone unturned to be reunited with her daughter.

Resolved once again, Naomi turned her attention back to the file Michael Donnelly had given to her before she'd left Eden. He'd provided a detailed account of all his activities and the interviews he'd conducted since she'd hired him, and as Naomi scanned his notes, she found it odd that no one remembered anyone accompanying Aubree that night. She'd shown up at the hospital in the middle of the storm, much as Naomi had, in the throes of hard labor. But Naomi was from Eden. What had Aubree been doing so far from her home?

As she read through Donnelly's account of that night, Naomi's mind drifted backward in time. She remembered racing to the hospital, trying to outrun the tornado, trying desperately to get help for her babies. And when she was finally there, the nurses had wheeled her into delivery. Their actions had been harried, their expressions worried, but not for Naomi.

"We've got the other mother prepped, but we still haven't heard from Dr. Simms."

"How's she doing?"

"Not good. We're having trouble finding the baby's heartbeat—"

That woman, Naomi now realized, must have been Aubree DeWitt. Her baby had died that night, and someone had taken one of Naomi's babies to replace her. But who? Who had been at the hospital with Aubree DeWitt on that night? Who had persuaded Willa Banks to swap the two babies?

No one at Eden Memorial had known who Aubree was when she was first admitted. It was only after she'd been taken to County hospital that someone had supplied the admittance desk with her name and address. Which proved that someone had been with her. The same someone who had stolen Naomi's baby?

Donnelly had included very little about Aubree DeWitt's murder because he'd used the limited resources provided by Naomi to investigate the events that had occurred on the night she'd given birth to her twins. He'd done exactly what she'd asked him to do—he'd found her daughter—but now, suddenly, Naomi was consumed with curiosity about Aubree DeWitt. She felt an odd connection with the woman, probably because Aubree had raised Naomi's child as her own.

But was it more than that? Having met Alex DeWitt,

was she more than a little curious about the kind of woman he had married?

She closed the folder and rubbed her eyes, then got up and walked over to the window. Opening the French door, she stepped out on the tiny balcony that overlooked Royal Street. It was still early, just after seven, but the coming rainstorm had chased most of the tourists inside. The few scattered pedestrians were locals, accustomed to New Orleans weather. They leaned against buildings, lingered on street corners, nowhere to go, no one to see. Just another rainy twilight in the Big Easy.

Now and then Naomi caught the faint sound of music, a saxophone, she thought, but the mournful notes were as elusive as dreams in the falling darkness.

And through the quiet came another sound, whispering along the rooftops. Rain began to fall, gently at first, and then with a steady drumbeat on the sidewalks and streets until even the locals sought shelter in recessed doorways and under awnings.

Droplets splashed against the ornate black railing on the balcony where Naomi stood, but instead of stepping back, she leaned forward, eyes closed, letting mist from the falling rain settle on her face. She felt tired suddenly. Overwhelmed. In spite of her best efforts, it was hard on evenings like this not to dwell on her losses. Not to succumb to the despair.

It was hard not to think of Sadie.

Naomi sometimes wondered if she and her daughter would have remained in Eden if Sadie hadn't disappeared. Naomi had been an unwed mother in a small Southern town, and even fifteen years ago, that status carried a stigma. Sly looks, gossip. It hadn't always been easy. She and Sadie might have been better off making a fresh start somewhere else, perhaps even here in New Orleans, a city that had drawn Naomi unaccountably for years. But she'd only been eighteen when her daughters were born. She'd needed her mother's help.

So when she'd left the hospital, she'd gone back to her mother's house where she and Sadie had shared a bedroom until Naomi's sister had eventually moved into town when she'd gone to work for the Jefferson County Sheriff's Department. Sadie had inherited Abby's old room, and then one day she hadn't come home from school.

As the years passed, Naomi had stayed on in her mother's house, even after her mother died, because that was the only home Sadie had ever known. That was the place she would come to if she could somehow find her way back.

But in ten years, she hadn't come back. Now Naomi was searching yet again, this time for another daughter, and she shivered as a strange uneasiness settled over her.

The rain had eased up, but the chill inside Naomi deepened. Suddenly she couldn't seem to stop trembling. She wore a sleeveless light blue shell and slim black pants with sandals, and for a moment, she thought about going back inside for a sweater. But it wasn't the weather that had caused her blood to go cold. It was the dart of an image, like the lunge of a sleek panther, through her mind.

Unbidden, Alex DeWitt was back inside her head.

To be truthful, he hadn't been far from Naomi's thoughts all afternoon. That look of suppressed rage in his eyes. The warning note in his voice. *"If you try to*

*harm my daughter in any way, I will make your life a
living hell.''*

Had he made his wife's life a living hell before he'd
killed her?

That's not fair, Naomi immediately admonished herself. He'd never been charged or convicted of anything.
As far as she knew, he'd never even been a suspect.
She'd been the subject of gossip herself so she knew
how rumors could get started. A rich wife. A troubled
marriage. A handsome husband who could have his pick
of any woman he wanted.

Yes, Naomi thought, a man like Alex DeWitt invited
talk. Dark and brooding, he wouldn't take the time to
disavow the rumors. More than likely, he would simply
mock them.

Had he loved Aubree? Had he been devastated by his
wife's murder? Had he tried to move heaven and earth
to find her killer?

Even after all these years, was he gripped in the middle of the night by the same loneliness that plagued
Naomi?

Somehow she doubted it.

According to Michael Donnelly, Alex DeWitt had
come back to the States only long enough to collect his
daughter before heading back to London, where they'd
remained for nearly ten years. Why, after all this time,
had he decided to move back to New Orleans? Because
he thought the talk would have died away by now?

Because the murderer always returns to the scene of
the crime? Naomi shivered again.

And what about Aubree's parents? Donnelly had told
her that the Bellamys had tried to get custody of Taryn
before Alex had swept her off to England. Had his been
the action of a desperate father or a guilty conscience?

Naomi stared down at the glistening sidewalk, her disquiet suddenly turning restless. The rain had stopped, and people were coming back to the streets, materializing from doorways and shops and alleys deep with shadow. She had the sudden urge to be out among them. To pretend for a little while that she belonged here, that she had no greater care in the world than to decide where to have dinner.

Turning, she went inside and closed the door behind her.

THE LAW OFFICES of Brown, Jenrette and Boudrieux were located in an old warehouse on North Peters, on the French Quarter side of Canal Street near the waterfront. On the easy side of Canal, some would say.

The location was not an accident. The laid-back style of the Quarter mirrored the relaxed and somewhat unorthodox approach to the law shared by the firm's three partners—Danny Brown, Wilson Jenrette and Foley Boudrieux. An approach that had made them, to no one's greater surprise than their own, all highly successful attorneys and wealthier than any of them had dared dream of back in law school. The hustle and bustle of the Central Business District, the location of the world headquarters of Ventura Oil, was only a short distance away, but it might have been a world away.

Alex found a parking spot, got out, then glanced up at the faded warehouse as he strode across the street. From the outside, the old brick building retained a crumbling facade that gave the impression of having been forgotten by both time and progress, but like most of the other warehouses in the area, including the famous Jax Brewery, the building had been given a thorough makeover inside.

A freight elevator carried Alex to the second floor, where he stepped into a world of buttery leather sofas in soft autumn colors, teak floors that gleamed beneath Oriental rugs, and lush oil paintings by talented local artists tastefully displayed in exotic wood frames.

The receptionist had already left for the day, but Foley Boudrieux was expecting him. When Foley heard the clamor of the elevator, he stuck his head out his office door and motioned Alex down the hall.

The proclivity for trouble that had almost been his downfall in college still gleamed in Foley's eyes, but he'd made an effort over the years to look, if not always act, the part of successful attorney—jacket and silk tie in respectable shades of gray; tasseled loafers buffed to a high sheen; crisp Egyptian cotton shirts in white or light blue. His hair was the color of red Georgia clay, his eyes the brilliant, piercing blue of a summer sky. He had been Alex's closest friend since their college days at Tulane, and it was for this reason, as much as for his professional expertise, that Alex had called him after Naomi Cross's visit that afternoon.

And, too, Alex had been reluctant to consult with the firm of attorneys retained exclusively by Ventura Oil because he wanted to keep this matter as private as possible. A mute point, he conceded, if Naomi Cross had been sent by Joseph Bellamy.

"So let me get this straight," Foley said, once they were settled. He'd offered Alex a whiskey, which he'd declined, but Foley had poured himself a bourbon from the bar he kept concealed and stocked behind a bookcase.

Relaxed and in no particular hurry to get to the point, he leaned back in his leather chair and propped his feet on his desk, sipping his drink. He'd shed his jacket sometime earlier, and his red suspenders, a glimpse of the real Foley Boudrieux, fairly glowed against the snowy background of his shirt. "Some woman showed up out of the blue at your office today claiming you stole Taryn from her."

"Those weren't her exact words," Alex said dryly. "She said that her baby had been stolen fifteen years ago from that hospital in Eden, Mississippi, where Aubree had Taryn."

"*Eden,* Mississippi?" Foley lifted his drink. "Where the devil is that?"

"North of Jackson, I think. Anyway, she says that Aubree gave birth that same night in the same hospital."

Foley peered at him over the rim of his glass. "Is that true?"

Alex hesitated, frowning. "I guess it could be. Aubree went into labor while she was driving from New Orleans to Memphis, but I never could figure out what the hell possessed her to take off on a road trip so close to her due date."

Something flashed in Foley's blue eyes. He set aside his drink and regarded Alex across the expanse of his desk. "Maybe she was running from you."

"What?"

Foley shrugged. "She knew you were coming back to New Orleans for the birth of your baby. Maybe she wanted to make you come look for her."

"That would have been like her," Alex muttered. Impulsive. Eager to make him worry with no thought to the baby's safety. He shifted uncomfortably. "This woman, Naomi Cross. She said she'd been told that one of her babies had died that night."

"One?"

"She had twins."

One auburn eyebrow lifted slightly, but Foley said nothing. Behind him, through long windows, city lights twinkled in the wet twilight.

Somewhere out there, Naomi Cross was probably plotting her next move, Alex thought grimly. His frown deepened as he tried to imagine what that move might be. "She said recent events in Eden had led her to believe that both her babies had, in fact, been born healthy that night. It was Aubree's and my baby who had died. Someone swapped the babies—"

Foley swore so viciously that Alex stopped, stunned. The lawyer's blue eyes blazed with anger. His expression was usually so benign that it was off-putting to see him suddenly so furious. "That's the most ludicrous story I ever heard tell. Anyone whoever saw Aubree with that baby would never believe such nonsense. Say what you will about her, but she adored that kid."

"I've never denied that," Alex said quietly. He'd long suspected Foley of having deep feelings for Aubree, but he'd never confronted him, perhaps because he'd been unwilling to lose his best friend. Besides, Aubree had never shown the slightest interest in Foley, other than as a friend, someone like all the others in her entourage she could use and manipulate to her own selfish end. If Foley had fallen in love with her, Alex felt nothing but pity for him.

Foley studied the corner of his desk for a moment, as if reluctant to meet Alex's gaze. "This woman's obviously after something. Money, would be my guess."

"That's what I thought, too, only…"

"What?" Foley demanded

Alex shrugged. "She seemed so sincere."

Foley snorted in a very unlawyerlike fashion. He

picked up his drink. "Convincing actresses are a dime a dozen, my friend. I've run up against a few myself."

They both had, Alex thought, Aubree being the most convincing of them all. Until she'd finally shown her true colors.

"Look, Alex." Foley sat forward, his eyes gleaming with indignation, anger and something else Alex couldn't quite define. "You can't believe there's any truth to this woman's claim. What proof does she have?"

"None, that I know of."

"Then stop worrying."

Alex ran a hand through his dark hair. "I know what she says can't be true, okay? Taryn is my daughter. I don't have a single doubt about that. But there's something about this woman…I can't explain it." He got up and walked to the wall of windows to stare out.

The pavement below glistened in the aftermath of the rainstorm, and a mild breeze fluttered the umbrellas of an outdoor restaurant across the street. In the distance, the river was a wide, shimmering ribbon, trimmed by lights on both levees. Somewhere out on the water a tugboat horn sounded in the darkness as it guided a swollen freighter to its dock. The sound was mournful, lonely. For no accountable reason, it made Alex think of Naomi Cross.

There was something about her that was too beguiling. A quality that was almost hypnotic. Alex had known beautiful women before. Naomi's appeal was far more than physical. She exuded a kind of moral strength and inner courage that was rare enough to find these days. And in the depths of those lush brown eyes lurked an infinite sadness that had touched Alex in a way he couldn't name.

He frowned, steeling his resolve. Whatever her reasons, Naomi Cross was out to make trouble for him and Taryn, and he would do well to remember that fact. He turned now and faced Foley. "I don't think she's an actress. I wish it was nothing more complicated than that." A fraud he could handle. "What worries me is that she seems to believe her own story. I'm afraid someone has gotten to her, and they've somehow convinced her that her daughter and mine were swapped at birth fifteen years ago."

Foley gave him a measuring look. "You mean someone like Judge Bellamy."

"He denies it, but can you think of anyone else who would want to cause me trouble?" Alex strode back across the room and sat down near Foley's desk, but almost at once, he rose again and began to pace the ivory Berber carpet.

"Now, just calm down," Foley advised. "You have absolutely no proof that this woman is connected to Judge Bellamy. What we need to do is find out exactly who she is and what she wants."

Alex stopped pacing. "I know what she wants," he said angrily. "She wants my daughter."

"Somehow I think we're going to find out there's a lot more to her story than she's let on." Foley glanced at his watch. "It's late, but let me see what I can find out. I've got some connections in Mississippi. You say she's from a place called Eden?"

"That's right."

"A lady from paradise," Foley murmured.

"Wait until you see her," Alex said grimly.

Foley glanced up. "That good, huh?"

"She gives new meaning to the word temptation."

A little smile played across Foley's lips. "In that

case, maybe I should check her out for myself," he drawled. "You know, as a favor to an old friend."

Alex clenched his jaw. "If you want to do me a favor, help me find a way to get rid of her."

Foley's smile disappeared. "The first thing you need to do is stop throwing around phrases like that. If she were to turn up dead, it wouldn't look too good, buddy."

Alex stared at him in shock. "Dead? That never crossed my mind—"

Foley put up a hand. "I wasn't suggesting that it had. All I'm saying is that given your history in this town, you need to be careful, especially where this woman is concerned. You don't know who her friends might turn out to be. Or her enemies, for that matter."

A KIND OF HUSHED QUALITY had fallen over the French Quarter since the rain, and a fine mist blurred the sharp edges. Even the garish neon signs advertising exotic drinks and topless dancers took on a dreamlike quality that made Naomi feel as if she were almost floating along the sidewalks.

She wasn't at all apprehensive on the streets. It was still early, and now that the rain had stopped, both locals and tourists alike had come back out. In spite of the Quarter's reputation, Naomi had never been frightened of it.

Leaving Royal Street, she turned right on St. Peter, and as she neared Bourbon Street, the crowd thickened, spilling from the sidewalks onto the street. Rock music blared from open doorways, and Naomi was momentarily jostled by a group of students crossing the intersection, in a hurry to get to the next bar.

"Laissez rouler les bon temps!" they called to her.

Naomi smiled and nodded politely, declining their impulsive offer to join them at Pat O'Brien's for a round of hurricanes. After that, she tried to keep to the inside edge of the sidewalk, blending as best she could into the shadows of the buildings.

After a while, she began to feel hungry, and she found a quiet little restaurant that advertised filé gumbo and crawfish étouffée on its windows. She took a seat in a corner, facing the door, and watched the street as she waited for her order.

A man came in after her, brushing raindrops from his dark hair. He was tall and thin, but muscular, as if his job required him to keep fit. He wore jeans, a black T-shirt, nondescript except for a serpent tattoo that ran all the way down his bulging forearm to coil around his wrist. His gaze brushed Naomi's, then moved on, but in the instant when their eyes met and held, a chill like nothing Naomi had ever experienced swept through her.

Someone walking on your grave, Grandma Eulalia would have told her.

Only a handful of customers were seated at the tables, but the man found a place at the bar. His back was to Naomi, but she had the uncomfortable notion that he was watching her in the mirror, that if she looked in his direction, their gazes would meet again in the glass.

She wanted to get up and leave, but just then the waitress brought her food, a steaming plate of rice and spicy jambalaya. The aroma was so enticing that Naomi decided she would be foolish to let herself be chased away by a man who had followed her into the restaurant with no more sinister purpose than to have a beer and strike up a flirtation with the cute blond bartender.

The young woman seemed to know him, and Naomi began to relax. She was letting her imagination run away with her. Letting the ambiance of the French Quarter get to her. The man was obviously someone who came in here often.

Putting him out of her mind, Naomi ate her food, sipped her iced tea, and after a while the soft murmur of voices around her began to lull her. Resisting the lethargy, she tried to plan her next move, but in truth she had no idea what she would do if she couldn't appeal to Alex DeWitt's sense of justice. If she couldn't somehow convince him that she had given birth to the daughter he thought was his.

Naomi tried to put herself in his position. It wasn't difficult. She knew what it was like to lose a child. She'd lost two daughters. No one knew better than she how blindsided Alex DeWitt must have felt earlier in his office. How threatened.

As she lingered over her tea, Michael Connelly's words came back to her. *"I don't know if Alex DeWitt was involved in his wife's murder or not. No one does. But I can tell you this. A man who kills once, even in passion, usually finds it much easier to kill a second time if he feels threatened."*

Naomi tried to shove the warning aside. She didn't want to speculate about the night Aubree DeWitt had been murdered. She didn't want to contemplate how dangerous Alex DeWitt might become if she persisted in her mission. She didn't want to think of him as a murderer, she realized, and it wasn't just because of the danger he could pose. Alex DeWitt, for all the harshness of his words and the coldness in his eyes, had touched something deep inside Naomi that no man had ever touched before.

Oh, she'd fallen for Clay Willis in a big way, and she'd given herself to him one rainy April night because he'd been good-looking and charming and, to be truthful, Naomi had been curious and too impulsive by half. She'd also been a romantic back then, and a dreamer.

She'd made love a half dozen times with a boy who couldn't leave town fast enough once he'd learned she was pregnant. But she'd never been with a *man,* and that fact had never hit her more forcibly than the moment Alex DeWitt had looked up from his desk and seen her.

Unsettled by the thought, Naomi paid her check and left the restaurant. She turned right on Dumaine, strolling past the Voodoo Museum, closed now for the evening. Some of the shops along the street were dark as well. The carving of an ebony cat, blending almost seamlessly with the shadowy interior of a small art gallery, stared at her balefully from the window. Naomi stopped to admire the piece, and when the amber eyes blinked, she jumped, realizing belatedly the animal was real. The cat yawned, stretched, then settled back down to his perch in the window. And Naomi moved on, slightly unnerved by the encounter.

As she turned on Royal, the crowd on the streets thinned, but she still wasn't afraid. The hotel was just a short distance away, and she kept to the outer edge of the street now, avoiding the dark, shadowy doorways and alleys where someone might lurk.

A few stores down, a group of middle-aged female tourists were peering into the window of a jewelry shop, oohing and aahing over the contents. When they moved on, Naomi stopped to see for herself what had drawn their attention. Nestled on a bed of black velvet, an array of colored gemstones—tanzanite, pink tourmaline, and green garnet—set in heavy, ornate gold glowed softly behind the plate glass window protected by wire mesh.

Naomi had no idea whether the jewels were real or not, but they were certainly beautiful, and like any woman, she took a moment to admire them, although she knew they were as far out of her reach as the moon. The only jewelry she'd ever owned, other than several pairs of inexpensive earrings and a string of faux pearls she'd purchased from a clearance table at Lawson's Department Store in Eden, was a tiny gold and topaz ring left to her by Grandmother Eulalia.

Naomi didn't consider herself poor. She'd inherited her home when her mother died, and even though the salary she drew from her position as one of the directors of the Children's Rescue Network was meager—she and the other directors would have it no other way because every spare dime went into the search and rescue of missing and exploited children—it met her living expenses in Eden. And if there was no money for extras, well, finding a single clue that might help track down a missing child was far more precious to Naomi than any diamond.

She started to turn away from the jewels, but a movement inside the shop stilled her. Remembering the cat moments earlier, Naomi wasn't overly alarmed, but then, as she peered into the window, she realized that the motion hadn't come from within, but from somewhere outside.

Her pulse quickened as a man's reflection materialized in the glass. He was standing behind her at the edge of the street, staring at her reflection in the glass. As their gazes met, he lifted a cigarette to his mouth, and Naomi could see the glowing tip reflected in the window.

Fear darted through her even as she reminded herself that there were a lot of people on the street. A man standing on the sidewalk smoking was hardly cause for alarm. But…there was something familiar about him.

The image of the tattooed man at the restaurant immediately leaped to her mind, and Naomi whirled, her heart pounding in her throat.

Chapter Four

He was walking off, his back to Naomi. She could see
smoke from his cigarette drifting on the night air as he
approached the crowd of tourists who'd wandered on to
the next store window. He said something to one of the
women, and they all laughed, as if whatever he'd told
them had been very clever and amusing. Then he moved
around them and continued down the street.

He never looked back. Naomi never saw his face. She
couldn't say with any certainty that he'd been the man
she'd seen earlier at the restaurant. But an uneasiness
crept over her just the same, and she turned, hurrying
toward the lighted flags that marked the front entrance
of the Spencer.

Her footsteps echoed hollowly on the pavement, and
a chill ran down her spine. Suddenly Naomi couldn't
shake the notion that she was being followed. She could
feel a dark gaze on her, and the hair at the back of her
neck prickled in warning. She even thought she could
smell cigarette smoke.

She spun, searching the street behind her, and she
saw a brief flurry of movement as someone darted into
a recessed doorway.

In a full-blown panic now, Naomi whirled, and abandoning all pretense of calm, sprinted toward her hotel, resisting the urge to glance over her shoulder yet again. She knew he was behind her, perhaps gaining ground. She couldn't spare even one precious second. She had to make it to the hotel—she had to get inside...behind locked doors.

A couple came out of the wrought iron gate of the hotel's courtyard and turned up the street toward Naomi. When they saw her, breathless and running, they stopped, giving her a curious glance as she flew by them. She slowed and glanced back. They were still gazing at her, but beyond them, the sidewalk was empty.

Naomi nodded to the couple briefly before disappearing through the gate. She hurried through the courtyard, then entered the hotel through a side entrance.

Waiting for an elevator, she let her gaze scan the narrow lobby. The dark, heavy antiques and luxurious damask drapes evoked a different era. Naomi could easily imagine hoop skirts swirling through the tall, arched doorways and jewels glittering beneath the crystal chandeliers. But at the moment, she was too caught up in her own anxiety to fully appreciate the grace and Old World charm of the Spencer Hotel. She was sure someone had followed her, but if he watched her now from behind one of the potted palms, Naomi couldn't spot him.

The bell sounded, and as the elevator doors slid open, she stepped quickly inside. Staring straight ahead as she rode up to the fifth floor, she caught a glimpse of her reflection in the mirrored walls. Her short dark hair was all askew, and her cheeks were flushed with color. After all these years, she hardly noticed the haunted look in her eyes anymore.

Fluffing her hair as she tried to calm her nerves, she left the elevator and strode down the hall, inserting the card into the lock and then slipping inside her room. She threw down her purse and key, and was just about to draw a breath of relief when someone rapped sharply on the door.

Naomi jumped as her gaze shot to the dead bolt. She'd turned it, hadn't she?

She walked over to the door as the knock came again. Whoever stood outside in the hallway was growing impatient.

"Miss Cross? I know you're in there. I saw you come in. Please open the door. I need to speak with you."

The deep voice, muffled through the heavy wood, was unnervingly familiar, and Naomi knew it at once. She glanced through the peephole anyway. Alex DeWitt was standing just outside her door, and Naomi's heart gave another painful thud.

He'd seen her come in, he said. Was he the one who had been following her?

Fear prickled down her nape. A shiver of something else slid along her backbone.

In spite of the warning bells that sounded inside her, Naomi reluctantly drew back the door.

He seemed to suck the air right from her lungs, and she found herself clutching the door, torn between running away from her fears and standing firm against them. She chose the later. After all, this was the man who stood between her and her daughter.

She moved aside to allow him to enter. "How did you know where to find me?" she asked, closing the door behind him.

"I have very resourceful friends." Rain glistened in his dark hair, as if he had been out walking in the downpour. Again Naomi remembered the reflection in the store window, her certainty that someone had followed her.

She was a tall woman, but he towered over her. Beneath the starched fabric of his white dress shirt, she could imagine the ripple of lean muscle across his chest and abdomen. He looked strong, powerful. Sleek as a panther and perhaps just as dangerous.

And she was alone with him in her hotel room.

At thirty-three, Naomi had never been alone with a man in a hotel room. She had rarely been alone with a man at all. The Cross women had a penchant for picking mates who took off and left them when the going got tough. Her grandfather had never married her grandmother Eulalia. Her father had left when Naomi's sister, Abby, was just a baby. And then, of course, Clay Willis had joined the army to avoid marrying Naomi. Of all the Cross women, only Abby had been smart. Only Abby had chosen a career instead of a man until the right one had come along.

Sometimes Naomi couldn't help but envy her sister. Abby had it all now. A fulfilling career. A man who adored her. But that was all another story, and Naomi didn't have time to dwell on the what-ifs or the what-might-have-beens. Not when Alex DeWitt was looking at her with what she could only surmise was suspicion. And anger.

He walked over and tossed a folder onto the cherrywood desk. The sound seemed to echo in the silence of the room. Then he turned slowly toward her. "I know who you are."

The nerves in her stomach rippled uncomfortably. "I told you my name this afternoon."

"That's not what I mean." He nodded toward the file. "Take a look."

Naomi walked over to the desk and flipped open the folder. Her breath caught in her throat as she quickly scanned the faxed pages.

Beside her, Alex DeWitt said softly, "You founded the Children's Rescue Network in Mississippi after your daughter, Sadie, was kidnapped ten years ago. You still work there as one of the directors and as their spokeswoman. Over the years you've appeared on a number of programs dealing with missing persons. One might even say you're an expert on the subject. A lot of things make sense now."

She glanced up quickly. "Like what?"

His gaze on her deepened. "I understand now why you're doing this."

Naomi's heart was pounding so hard she could barely speak. Alex DeWitt was such a commanding presence she had a hard time meeting his gaze, speaking to him at so close a range. She turned away from him, giving herself a moment to collect her thoughts. Then, as it had earlier that day, her anger came to her rescue.

She spun back toward him. "You think I'm doing this because of what happened to my daughter? To my *other* daughter? You're wrong. My being here has nothing to do with Sadie. Not in the way you mean."

Something flickered in his green eyes, something that might have been pity if he were the type of man who seemed capable. "You've lost two children. I can't imagine what that must be like. I don't blame you for wanting to believe that one of your daughters is still alive."

"You can't possibly know how I feel," Naomi said, her hands balling into fists at her sides.

One dark eyebrow arched slightly. "I'm a father, Miss Cross. I know how I would feel if I lost my daughter. I'd rather have my heart ripped out."

Naomi closed her eyes for a moment as the force of his words hit her. He didn't know how she felt. No one did. But as a parent, he could imagine, and she heard in his voice that same sense of dread, a hint of the terror that was every parent's nightmare. Maybe it *had* been pity she'd seen in his eyes, or something very close.

"I don't blame you for grasping at straws," he said quietly.

"That's not what I'm doing." She glanced down at the folder, wondering what else he'd learned about her since she'd left his office earlier. "Maybe I'd better explain to you how I came to find out about my...about Taryn."

A frown flickered across his brow, but he nodded. "That might be helpful."

She gestured toward the peach sofa in the sitting room. "Please sit down."

After waiting until she'd seated herself in one of the armchairs near the window, he sat down, gazing at her with icy green eyes.

Naomi's hands curved around the arched swans' necks that formed the arms of her chair. She couldn't seem to tear her gaze from Alex DeWitt. He looked every inch the successful oil executive. His dark suit, the same one he'd been wearing earlier, was elegantly cut, his white shirt impeccable. His black hair, though mussed slightly from the rain, was cut in a style that was very flattering. She thought, as she had that afternoon, that he was a very handsome man. Mesmerizing, even, but cold.

He cocked his head slightly. "You were going to explain how you happened to come and see me."

Naomi cleared her throat, slightly embarrassed at her lapse. "It's just that I hardly know where to start."

"Perhaps on the night your daughter was born might be the best place."

"Daughters," she corrected him. "Taryn was a twin."

Again something flickered in his eyes, this time a look of anger. "You gave birth to twin daughters that night. One of them was Sadie, the little girl who disappeared ten years ago."

"Yes." *My precious Sadie,* Naomi thought with the same rush of emotion she always felt when her daughter's name was mentioned. After all this time, the pain had never lessened. "There was a storm that night," she said softly. "Two tornadoes ripped through Eden, destroying lives, homes." She shuddered, remembering. "I was home alone when the storms hit. My mother and sister were away."

"And your babies' father?"

Her gaze on him faltered. "He left town when he learned I was pregnant." Naomi stared down at her hands. "I went into labor three weeks early. The doctor had warned me that multiple births were risky, so I knew I had to get to the hospital. The phone lines were down. I couldn't call for an ambulance so I drove myself. By the time I got to the hospital, I was…something had gone wrong. I was bleeding. But there were so many other people who had been hurt in the storm. The emergency room was in chaos.

"The last thing I remember as I was being wheeled to the delivery room was overhearing the nurses talk about another mother who was in labor. The nurses were worried because they couldn't find her baby's heartbeat.''

His gaze on her darkened, but he said nothing.

Naomi leaned toward him slightly. "Why was your wife in Eden, Mr. DeWitt?"

"I told you. She was driving from New Orleans to Memphis."

"So far along in her pregnancy?"

"Aubree could be…impulsive."

"Is it possible that…" Naomi trailed off, not quite knowing how to ask what she needed to know. "Is it possible she wasn't alone? Could someone have been traveling with her?"

"If someone was with her, she never told me." Abruptly Alex DeWitt got up and strode to the window to stare out. After a moment, he opened the door and stepped out onto the balcony, as if the room had suddenly become too confining for him. Naomi didn't know what else to do so she got up and followed him.

They stood side by side at the railing. Not talking. Not looking at each other, just gazing off into the night. Dark clouds lingered over the city, like a curtain that couldn't fully be lifted, and Naomi could smell the rain. She'd always loved the scent.

After a while, she turned to Alex. "Do you want to hear the rest?"

He lifted his shoulders. "If I said no?"

She swallowed. "It's up to you. But my mother always said that burying your head in the sand doesn't change anything. It only prolongs the inevitable."

"Your mother was probably right," he said with a bitter edge to his voice. "But nothing you say is going to change things, either. Taryn is *my* daughter."

She's my daughter, too, Naomi wanted to argue, but

instead she turned to stare down at the street. Colors glistened in the wet pavement, like a child's finger painting. The kind a mother hangs on her refrigerator door, Naomi thought, as the ache inside her deepened.

"You may as well tell me the rest," he said grudgingly.

"I don't remember anything after I was wheeled into delivery," she said, "but I was told later that I lost a great deal of blood that night. I went into shock. I guess I almost died. Two days later, when I finally came to, there was a moment when I wished I had."

Alex turned at that, his gaze meeting hers in the darkness. "You found out one of your babies had died."

She nodded, a lump rising in her throat. Lightning flashed overhead, illuminating his face for a moment so that she could see the intensity of his stare. Naomi shivered, wrapping her arms around her middle. "I blamed myself. If I'd gotten to the hospital sooner…if I'd taken better care of myself…if I'd had a husband…" She trailed off. "But no amount of self-recrimination was going to bring my baby back, and eventually I realized I was lucky to still have one healthy baby when so many others had lost everything that night."

"And the other woman? The other mother who was in labor?"

"I never knew what happened to her. In fact, I'd forgotten all about her until recently. We were both moved to a different hospital after the second tornado hit. You can imagine the confusion that night."

His eyes told her he knew exactly what she was getting at. "Did you—" He broke off and stared up at the sky. "I don't know how to put this without seeming insensitive—did you see your baby?"

"Both of them, you mean?" She shook her head.

"The town held a mass funeral at the high school for the tornado victims. There were so many of them. My baby...the baby that I was told was mine...was buried before I ever regained consciousness." Naomi heard a muffled sound, like a dozen whispers, and then the rain came down again. For a moment, neither of them said anything, they just stood there watching the rain shower.

Then Naomi felt his hand on her arm, and a deep shiver tingled through her. "I'm sorry," he said. "I really am."

"It was a bad time for me." She moved away from him slightly, holding her hand out to catch the rain, as she and Abby had done as children. As Sadie had once done. As Taryn had undoubtedly done. "But I survived. And then five years later, when my other daughter was kidnapped, I managed to survive that, too. I've been through a lot, Mr. DeWitt. More than you can imagine. I've spent the last ten years looking for missing children, trying to offer comfort to their parents. The position at the Children's Rescue Network has toughened me, made me learn how to fight." She drew her hand back from the rain and turned to face him. "Do you understand what I'm saying?"

"Yes, I'm afraid I do."

She nodded, as if they'd come to some kind of important agreement. "Just over a month ago, a little girl was kidnapped on the anniversary of Sadie's abduction. She disappeared from the same school playground where Sadie was taken ten years earlier. I became involved in the case through my position at the CRN."

"But the second little girl...she was found unharmed."

"Yes. She was taken by a nurse who worked at the

school. Her name was Willa Banks.'' She glanced up at him. "Does her name ring a bell?''

He frowned. ''No. Should it?''

''She used to work at Eden Memorial Hospital. She was on duty the night my babies were born. The night your wife also gave birth.''

His expression hardened. Naomi could see the rigid line of his jaw even in the darkness. ''And for some reason, you think she switched the babies. You think it was my baby who died.''

Naomi nodded.

He glanced away. ''I don't believe that. I won't believe it.''

''I know it's difficult—''

He turned back to her, his gaze bleak, unyielding. ''Why would she do that? What earthly reason would this woman...this Willa Banks have for swapping those babies?''

''Someone obviously persuaded her to.''

''Persuaded her how?''

Naomi shrugged. ''Money? I don't know. What I do know is that her guilt ate away at her for years. When Sadie was kidnapped, she couldn't stand the thought that I'd lost both my children, and that she had been the cause of one of my losses. I guess her mind began to go, though no one knew it. Not until ten years later, when she saw another little girl on the same school playground and thought she was Sadie. She thought that by taking that little girl and returning her to me, she could make up for her part in swapping my baby.''

Alex rubbed a hand across his chin. ''This is the most bizarre story I've ever heard.''

''I know,'' Naomi said. ''But it's all true. Every word I've told you.''

"Why should I believe you?" he asked coolly. "You've yet to give me one shred of proof. And I suspect that's because there isn't any. By your own account, this Willa Banks is...shall we say?...not of sound mind. Yet you seem all too willing to take her word for events that supposedly occurred fifteen years ago. You would have no objection, I take it, if I were to talk to this woman myself?"

"I wouldn't, except for one thing. She's dead."

"That's rather convenient, isn't it?"

Naomi said defensively, "I suppose it depends on your perspective. It would be more helpful to me if she were still alive because there are still too many unanswered questions. My baby was stolen from me. Someone came to the hospital that night and persuaded Willa Banks to take her. I'd give a lot to know who that person was."

"Assuming the story unfolded as this woman claimed it did."

"I believe it did," Naomi said fiercely.

"But you have no proof."

His condescending tone was even more infuriating. "I know it's true," Naomi said stubbornly.

His tone, if possible, grew even colder. "What is it you want from me, Miss Cross? What is it you expect me to do with everything you've told me?"

Naomi lifted her chin. "I want you to allow Taryn to have a DNA test."

He didn't say a word, but the look on his face...the flash of rage in his eyes, sent a chill racing down Naomi's spine. Had she made a terrible mistake in allowing Alex DeWitt into her hotel room?

He moved toward her, so swiftly Naomi hardly had time to draw a breath. He reached out, grasping her forearms in his hands, and though he held her lightly, Naomi had no doubt that she was trapped. If she moved, he would tighten his grip. If she tried to get away, he would stop her.

It might have been her imagination, but the rain seemed to fall harder as he held her, the steady downpour loud enough to drown out even a scream. Naomi was suddenly, painfully conscious of the pavement five stories below her.

"Why would I do that?" he demanded angrily. "Why would I put her through that?"

"She wouldn't have to know—"

"You want me to lie to her?"

"I didn't come here to make trouble for Taryn," she said shakily, finding the courage to somehow meet his gaze. "That's the last thing I want. But I have to *know*. Can't you understand that?"

"And then what?" His voice rose slightly over the rain. "Supposing I did agree to a DNA test, and supposing you found out that you gave birth to her. Do you really expect me to believe that would be enough for you? That you would disappear from our lives forever?"

He released her then and turned toward the open French door. Glancing over his shoulder, he said darkly, "There will be no DNA test. Taryn is my daughter, and nothing you or anyone else can say or do will ever change that."

"I don't want to take her away from you," Naomi said, following him back into her suite. She watched as he strode toward the door. "I don't want to hurt either one of you. I just want the truth."

His voice lowered menacingly as he paused with his hand on the knob. "You want a great deal more than that, or you never would have come to New Orleans."

Chapter Five

Alex went around to see Foley again the next day. He'd managed to postpone his trip out to the offshore drilling sites until the following week, even though he knew he was going to catch flak from his superiors. But he couldn't be concerned about that. He wasn't going to leave town, even for a day, while all this business with Naomi Cross was still up in the air. No telling what she might try to do while he was gone. No telling what Joseph might do, because Alex still wasn't entirely convinced Aubree's father hadn't somehow orchestrated all this, maybe even without Naomi's knowledge.

"I spoke to the Jefferson County sheriff this morning," Foley informed him, drawing Alex out of his reverie. "His name is Mooney, and his office is right there in Eden."

"What did he say?" Alex asked anxiously.

"He pretty much confirmed Naomi Cross's story."

"So it's true." Alex felt more numb than surprised. Ever since he'd left Naomi's hotel room last night, he'd been bracing himself for this moment, even as he told himself her story couldn't possibly be true. No way on this earth Taryn could be her daughter. Because if she was…if Naomi had given birth to her, that meant Taryn couldn't be his. That meant his and Aubree's baby was dead.

But Taryn *was* his daughter, Alex thought fiercely. She was his daughter in every way that counted. He'd raised her, dammit. He'd sat up with her when she was sick, held her when she'd awakened from her nightmares. Ever since Aubree's death, Alex had tried desperately to make up to Taryn for those years when he hadn't been there for her. But maybe that was impossible. Maybe he couldn't make up for it, and this was his punishment.

"Look," Foley said, setting aside his notes. "I can see you're worried about this woman, but I think you should try to relax. From what I've been able to gather, she doesn't have a case."

"You sure about that?" Alex sat forward, his hands clenched around the arms of his chair.

"Absolutely. Sheriff Mooney admitted there wouldn't even be an investigation unless Naomi Cross pressed for one. And she hasn't."

"That's because she decided to come here and investigate for herself."

"Yes," Foley agreed. "She's desperate. Sheriff Mooney made no secret of the fact that his department has their hands full right now, what with two kidnapping cases, an attempted murder, and God only knows what else going on up there. They're not about to open up a fifteen-year-old can of worms based on a crazy woman's deathbed confession, especially considering there are no hospital records, no witnesses, no evidence of any kind to back up her claim. It's a dead end as far as they're concerned."

Alex wished he had as much confidence as Foley seemed to that this whole thing would just dry up and blow away in a matter of days. But Foley hadn't seen the look on Naomi's face last night when she'd talked about her daughters. Alex had, and he knew there was no way in hell she would give up that easily. Evidence or no, she would find any means possible to keep her hope alive. Because she had to.

"It isn't going to be that easy," he said with a sigh. "Naomi made it clear last night that she isn't going away."

Foley's auburn brows lifted slowly. "Naomi?"

Alex shrugged. He'd surprised himself a little by referring to her by her first name, but it had just slipped out. A little too easily, perhaps. "She's pushing for a DNA test."

"She can push all she wants, but that doesn't mean you have to agree." Foley shrugged. "You're holding all the cards here whether you realize it or not. If you don't agree to the test, then it's all over. The problem goes away."

"I'd like to believe you, but you haven't met Naomi Cross." Alex left his chair, sliding his hands into his trousers pockets as he moved to the windows. "She won't go away. She's convinced Taryn is her child, and if I don't agree to the DNA test, I'm afraid she may try to get to Taryn. She doesn't need that kind of confusion in her life right now, Foley. *I* don't need it."

The lawyer nodded sympathetically. "Then as I see it, you've got two options. You can agree to the DNA test—" He raised a hand to cut off Alex's protest. "You can agree to the DNA test and if the results disprove Miss Cross's accusations, as we both know they will, then she'll have no recourse but to leave you alone."

"And just what do I tell Taryn?" Alex asked angrily.

"Don't tell her anything. There are a number of ways to get a DNA sample without anyone being the wiser."

Yes, Alex thought. Naomi had suggested much the same thing to him the night before, but it still seemed deceptive, another potential for driving a wedge between him and his daughter.

He'd known Naomi for less than twenty-four hours, and already she'd wreaked havoc in his life. "I don't like being put in the position of having to deceive my daughter."

"I realize that, but it might be the best way to get Naomi Cross off your back," Foley pointed out.

"You said I had two options," Alex said grimly. "What's the other?"

"We could file a restraining order against her. That would keep her away from Taryn—and you—until she gives up and goes home. Of course, it would also be a matter of public record. No way to keep it a secret."

Alex turned to stare out the window. In the distance, sunlight glinted on the river, and he could just make out the silhouette of a lone barge steaming downstream. The city looked beautiful today, all golden and sun drenched. This was the New Orleans he'd remembered on those cold, rainy days in London.

There'd been a time when Alex couldn't wait to get out of New Orleans, when he'd thought this was the last place he could ever make his home. He'd thought this city had been ruined for him. But even though his parents were dead, he had roots here, and if he were honest with himself, he'd have to admit that his daughter wasn't the only reason he'd wanted to come home after ten years. He'd been in exile, if only in his own mind, for nearly a decade, and Alex had come to a point in his life when he'd decided it was finally time to put the past to rest. To finally put Aubree's memory behind him.

Sometimes he still had a hard time understanding how things had gone so wrong between them. They'd married too soon, he supposed, still believing that the physical attraction that had been almost overwhelming between them could overcome any obstacle.

It was an old story. They'd been young and stupid, mistaking lust for love, and when the bloom had faded from the romance, there'd been nothing much left but bitterness. And an innocent child caught in the middle. A beautiful little girl who'd deserved so much better than either of them had given her.

He couldn't help comparing his and Aubree's selfishness to the way Naomi Cross had looked last night when she'd talked about her children—the baby she'd thought had died at birth and the other little girl who had been abducted from a school playground. No question that she'd loved them. No question that she would have sacrificed anything, even her own life, for them.

Alex couldn't imagine anyone going through what she'd been through in her life, and yet the ravages of her despair had left her face oddly untouched, except for her eyes. Her eyes betrayed her sadness, her vulnerability, and somehow that made her even more appealing.

She had the power to bring him and his daughter great pain, but Alex couldn't find it in himself to wish her any harm.

He returned to his chair and sat down. "Hold off on the restraining order," he told Foley. "Let me try talking to her again."

"Maybe you should let me talk to her," Foley suggested.

"I'll think about it."

Foley gave a brief nod. "You do that. In the meantime, I'm afraid you've got bigger problems than Naomi Cross."

Alarm traced up Alex's backbone. "What are you talking about?"

"You're not going to like this," Foley said grimly. "But I was at the Barrister's Club last night," he said, referring to an exclusive private institution whose membership had boasted, for over a hundred years, the most prominent lawyers, judges and politicians in the city. "Brace yourself, Alex, but it looks like Joseph Bellamy may be preparing to go after custody of Taryn again."

Alex swore violently. "How can he do that? On what grounds? Taryn's been with me for the past ten years. What judge in his right mind would award custody to Bellamy?"

"I don't have to remind you of the clout that old man still wields in this town." Foley glanced toward the door, as if afraid someone might be standing just outside, eavesdropping. He leaned toward Alex, lowering his voice. "Listen, this is strictly on the q.t., you understand? There's an unspoken gentlemen's agreement that nothing, and I do mean nothing, that goes on inside that club ever leaves those sacred halls. Wilson used his family connections to get me in. If word gets around that I've got a problem keeping my mouth shut, we'll both be booted out. And that, my friend, would be very bad for business."

Alex thought it all sounded like a bunch of childish nonsense, but he'd been in the corporate world long enough to recognize the value of social clubs and high-powered cliques. The oil business wasn't all that dif-

ferent. "All right," he said impatiently. "Just tell me
what you heard."

Foley cast another glance toward the door. "Apparently, Judge Bellamy has been spending a great deal of
time sequestered in meetings with the other senior partners at his firm. Some of the associates at the lower end
of the food chain over there seem to think time and
resources are being diverted from other, more important
cases in order to mollycoddle one of the founding partners."

Alex didn't doubt it. Joseph Bellamy was used to
getting his way, no matter who else had to suffer. Aubree had come by that trait honestly.

"Yesterday, they had another closed-door conference
with an outside attorney named Griffin Douglas," Foley
said. "Name ring a bell?"

Alex frowned. "No, should it?"

Forgetting to worry about eavesdroppers, Foley settled back more comfortably in his chair. "Griffin Douglas has testified numerous times before congressional
committees on Capitol Hill regarding the rights of
grandparents in cases of divorce, parental neglect and
abuse. Last year, he lobbied in Baton Rouge to get a
bill passed here in Louisiana that would guarantee
grandparents visitation rights. He's devoted his entire
professional career to this cause. There's no one in the
country more savvy—or more ruthless—on the subject.
If he's agreed to take the case, then the judge has called
in some major markers."

Alex experienced a sinking sensation in the pit of his
stomach. "He's that good?"

"The man's brilliant. You put his expertise with the
judge's connections and you've got trouble, Alex. Big
time. Bellamy is on a first-name basis with every trial

judge in Orleans Parish. With Griffin Douglas on board, this could get ugly.''

Alex rose again, but instead of going to the window, he started pacing back and forth across the thick carpet.

"There's something else."

"God," Alex said, shoving his hand through his hair. "What else could there be?"

Foley's expression had grown very sober. "One of the associates let slip that all that old business about Aubree's death is going to be dredged up. Designed, of course, to assassinate your character."

Anger warred with desperation. "That was ten years ago, for God's sake, and I was cleared. I wasn't even in the country. Doesn't anyone is this damn town ever forget?"

"You know better than that," Foley chided. "In New Orleans, everyone knows everyone else, and they don't forget a damn thing about your past. At least not for long," he said with a touch of irony.

"I guess I'm beginning to realize that," Alex said bitterly.

Foley's gaze was sympathetic. "If you were the child's mother, we wouldn't even be having this conversation. Paternal rights have come a long way, but there are still some old-fashioned judges down here in the South who think a child, especially a teenage girl, would be best served in a stable home with a female role model. Someone who is the epitome of propriety. Someone, say, like Gwen Bellamy."

Alex stared at him in shock. "You've got to be kidding. Let me remind you that Gwen Bellamy was Aubree's stepmother. The two of them couldn't stand each other, and she's never shown the slightest interest in

Taryn. On top of that, the woman is neurotic, a chain-smoker and a habitual liar.''

"None of which is going to matter one bit when Griffin Douglas gets through with her. She'll come off like the reincarnation of Mother Teresa."

"You make it sound hopeless," Alex said gloomily. "Like there's no way to fight this."

"Oh, we'll fight it all right," Foley assured him. "Make no mistake about that. But in the meantime—" he hesitated for just a heartbeat "—ever given any thought to remarrying?"

Alex gave him a quelling look. "Very funny."

"It wasn't meant to be." When Alex glared at him, Foley shrugged. "All I'm saying is that if you could provide the same kind of home situation for Taryn that the Bellamys are offering, the judge might have a harder time convincing even one of his buddies on the bench to remove her from your custody. Think about it for a minute, Alex. Aside from all that old business about Aubree, you're a single man who's dragged your daughter halfway around the world and back for nearly ten years. That's not a stable environment."

"We lived in London," Alex said through gritted teeth. "That's hardly dragging her halfway around the world."

"But you weren't just in London," Foley reminded him. "Your job required a fair amount of travel."

"And I always took Taryn with me."

"What about when she started to go to school? You had to leave her with Louise then, didn't you?"

Louise Wheeler had been Taryn's nanny since birth, but as Taryn had grown older, her role had developed into that of housekeeper. She'd worked for the Bellamys for years, had, in fact, been Aubree's nanny. When Alex had made plans after Aubree's death to take Taryn back to London with him, Louise had offered her services. Everything considered, it had seemed like a good idea to Alex not to separate his daughter from everyone she knew, even though he'd been worried that Louise's first loyalty would always remain with Joseph Bellamy. However, her devotion to Taryn was undeniable, and she'd been a godsend during those first difficult months when Taryn had such a terrible time accepting her mother's death.

"I left her with Louise on occasion, but never for more than a few days at a time. I had to make a living," Alex said in exasperation. "I'm a single parent—"

"My point exactly," Foley cut in. "Look, Alex, you don't have to convince me you've been a good father. I know you've done right by Taryn. But I'm just trying to give you a taste of what to expect."

"Thanks," he said dryly.

"And that's not all. If you've got women in your past, and somehow I doubt you've been celibate for the past decade…" Foley trailed off, giving Alex a knowing look. "Then you can bet they'll be paraded across the witness stand to your detriment. While Gwen Bellamy is portrayed as a saint, you'll come off looking like a cross between Don Juan and the Marquis de Sade. And that's if you're lucky, my friend."

NAOMI STOOD across the street, catty-corner from St. Anne's Academy for Girls and watched the parade of luxury automobiles inch around the circular driveway as parents and nannies picked up their children after school. It would seem to the casual observer that all the students at St. Anne's came from well-to-do backgrounds, but Naomi knew that appearances could be deceiving. Even though she'd had to scrimp and save to afford the tuition, she'd sent Sadie to Fairhaven Academy because she'd wanted her child to have not only a good education, but a safe environment.

Even ten years later, the irony of her decision was devastating. It was still hard for Naomi not to blame herself for what had happened. If she'd sent Sadie to a different school, if she'd been there that afternoon to pick up her daughter the moment class was dismissed…

She tried to block out all those painful images as she watched the school. St. Anne's was located in historic Uptown, a few blocks over from Tulane University. Naomi had parked half a block away and walked to her current observation spot, where she could see not only the front of the school but the wrought iron pedestrian gate that opened directly onto a shady side street. A park, dotted with dozens of statues and historic markers, as well as pigeons, was located directly behind her, and she could hear children laughing somewhere in the distance. Naomi didn't think anyone would take much notice of a lone woman milling about.

Several kids had already exited through the side gate of St. Anne's, heading off in various directions, but after a few moments, pedestrian traffic, as well as the line of cars in front of the school, started to thin, and Naomi had still seen no sign of Taryn.

It was possible, of course, that her daughter had come and gone and Naomi hadn't recognized her. She'd seen only one picture of Taryn, but she'd been certain she would be able to spot her, even in a crowd of students dressed in identical school uniforms.

In spite of all the trees, it was hot on the sidewalk and Naomi could feel her cotton blouse sticking to her back as she waited. After another few minutes passed and the last car had driven away from the school, she decided she might as well go back to her air-conditioned suite at the Spencer. For whatever reason, she'd missed Taryn, and there was nothing she could do now but come back tomorrow.

But just as she started to head back to her Jeep, the wrought iron side gate swung open and a girl stepped through. Naomi couldn't see her face clearly, but she knew instinctively it was Taryn.

The girl was tall and slender, with a sweep of glossy dark hair and a natural grace that made her seem older than her years. She was very beautiful. To Naomi's eyes, she was perfect.

Her heartbeat quickened at the sight of her. Overcome with sudden emotion, Naomi had to blink back tears. This was her daughter. Her baby. A miracle when Naomi had given up believing in miracles a long time ago.

As if sensing her scrutiny, Taryn glanced across the street, her gaze, it seemed to Naomi, meeting hers. For a moment, she wondered what she would do if Taryn came over to her. Would she blurt out the truth? Make up some lie?

Naomi almost wished Taryn *would* come to confront her, so that she could see her up close. So that she could reach out and touch her. So that she could whisper on a tremulous breath, "I'm your mother, Taryn, and I'll never leave you."

But now was not the time for such a stunning revelation. Taryn could not be made to suffer for Naomi's impulsiveness. Everything would have to be handled just right if Naomi were to have any kind of relationship with her daughter in the future.

Taryn's gaze scanned the park behind Naomi, then

moved up the street. She appeared to be waiting for someone. There was a bus stop on the opposite side of the street from the school and, after a moment, Taryn crossed the intersection and sat down on the bench.

She was even closer to Naomi now. All Naomi had to do was cross the street, too, and sit down on the bench beside her. She could pretend to be waiting for a bus. She wouldn't stay long, just a few moments, just long enough to say something to Taryn so that she could hear her daughter's voice. What harm would there be in that?

Her heart thudding in anticipation, Naomi stepped into the street, then jumped back, startled, when a city bus lumbered up to the intersection and stopped. On the street to her left, mere inches from where she stood, a car screeched to a halt, as if abruptly caught by the light. Naomi automatically turned at the sound.

It was only later that she reflected on how perfect the timing had been. The bus chugging across the intersection had completely cut her off from the activity on the other side of the street. There was no one to witness, no time to even scream, as a man came out of the park and grabbed her from behind.

Chapter Six

Stunned, Naomi tried to fight him off, but the surprise of his attack had caught her off guard and crippled her reflexes. Before she even knew what had happened, he'd gripped her tightly around the waist and clapped a hand over her mouth. He shoved her toward the curb, where the back door of a car stood open. Thrusting her inside, he slammed the door in her face.

Heart pounding in terror, Naomi jerked frantically at the door handle, then threw her whole weight against the door. *Oh, God, oh, God, oh, God,* she thought. Is this what Sadie had felt? This mind-numbing terror? The disbelief? She'd been just a child when she'd been abducted, helpless and tiny...

A tinted Plexiglas panel separated the front seat from the back, and Naomi pounded on the divider with both fists. "Let me out! Please!"

But the car pulled away from the curb, and for the first time, Naomi realized she wasn't alone in the back seat. An older man, as silent and still as a statue, watched her from the shadowy corner. Something about his silence, the way he stared at her without blinking, made fear bubble up inside her again.

Naomi glanced around, frantic to find a way out. She

beat on the Plexiglas divider again. "Stop this car!" she screamed. "Let me out!"

She turned back to her silent captor. "Who are you?" she asked desperately. "What do you want with me?"

Still he said nothing, just continued to stare at her until gooseflesh prickled along Naomi's arms.

As the car raced through the intersection, she threw herself against the door again. The bus had pulled away, and she could see Taryn still sitting on the bench. For a moment, Naomi could have sworn their gazes met, lingered, but then the car whisked by, and Taryn was lost from her sight.

"She's a beautiful girl, isn't she?" The man's voice was deep and well modulated, a cultured drawl, but there was something unpleasant below the surface. Something dangerous.

Naomi's hand gripped the door handle, even though she knew it was hopeless. The door was locked in such away that it couldn't be opened from the inside. And even if she could somehow disengage the mechanism, the car had picked up speed. To jump from a moving vehicle would be risking life and limb, but given the opportunity, she thought she just might take that chance.

"Who are you?" she asked again, trying to hide the tremor of fear in her own voice.

"My name is Joseph Bellamy. Ah," he said, when he saw her react. "I see you've heard of me. But then, I expect you checked this scam out thoroughly before you tried to pull it off."

Naomi gaped at him. "I don't know what you're talking about."

He cocked his head slightly, regarding her. "Spare me the denials. Your ilk used to pass through my court-room every single day, Miss Cross. Con artists. Petty thieves. I granted them the same mercy they had bestowed upon their victims. Which is to say, none.'' His gaze met hers again, and a shudder ripped through Naomi.

They turned down a main thoroughfare, and as they left the shade behind, sunlight filtered in through the tinted windows. She could see him clearly now, the prominent nose, the once strong jawline now sagging with age. His eyes were the color of a frozen pond in the dead of winter, his hair a slightly darker shade of silver. On first glance, Joseph Bellamy was a handsome, distinguished-looking man, but a closer scrutiny uncovered the cruelty in his mouth, the arrogant set of his jaw and chin.

Naomi's stomach started to churn. How did he know her name? How had he known where to find her?

"What do you want from me?" she demanded.

"I want to have a few words with you. In fact, I'd like to tell you a little about my family if you'd indulge me.''

What choice did she have?

Think, Naomi, think! She had to find a way out of this. She had no idea what Joseph Bellamy had in store for her, but she didn't think it was going to be pleasant.

As if her desperation had communicated itself to him, he smiled slightly. "You won't be harmed. You have my word on that.''

Small comfort, Naomi thought.

"Since you've undoubtedly done your research on my family, you may already know that the Bellamys have a long and distinguished history in Louisiana. My grandfather was a two-term governor, my father a U.S. senator. I was groomed at an early age to carry on the tradition, but I was never cut out to be a politician.''

He sighed heavily, as if the burden was still something he hadn't gotten use to carrying. "I couldn't win over the crowds the way my father could, and the way his father had before him. I had no charm, no charisma as the truly great politicians all have in abundance. My father used to say that I didn't have the magic." Something flashed in his eyes, a curious mixture of regret, anger and shame, but then his gaze came back immediately to settle on Naomi. "I didn't have the magic, but my daughter did.

"Aubree was a natural. Smart, beautiful, glamorous. She could work the crowds like no one I'd ever seen before. They worshiped her, adored her, and she loved them. She had a glorious future ahead of her, and then she met Alex DeWitt."

Naomi had never heard mere words convey such contempt. He had all but spat Alex's name.

"Everything changed when she met him. She dropped out of law school to pursue him, that nobody who came from nowhere. She gave up everything for *him*." He drew a quick breath, as if trying to beat back a rage that had been building for years. "The marriage was a mistake from the first. They both knew it. When Alex went off to London, I thought that would be the end of it. Aubree would be rid of him forever, but she was as willful as she was beautiful. She wouldn't let go. She allowed that man to destroy everything that was good in her life. And then he destroyed her."

He fell silent then, and the car was so well insulated that all Naomi could hear was the sound of her own pulse pounding in her ears. *"And then he destroyed her."*

"When Aubree died, she took everything with her," Joseph said softly. "My hopes, my dreams. I once aspired to the Supreme Court, and when a new administration took office, my name was mentioned as a possible nominee. I was no politician, but I could have had power and fame. I was destined for greatness in my own right, but without Aubree to carry on the dynasty, it seemed…pointless. My wife, Gwen—'' He flicked his wrist, an unconscious gesture of dismissal that spoke volumes. ''She was happy here in New Orleans, so I retired from the bench and prepared to settle into my old age. To eventually die still mourning the loss of my daughter.''

Naomi didn't know what to say. Given her own circumstances, she could almost feel sorry for him except that Joseph Bellamy was not the sort of man to engender pity. Naomi suspected he used emotions the way he used everything else—to his own advantage.

''I thought my life was over,'' he said, ''but then one day, a miracle happened. I saw Aubree in Taryn. She has the same beauty, the same grace and natural charm. Oh, she's rough around the edges. I'll admit that. I wouldn't expect anything else being raised by Alex DeWitt. But she is her mother's daughter, and someday she'll fulfill the destiny that Aubree never got the chance to fulfill.''

So that was it, Naomi thought. He had plans for Taryn. He had her future all mapped out. She would carry on his family's tradition. She would do great things in his name. She would accomplish what he had never been able to do.

But in all his glorious scheming, he'd never once mentioned the word *love*.

No wonder Alex had taken his daughter to London, far away from Joseph Bellamy's twisted sense of family and destiny. Naomi felt that same protective instinct rise inside her, and she knew she would do anything to protect Taryn, to keep her from falling prey to this cruel man's manipulations.

Naomi's hands curled into fists at her sides. "I don't know how you found out about me," she said coldly. "But if you know my name, then you also know why I'm in New Orleans. Fifteen years ago, my baby was given to your daughter. I don't think she ever knew. I think she always believed that Taryn was hers. But the truth of the matter is, Taryn is *my* daughter, and nothing you say is going to change that."

The car had pulled alongside Naomi's Jeep, and Joseph Bellamy leaned forward to rap sharply on the divider. The man on the passenger side got out and opened the door. But before Naomi could slide out, Joseph Bellamy's hand closed around her wrist. His grip was surprisingly strong, his fingers like an icy vise against her skin.

"How much do you want?"

Naomi shuddered at his touch. "What?"

"You came here looking for money, so name your price."

"There isn't enough money in the world to keep me from my daughter." She tried to jerk her hand away, but his grasp only tightened.

"Taryn is all that I have left of Aubree. If you try to take that away from me, I will destroy you. That's not a threat, Miss Cross. It's a promise."

As Alex sat across the table from Taryn at dinner that night, he wondered again what had happened to his daughter. Who was this brooding, dark-eyed stranger who had stolen his daughter's sunny disposition, her natural optimism, her contentment in spending a few quiet hours with her old man?

She was growing up too damn fast, and changing so rapidly, both inside and out, that he couldn't keep up with her. Didn't want to, he had to admit. There were times lately when he would give just about anything to turn back the clock to the happier times he and Taryn had shared in London. Or even farther back than that, so that he could undo the time he'd missed with her.

But there was no going back, and even if they left New Orleans and returned to London, or someplace else, Alex didn't think anything would ever be the same again. Taryn was going through something he couldn't be a part of, and instinct told him it would be wise to give her some space. To be patient. But no matter what he did, he had an uneasy feeling that he was going to lose a part of her forever.

Their relationship was so fragile these days, the last thing he wanted to do was start a fight, Alex thought wearily. But he had parental responsibilities that couldn't be ignored.

He laid aside his knife and fork. The glazed pork roast Louise had prepared for dinner was tender and succulent, but he didn't have an appetite. Too much going on in his life, he supposed. Or perhaps it was something Foley had said to him earlier that had left him so unsettled.

"Ever given any thought to remarrying?"

No, Alex thought bitterly. One marriage was quite enough, thank you.

He picked up his wineglass. "So where were you today?" he asked Taryn.

She glanced up, immediately wary. Her dark-rimmed eyes narrowed on him, and Alex's first inclination was to stop the conversation right then and there and demand that she go upstairs to scrub her face. When he'd agreed to the makeup, he'd made it clear he was giving permission for only the lightest shades of lipstick and eye shadow. She was far too young, in his opinion, to wear black eyeliner and heavy coats of mascara, but if he'd learned anything in the past few months in dealing with a rebellious teenager, it was to pick his battles carefully. Wage them one at a time, and tonight he had a more pressing issue.

Taryn flung her dark hair over her shoulder. "I was at school. Where do you think I was?"

Alex sighed. "I'm talking about after school. Louise went to pick you up and you weren't there."

"I tried to call her," Taryn said defensively, "but she wasn't home so I left a message. Crystal invited me to go home with her so we could study for a Spanish test tomorrow. Her mother picked us up."

Alex took a careful sip of his wine. "So you just decided to go to Crystal's even though you knew Louise might be worried."

"I *said* I called."

"Yes, and when you couldn't reach Louise, you should have waited for her at school," Alex said sternly. "But you thought nothing of worrying her, let alone wasting her time, did you?"

Taryn gave an exasperated sigh. "I didn't think it was going to be such a big deal. She gets paid whether she picks me up or not."

"That's not the point." Very deliberately, Alex set his glass aside, trying to curb his irritation. "You know Louise worries when she doesn't know where you are. Just as I do."

"Here we go," Taryn muttered. "Pack your bags because we're going on a guilt trip."

"That attitude is not helping your cause," Alex warned her. He stared at her for a moment, but she refused to meet his gaze. "At any rate, you didn't go home with Crystal. I called her mother to check."

Something that might have been fear flickered across Taryn's face before it was replaced almost immediately by defiance. "So you're *spying* on me now?"

Alex glared at her. "It seems I have to. It's bad enough that you went off somewhere without seeing fit to tell us where you were going, or who you were going with. But I won't tolerate lying, Taryn."

"It's not a big deal!" she insisted. "I went shopping with a friend."

"What friend?"

She hesitated. "No one you know."

"Oh, that's just great."

Taryn rolled her eyes. "I'm fifteen years old, Dad, and it was broad daylight, for crying out loud. And besides that, his family lives only a few blocks over from here. They just moved in, and I was showing him around town. You know, being a good neighbor. Okay?"

"No, it's not okay." Alex tried to hang on to his temper, but it wasn't easy. His daughter had gone off with a boy. No way in hell was he ready for that. "Until I tell you otherwise, you'll wait after school for Louise to pick you up, and you'll come straight home with her. No TV, no phone calls, no Internet, and no friends over. You understand?"

A look of complete disbelief swept over her features. "What about this weekend? Grandfather invited me to

his house. He said he would call and talk to you about
it."

"Well, he didn't," Alex said, wincing at the thought
of Joseph Bellamy contacting Taryn behind his back.
"And I'm afraid you won't be going anywhere without
Louise or me for quite some time."

Taryn flung her napkin to the table as she scooted
back her chair. "That's not fair! You're just doing this
to keep me away from my grandfather! You hate him!
I know you do!"

"Taryn—"

"You hate him just like you hated my mother!"

Stunned, Alex stood and faced her. "That's enough,
young lady. I think you'd better go on up to your room
and think about all the trouble you're in. Then maybe
afterward, you'll decide to come down here and apol-
ogize to me for this outburst."

"Don't hold your breath," she lashed out at him.

Alex shrugged. "That's up to you."

They stared at each other for a long, stony moment
before Taryn's rigid expression finally wavered. "Why
are you doing this to me?" she asked in a tiny voice.

Alex's heart melted. He had to swallow past the sudden lump in his throat. "Believe it or not, I'm trying to
protect you, Taryn. I'm trying to do what's best for
you."

"Like you even care," she said sullenly.

"I do care and you know it."

"If you cared so much, why did you take me away
from New Orleans after my mother died? Why did you
take me away from the people who loved me?"

It was Taryn who was speaking, Taryn who glared
up at him angrily, but it was Joseph Bellamy's embit-
tered words Alex heard.

"If you cared about me, why weren't you around when I was little?" she taunted. "You weren't even there the night I was born, that's how much you cared. You didn't want me back then, so why pretend you do now?"

NAOMI SAT AT THE DESK in her hotel room. It had been hours since her confrontation with Joseph Bellamy, but she was still shaken by the cold hatred in the man's eyes, the threat she knew he had every intention of carrying out. *"If you try to take that away from me, I will destroy you."*

Naomi shuddered, knowing he meant every word, but if he thought he could frighten her away, he was dead wrong. If anything she was more determined than ever to prove that Taryn was her daughter. She didn't have Joseph Bellamy's power or Alex's money, but she could give Taryn something that no one else could—a mother's love. And she had so much love to give, Naomi thought.

Blinking back tears, she stared down at the last picture of Sadie that had been taken before she'd gone missing. In the days following her disappearance, that photograph had been printed on thousands of flyers that were distributed all over Jefferson County, and it had run in newspapers and on news broadcasts for days on end. That same picture had been blown up into posters and sent to law enforcement agencies and missing persons organizations all over the country.

As the years had gone by, Naomi had stared at the picture a million times, but never with more sadness than she had during these past several days when she'd first learned of the remains that had been uncovered in Grover County.

She'd called the sheriff's office in Eden an hour or so ago after arriving back at the hotel, but there was still no news. It could take several more days, or even weeks to complete all the tests, and even then, a positive identification might never be made, although with current technology, including DNA, that seemed less likely. But somewhere deep inside Naomi, she already knew the truth. After all these years, her daughter had finally been found.

With her fingertip, she traced the shape of Sadie's precious face, her eyes, her nose, her mouth, while in her mind, she could still hear that sweet little voice telling her goodbye on that fateful morning.

"Bye, Mama."

"Bye, bye, Sadie Belle. Have a good day, you hear?"

"I will." Then, as if she'd had a premonition, Sadie slid back across the front seat and threw her arms around Naomi's neck. "Love you, Mama."

"I love you, too, Sadie Belle. So, so much." Naomi had touched her fingertip to Sadie's dimple, and they'd both laughed before Sadie climbed out of the car and ran happily toward her teacher.

That was the last time Naomi had seen her daughter.

When she got to school that afternoon a few minutes late, no one could find Sadie. She'd disappeared while playing a game of hide-and-seek with the other children. At first, everyone thought she'd just hidden too well. But as the minutes crept by, and then the hours, the horrible truth had gripped them all. Sadie had been taken by a stranger.

What happened afterward was a haze. The hours of frantic searching. The countless interviews with police and the media. The fear, the nightmares, the endless, endless waiting.

And still Sadie hadn't come home.

For ten years, the waiting had gone on. For ten long years Naomi had existed in the awful purgatory of not knowing. Her life had been put on hold the day her daughter had disappeared, and for the past decade, Naomi's sole purpose for existing was to find her daughter.

But now she had a new purpose.

She touched her fingertip to the dimple at the corner of Sadie's mouth, then lifted the photograph to her lips. "I love you, Sadie Belle. So, so much. That's never going to change."

There would always be a hole in her heart where Sadie had been taken from her, a wound in her soul that would never heal. But she had another daughter to think about now. Another daughter who needed her.

Naomi hadn't been there ten years ago to protect Sadie from that terrible evil, and for that, she'd never forgiven herself. She hadn't been there when her daughter needed her the most, but she wouldn't make that same mistake twice.

Taryn was a girl in trouble. Naomi knew that without a doubt. And if it was the last thing she did, she would find a way to help her.

ALEX SAT ALONE in his study, briefcase open, a stack of contracts on his desk. He ignored the work, however, as he turned his chair and stared with a brooding frown out the window.

He wanted to go up and talk to Taryn, try to make things right between them, but he didn't know how. Everything he said lately was the wrong thing, and each confrontation drove her a little farther away from him.

He didn't understand what had happened. Except for those first few months following her mother's death,

Taryn had been a happy child. Then, when he'd been transferred back to New Orleans, everything had changed. Taryn had never been especially curious about her mother, but suddenly, in the past few months, Aubree had become this beautiful, mysterious entity who seemed bent on destroying the fragile relationship Alex had worked so hard to build with their daughter.

It wasn't Aubree's fault, of course, although sometimes Alex had the notion that if she could see them now, she'd be applauding her father's efforts to turn Taryn against him. No, if anyone was at fault for Taryn's current confusion, it was Alex. He had no one but himself to blame for the influence Joseph Bellamy had over her. It all came back to those first few years when Alex had been AWOL from his daughter's life.

He'd had a misguided sense of responsibility back then, and nothing he could do now would make up for those years. But he did love his daughter, more than anything in this world. He couldn't lose her now. He couldn't.

A soft knock on his door drew his attention, and he turned his chair, hoping against hope it might be Taryn. That she would come running to him the way she had when she was little and throw her arms around his neck. "I'm sorry, Daddy. I didn't mean to be bad. Please don't be mad at me."

As if he ever could be, when she'd looked up at him with those big brown eyes set in that solemn little face.

It seemed like forever since she'd called him Daddy.

"Come in," he called.

The door opened, and Louise Wheeler stuck her head around the door. She was an older woman, well into her fifties, with a tall, whip-thin body she carried ramrod straight, and a stern countenance that was rarely softened by a smile. She was not an especially easy person to be around, but she had her good points. She adored Taryn, and that was really all that mattered to Alex.

He remembered Aubree telling him once that Louise had had a difficult life before she'd come to live with the Bellamys. Her mother had died, her father had been in prison and she and her siblings had been left to the streets. She'd been in and out of trouble for years, and might have done some serious prison time herself if Joseph Bellamy hadn't seen something in her that no one else had.

He'd successfully defended her, pro bono, on a shoplifting charge, and then he'd taken her home, cleaned her up, given her a job and a place to live. She'd done odd jobs around the house at first, but then, after the first Mrs. Bellamy died, she'd become Aubree's nanny. The two were devoted to each other, and Louise was the only person Alex knew that Aubree had ever felt a smidgen of loyalty to. When they'd moved into the house in Metairie, a cramped bungalow barely big enough for the two of them, Aubree had insisted that Louise come to work for them.

"Are you crazy?" he'd asked her. "We can't afford a housekeeper on my salary."

"You don't expect me to leave her in that house with Gwen, do you? You know she can't stand Louise. She'll kick her out the moment my back's turned, and Louise has nowhere else to go. She's scared to death she'll end up back on the streets."

That hadn't happened, of course. Joseph had interceded on Aubree's behalf, as he always did, and Louise had remained safely ensconced in the mansion on River

Road until Aubree had left Metairie for the house off
St. Charles.

"Mr. DeWitt?" She said his name softly, calling him
gently out of his reverie. She held a manila envelope in
her hand. "This just came for you."

"This late?" Alex said in surprise.

"It came by messenger service." She walked across
the room and placed the envelope on his desk, hesitating
as if there was something else on her mind.

Alex glanced up. "Something bothering you, Louise?"

"I was wondering if I should take some dessert up
to Taryn."

"She had a chance to eat earlier."

Louise's thin lips almost disappeared in displeasure.
"As you wish." She turned to leave.

"Louise?"

"Yes?" She paused at door.

Alex sat back in his chair and regarded the woman
carefully. They seldom spoke of Aubree. It was the only
topic he knew of that could elicit even a flicker of emotion in the woman's stoic features. It was also a topic
upon which Alex knew they disagreed. Louise had
adored Aubree. Alex's feelings toward his wife had
been…much more complicated.

"Do you have any idea what Aubree was doing in
Eden, Mississippi, the night Taryn was born?"

She blinked, as if she couldn't comprehend his question.

"I know she was driving from New Orleans to Memphis," Alex explained. "I know she was supposedly
going to visit a friend of hers in Germantown. But why
did she leave so suddenly? Why did she decide to take
a road trip when she knew the baby could come at any

time? I've wondered about that for years. You were closer to her than anyone, Louise. Can you explain it?''

She opened her mouth, but at first nothing came out. Then she said in a hushed tone, ''I'm not one to repeat things I see and hear. Not in the house where I work.''

Alex nodded. ''I appreciate that. And I understand why you still feel a sense of loyalty to Aubree. She was good to you. She probably treated you better than she treated anyone in the world, other than Taryn.''

A look of pain flashed across Louise's stern features, and she glanced away.

''I'm not asking you to betray her memory,'' Alex persisted. ''I just want to know why she was in Eden, Mississippi, that night. It's…important.''

Louise's gaze came back to settle on him. She seemed calm now, in control of her emotions. ''I can't say why she was in Eden, but I can tell you why she left New Orleans. It was Mrs. Bellamy's doing.''

''Gwen?''

Louise nodded. ''They had a bad fight. I never heard such screaming. Mrs. Bellamy said she'd found out some terrible things about Aubree, and as soon as she told Mr. Bellamy, he'd see that she wasn't the angel he'd always thought her. Aubree couldn't stand the thought of her father turning against her. She had to get away because she couldn't face him. I tried to stop her, but you remember how she was when she set her mind to something.''

Alex remembered only too well. He also remembered the lingering animosity between Aubree and her stepmother. The two of them were always at each other's throats about something, but then, Aubree had inspired strong sentiments in a lot of people.

"Do you have any idea what Gwen was threatening her with?"

"No," Louise said coolly, in a voice that seemed to hint she wouldn't tell him if she did. "Will there be anything else?"

"No, that's all." But when Louise would have turned toward the door again, Alex once more called her back. "Go ahead and take Taryn up a piece of that red velvet cake you made for dinner. I know it's her favorite."

Louise nodded, but her expression never changed. "Are you sure I can't get you anything? More coffee?"

"No, I'm fine."

"I'll say good-night, then."

"Good night, Louise." After she'd left, Alex glanced down at the envelope on his desk, certain someone burning the midnight oil at Ventura had decided some matter of extreme urgency couldn't wait until morning. But there was no return address on the envelope, which was curious.

If it hadn't originated at Ventura, Alex couldn't imagine who would go to the trouble and expense to have a letter delivered to his home this time of night.

Suddenly he was filled with a terrible dread. Could these be legal papers served by the Bellamys? A summons to appear in court?

With grim resolve, he sliced open the flap with a letter opener and extracted the contents.

For the longest moment, he stared at the picture of the little girl, recognizing every feature, right down to the tiny dimple at the right corner of her mouth. The photograph was very much like the one of Taryn at five years old that he carried in his wallet. It could have *been* Taryn except for the caption at the bottom that asked the terrible question: Have you seen this child?

This was a picture of a child who had been missing for ten years. A little girl who looked enough like Taryn to be her identical twin. There were differences, of course, but the similarities were striking.

This was a picture of Sadie Cross, Naomi's long-lost daughter.

Chapter Seven

Like the lobby of the Spencer, the bathroom in Naomi's suite reminded her of another era, and after a long, tiring—not to mention traumatic—day, she was anxious to try out the huge claw-footed bathtub. Adding a generous dollop of lavender bath oil supplied, along with a host of other toiletries, by the hotel, she tested the water with her toe. She was just getting ready to climb in when the phone rang. Turning off the taps, she went out into the bedroom to answer it.

"This is Alex DeWitt," the deep voice informed her.

Naomi immediately drew the fluffy white bathrobe more tightly around her. "I...wasn't expecting to hear from you so soon."

He paused for such a long time that Naomi wondered if he'd hung up on her. Then he said in a toneless voice, "We need to talk."

Naomi clutched the lapels of her bathrobe. "When? Where?"

"As soon as possible. Tonight."

She glanced around nervously. Not here in her suite, she thought. As it was, his powerful presence from the night before seemed to linger in the sitting room, on the balcony. The first thing on Naomi's mind when she'd awakened that morning was the way he'd looked at her before he left. The darkness of his eyes. The way his voice seemed to vibrate with warning.

She closed her eyes for a moment, trying to think. "There's a small restaurant across the street from my hotel. I don't remember the name, but it's never very crowded."

"I'll find it. I'll meet you there in twenty minutes."

After hanging up, Naomi went into the bathroom and pulled the plug on her bathwater. She barely had time for a quick shower, but she wasn't about to show up for her meeting with Alex DeWitt looking bedraggled and at her worst. She stood under the shower for several long minutes, letting the hot water brace her, and then, after she climbed out, she even took the time to dry her short hair and apply a little makeup. By the time she'd dressed in jeans, sandals and a cotton shirt, Naomi felt a little better. After all, what did she have to fear from Alex DeWitt? He was the one who had her child. He was the one who should be afraid of her!

Still, as she walked the short distance to the restaurant, Naomi knew her courage was false, and that she was badly deluding herself if she didn't admit that Alex still had the upper hand. Without a DNA test, she couldn't prove Taryn was her daughter, and without evidence that her baby had been stolen from the hospital fifteen years ago, she would have a hard time convincing a judge to compel such a test.

But Taryn *was* her daughter. Naomi never doubted that for a moment. If anything, her encounter with Joseph Bellamy this afternoon had convinced her even more. A man in his position didn't make threats unless he was worried.

Had he been the one who'd convinced Willa Banks

to take Naomi's baby? Had he been so concerned about creating a Bellamy dynasty that he'd been willing to steal another woman's child? Or had his motive been less selfish than that? Had he wanted to save his daughter the heartbreak and grief of losing her baby?

Of course, there was no proof that Joseph Bellamy had even been in Eden that night. Just like there was no real proof that Naomi's baby had been stolen. But she knew the truth, just the same.

Alex was waiting for her when she arrived at the restaurant. He'd been pacing up and down the sidewalk in front, but the moment he spotted her, he stopped, his dark gaze marking her progress as she approached him.

"Thanks for agreeing to meet me," he said.

She nodded. "We have a lot to discuss."

Anger flickered in his eyes and he opened his mouth as if to deny her claim, but instead, he tore his gaze away, scanning the street for a moment before he said, "Let's go inside and get a table. I could use a drink."

He asked the hostess to seat them on the patio, a tiny, shadowy area protected from the street by weathered brick walls. A fountain trickled somewhere nearby, and the air smelled lush and heavy with jasmine. The garden was a tiny, lovely oasis, one of dozens of such hidden places in the Quarter.

Even though the night was warm and balmy, only one other couple occupied the terrace, but they were engrossed in each other, taking no notice as Alex and Naomi were seated at a candlelit table nearby.

A waiter hovered, anxious to take their drink orders. Naomi's hair stirred in a mild breeze, and she carelessly shoved it behind her ears. "I'll have an iced tea," she told the waiter.

"Bourbon," Alex said. After the waiter left, he

leaned slightly toward Naomi, his dark eyes intense in the candlelight. "Why did you send me that picture?"

"Because I didn't know how else to convince you. I don't know what Taryn looked like at five years old, but I'm willing to bet she resembled the picture I sent you a great deal."

His expression hardened, but he waited until their drinks were placed on the table before he spoke again. "What is it you expect to come of all this, Naomi?"

It was the first time he'd used her first name, and a thrill shot through her. The way he said it, with the flicker of candlelight reflected in his eyes...

Under other circumstances, the tiny garden, the candlelight, the cozy table, could have been a very romantic setting. But these were not ordinary circumstances, and Alex DeWitt was certainly no ordinary man. He was the legal father of the child Naomi had given birth to. He was a man whose past seemed to linger in the shadowy depths of his eyes, in the stubborn set of his mouth and chin. He was a man who, some thought, might have killed his wife, and whether he had or not, the question remained as to why people who knew him had been willing to believe him capable of murder.

Naomi shuddered as the breeze picked up. "I told you last night. I want a DNA test."

"And then?"

She frowned. When she said nothing, he leaned toward her, the candlelight dancing wildly in his eyes. "What then, Naomi? You said you had no intention of trying to take my daughter away from me, but what if the DNA test proves you gave birth to her? Do you really think you could just walk away from her?"

"You asked me that last night."

"And you didn't answer. Tell me now. If you were

to learn, without a doubt, that you gave birth to Taryn, could you walk away from her?''

Naomi closed her eyes briefly. "No," she whispered. "I couldn't."

Alex sat back in his chair, his gaze dark and brooding. "I thought not. So we're back to my original question. What is it you want from me?"

"I don't know," she said almost angrily. "I don't have all the answers. All I know is that I had to come here. I had to find her. After that—"

"You could destroy her," he said with devastating simplicity.

"Taryn is all that I have left of Aubree. If you try to take that away from me, I will destroy you."

The memory sent a shiver coursing through Naomi. "I would never hurt her. You have to know that."

"Not on purpose. I believe that." Alex paused, taking a long sip of his drink.

It might have been her imagination, but Naomi thought his hand trembled slightly in the candlelight.

"Taryn's at a difficult stage in her life. She's had a hard time adjusting to being back in the States, back in New Orleans. Her grandfather—"

He broke off, his voice turning bitter, and Naomi glanced up quickly. "What about her grandfather?"

A mask came over his expression, as if to hide his true feelings. "He's exerting an influence over Taryn that I'm not convinced is healthy."

"But she is her mother's daughter, and someday she'll fulfill the destiny that Aubree never got the chance to fulfill." Naomi's frown deepened. "What kind of influence?"

Alex took another long drink of his bourbon, as if he needed to fortify his resolve. "Taryn's mother and I were estranged when she died. I worked overseas when Taryn was young, and she didn't really know me when I came back to New Orleans. She was traumatized after Aubree's death, and I was very worried about her when I took her back to London with me. But with the help of a very good child therapist, she got through the worst of it, and her nightmares gradually faded. We were eventually able to forge a strong bond, but it took a long time and a lot of work. I don't think it would have been possible at all if we'd stayed here. Joseph Bellamy wanted to raise her himself. For numerous reasons, I wasn't about to let that happen."

Thank goodness, Naomi thought. She couldn't imagine a more miserable childhood than to be burdened by the zealous expectations of an overbearing father. Or in Taryn's case, grandfather. She couldn't imagine a worse role model than Joseph Bellamy.

A chill slipped over her as their gazes met. For a moment, it seemed as if they were perfectly attuned to each other's thoughts and that, in this one instance, they shared a common goal—to protect Taryn from Joseph Bellamy's ambition.

"Those years in London were the happiest of my life, and I think, for the most part, Taryn was happy as well. But then I was transferred back to New Orleans, and everything changed."

"Her grandfather still wants her."

Alex's gaze on her narrowed suspiciously. "How did you know that?"

Naomi hesitated. "Because I met Joseph Bellamy this afternoon."

His shocked gaze met hers over the candle flame. "What? Where?"

Naomi hesitated again, not certain she wanted to admit to Alex that she'd been waiting outside Taryn's school to catch a glimpse of her. She shrugged. "I think he might have been following me. I have no idea how he even knew about me, but he...well, let's just say, he forced a meeting."

"What's that supposed to mean?"

Naomi shrugged. "It doesn't matter."

Alex leaned toward her over the table. "Did he hurt you?"

The undercurrent of violence in his voice took Naomi by surprise. "N-no."

"What did he want?"

"He wanted to warn me not to get between Taryn and her destiny."

"He said that?" A muscle in his jaw started to throb. "What else did he say?"

"He gave me a Bellamy family history lesson. He said that Aubree was destined for great things, and now that she's dead, it's up to Taryn to carry on the dynasty."

Alex swore. "I was afraid of something like this. I let her see him when we first moved back to New Orleans, even though I knew it was a mistake. He started filling her head with lies about the past, building Aubree up into this saintly image while he tried to tear me down in my own daughter's eyes. That's why Taryn is so fascinated by Aubree all of sudden. It's *his* doing."

"I suppose it's only natural that he would want her to remember her mother in a favorable light," Naomi said.

"Aubree had no favorable light."

Naomi was shocked by the bitterness in his voice. He must have realized how he'd come across, because he said in a conciliatory tone, "That wasn't fair. Aubree had her good points. She was beautiful and brilliant and she could be charming when the mood struck her. And she was a good mother. It's just that…'' He ran a hand through his dark hair. ''There was so much bitterness toward the last, it's hard to remember that there was once love between us.''

''I understand,'' Naomi murmured. She felt a twinge of something in her stomach that, if she hadn't known better, she might have thought was jealousy. *She was beautiful and brilliant…*

''I know Joseph has been phoning Taryn behind my back. I think she's even been sneaking off to see him. He's poisoning her mind against me, but if I try to keep her from him, I come off looking like the bad guy.'' He drew a long, weary breath. ''Joseph is planning something. I know that. I'm afraid Taryn is going to be caught in the middle of something very ugly. And now here you are, trying to claim a piece of my daughter, too.''

His words sent a dagger through Naomi's heart. ''I don't want to hurt Taryn.''

''So you keep saying,'' he said in frustration. ''But how do you think she'll feel if she learns that Aubree wasn't her birth mother—''

Naomi cut him off. ''You believe me,'' she said almost in wonder.

Alex, who had been lifting his drink, froze. ''I beg your pardon.''

''You believe me,'' she repeated. ''That's why you're so worried. That's why you're telling me all this. Down deep inside, you know Taryn is my daughter.''

Emotions, dark and primal, flashed across his features before he got himself under control. But there was still something in his eyes, something he couldn't quite subdue. "Taryn is *my* daughter. I will never believe anything to the contrary."

"Then why not agree to the DNA test? If you're so certain, what could it hurt?"

Angrily he waved off the waiter who had come to take dinner orders. "Haven't you heard anything I've said? What I've been trying to do is make you realize how vulnerable my daughter is right now. She doesn't need any more upheaval in her life. A DNA test is out of the question."

Now it was Naomi who leaned across the table toward him. "Please." Her hand reached out and closed over his on the table. For a moment, the feel of his skin against hers sent a thrill of awareness racing through her nervous system. But then he pulled his hand away, his gaze icy.

"You're asking too much of me," he said in a low, harsh tone.

Naomi sat back. "Think of it from my perspective. I didn't give my daughter up for adoption. I didn't abandon her. She was taken from me. Stolen from me. All these years I thought she was dead, and now to find out that she's alive, to know that I can see her, touch her, hold her in my arms..." She paused as emotions threatened to overcome her. "I know I'm asking a lot. But it's only because I've lost so much. This...hope is all I have left. *She's* all I have left."

For a moment, she thought, prayed, she'd gotten through to him, but then his mouth hardened as he glanced away from her. "I'm not without sympathy. Believe me, I'm not. And, yes, I can see your point. But think of this from Taryn's perspective. Would you take her away from the only family she's ever known? Would you do that to her?" When Naomi made a tiny sound of protest, his gaze swung back to hers. "That's what you're proposing, isn't it? That she give up everything for you?"

Naomi put trembling fingers to her lips. "You make it sound so selfish."

His expression seemed to momentarily soften. "I don't think you're selfish. Far from it. I just don't think you've taken the time to consider the whole picture." He paused, then said reluctantly, "What if I let you see her?"

Naomi's heart quickened with hope. "What do you mean?"

He looked as if he was already regretting his hasty offer. He frowned down into his drink. "I can arrange a meeting. A dinner. You can spend some time with her, satisfy yourself that she's a normal, healthy, teenage girl who's being well taken care of. Who has a father who loves her very much. Would that be enough?"

No, Naomi thought. It wasn't enough. Not nearly enough. But it was a start. And she would be able to see her daughter. Talk to her. A week ago, she would not have thought that possible.

Her throat ached with emotion, and she nodded. "I'd like that."

He drew a breath. "All right. I'll set something up for tomorrow night, on one condition. You have to give me your word that you won't say anything to Taryn. If you let something slip, even by mistake, she would be devastated."

"You must know I wouldn't do that," Naomi said, "or else you would never have agreed to let me see her."

WHAT THE HELL had he been thinking? Alex wondered the next evening as he drove toward the French Quarter. Why on earth had he ever agreed to let his daughter within a hundred yards of Naomi Cross? He had only her word that she wouldn't blurt something out to Taryn, and just because he'd trusted her last night to keep her promise didn't mean that he should have. Or that she would. He'd regretted his decision all day, but it was too late now to change his mind. If he backed out, there was no telling what Naomi might do.

And as for Taryn, her attitude did not bode well for a pleasant evening.

He glanced at her as she sat with a sullen frown, staring out the window. She hadn't wanted to come tonight, and when he'd finally put his foot down, she'd stomped off to her room to change, only to reemerge a few minutes later, defiant in low-cut jeans and a cropped shirt that not only revealed her bare, tanned midriff, but a belly-button ring Alex had known nothing about. He'd just about hit the roof over that one.

He'd ranted and raved and promised dire consequences to follow, but by then, they'd been running so late, all he could make her do was throw a jacket over her getup and hope for the best. As for her makeup—

Don't even get me started on that, Alex grumbled to himself.

He was badly losing control here, he thought as he found a rare parking place on the street and slid into it. Maybe Foley hadn't been so far off base the day before. Maybe Alex should have remarried a long time ago. Maybe a woman's influence was exactly what Taryn needed right now. She had Louise, of course, but the dour housekeeper was no substitute for a mother.

And if Aubree had lived? That was easy, Alex

thought grimly. He would have had absolutely *no* control over Taryn's life whatever. Joseph would have seen to that.

He glanced at her again, and in spite of their earlier blowup, a wave of tenderness rolled over him. She wanted so badly to grow up, to be independent, and he wanted just as fiercely to keep her a child. He didn't want to lose her. Not to Joseph Bellamy, not to Naomi, not to some young man who would one day steal her heart. He loved her, belly-button ring and all, and there was nothing she could do to ever change that.

Silently they got out of the car and walked down Decatur, toward Jackson Square. The streets, as always, were alive with people heading to the French Market or one of the dozens of restaurants in the area. As they walked along, Alex didn't much care for the looks Taryn received, the occasional catcalls that came her way, but she seemed to enjoy the attention, tossing her head so that her dark hair flowed over her shoulders. It was a practiced move, and one, to Alex's way of thinking, far too mature for a fifteen-year-old.

He had the urge to whisk her home, lock her in her room and not let her out until she turned twenty-one. Or thirty-five. But like it or not, his little girl was growing up and she was, to his chagrin, quite a knockout.

Naomi was already seated when they arrived at the restaurant, and she rose to greet them as they entered. Her gaze flickered over Alex in brief acknowledgment, then moved to Taryn and lingered. When she looked at Taryn, the expression on Naomi's face almost took Alex's breath away. It was as if someone had turned on a light somewhere inside her. She looked positively radiant.

He tore his gaze from Naomi and glanced around.

The attention Taryn had gotten on the street was nothing compared to the unsolicited admiration that came Naomi's way. Heads turned—literally—and although the clientele was much too refined for catcalls, Alex knew what every man in the place was thinking. *If only I had a woman like that waiting for me.*

She wore a simple black dress, unadorned and devastating on her tall, graceful frame. Her short dark hair had been combed until it gleamed in the restaurant's subtle lighting, and her brown eyes had been made up just enough to look intriguing, her lips just enough to look...kissable.

She was without a doubt the most gorgeous woman Alex had ever seen in his life. And she seemed completely unaffected by it, which only added to her appeal, her charm, and to the faintly resentful stares she received from women who were seated nearby.

Next to him, he saw Taryn stiffen slightly, as if, even at fifteen, she was already wary of competition. A frown flitted across her brow as she stared at Naomi, but then she tossed her head, flinging her hair, and allowed Alex to lead her to the table.

As they approached, Naomi seemed to melt back into her seat, as if her legs would no longer hold her. "Hello," she said in a soft, breathless voice that did unexpected things to Alex's insides.

He braced himself, his hand still on his daughter's elbow. "Hello," he said. "Naomi Cross, I'd like you to meet my daughter, Taryn."

Naomi put out her hand to Taryn and, after only a slight hesitation, Taryn accepted it. But then almost at once she drew her hand back and sat down. A waiter instantly appeared to take their drink orders.

"I'll have a bourbon," Taryn announced.

"Make that a Coke," Alex said dryly. "Naomi?"

"A Coke sounds good to me, too."

"I'll take the bourbon," he said to the waiter.

"Well," Naomi said nervously, glancing at Taryn. She didn't seem to know what to do with her hands. Finally she clasped them in her lap, but Alex noticed that they were trembling. This was not going to be an easy night for any of them. "You must be what, a sophomore in school, Taryn?"

When Taryn merely shrugged, Alex said, "She goes to St. Anne's Academy."

Something flickered in Naomi's eyes, but she smiled. "How do you like it there?"

"I hate it. It's an all-girl school." Taryn shot Alex a bitter look. "His idea, not mine."

"It's an excellent school," Alex said. "We were lucky to get her in. The waiting list is pretty formidable."

Taryn rolled her eyes, reaching for the bread the waiter had placed on the table. Rather than eating it, however, she plucked little pieces from the crust and left them on her bread plate.

"What's your favorite subject?" Naomi asked, obviously grasping for a connection. Alex almost felt sorry for her.

"Science, I guess," Taryn mumbled with a shrug.

Naomi brightened. "Really? I always loved science, too. In fact, there was a time when I wanted to be a doctor."

Alex felt something tighten inside him. Until recently, Taryn had always talked of being a doctor, too. Coincidence or genes that she and Naomi shared a common interest?

"So why didn't you? Become a doctor, I mean," Taryn asked reluctantly.

Naomi seemed at a loss for a moment. She shrugged her thin shoulders. "Things happened. My plans had to change. I never even went to college," she said with deep regret.

She'd gotten pregnant, Alex thought.

"Where do you plan to go to college?" Naomi was asking Taryn. "Or is it still too early to think about that?"

"I'm hoping she'll consider Tulane," Alex said.

"I'm not going to Tulane," Taryn announced flatly. "I may not go to college at all."

Alex fought back his irritation. There'd never been any question of her going to college. They'd talked about it for years, and she'd always been just as enthusiastic as he. He knew she was deliberately trying to goad him tonight, and he wasn't going to rise to her bait. "We'll discuss that later," he said. "Maybe Miss Cross would enjoy hearing about your hobby."

"Oh, I would." Naomi trained an expectant gaze on Taryn. "What kind of hobby do you have?"

"I raise butterflies."

Taryn's hobby usually elicited a host of delighted responses, but instead of exclaiming about the charm and novelty of such a pastime, Naomi didn't say a word as her face went almost completely white. She looked as if she'd just been given some devastating news, a piece of information she didn't quite know what to make of.

She lifted her hand, to do what, Alex had no idea, and her fingers bumped against her water glass. The glass tipped, but Alex's hand shot out to right it before more than a drop or two of water spilled. Naomi seemed hardly to notice.

She shoved back her chair and stood. "I...would you excuse me for a moment?"

Alex half stood, too, and nodded. "Of course. Are you all right?"

But Naomi turned and fled without a word. He watched her hurry toward the back of the restaurant, say something to a waitress, then moments later, disappear down a hallway that he presumed led to the ladies' room.

"Well," Taryn said beside him. "I guess she doesn't like butterflies."

"I guess not," Alex murmured, his gaze never leaving the spot where he'd last seen Naomi Cross.

Chapter Eight

Naomi barely noticed her elegant surroundings—the black marble sinks and floor, the gold and aqua wallpaper, the pale pink lighting. She sat down on a black-and-aqua striped stool and stared at herself in the mirror. But it wasn't her pale reflection she saw staring back. Her mind had gone backward in time, to a summer afternoon in her own backyard.

"Look, Mama! They came back!" Sadie called excitedly. "Just like you said they would."

Naomi smiled as she watched the orange-and-black Monarchs cluster around the butterfly bush she and Sadie had planted earlier that spring. "They always come back," she told her daughter. "Just like magic."

One landed in the palm of Sadie's hand, and her expression looked positively enraptured. "Aren't they beautiful, Mama?"

The memory faded away, and Naomi was left staring at her own reflection in the mirror. She blinked, barely recognizing the drawn, tense face, the shadowed eyes. Somehow, she'd expected to see herself the way she'd been that day with Sadie—young, carefree, happy. But ten years had passed since that day, a decade of pain that was now etched in Naomi's face. She closed her eyes.

The door opened and Taryn stepped through. "My dad sent me in here to make sure you're okay. Are you sick?" Her voice sounded more wary than concerned.

Naomi managed a weak smile. Her hands were trembling so she clasped them in her lap. "No, I'm okay. I just felt a little light-headed."

"Yeah," Taryn said dryly. "My dad seems to have that effect on some people." She walked over to the vanity and sat down on a stool beside Naomi.

Naomi's heart started to pound. She was so close to her daughter. So very close...

"You've noticed it, haven't you?" Taryn's gaze met hers in the mirror. "The way women stare at him, I mean?" She paused. "What's going on between the two of you?"

"Nothing...we're just...acquaintances."

"You're more than that," Taryn insisted. "He wouldn't have dragged me out to dinner to meet you if he didn't have a thing for you. And he sure wouldn't be sitting out there worrying about you."

Naomi's chest tightened and her stomach fluttered uncomfortably. The conversation had badly unnerved her. She didn't know what to say.

"Well," Taryn said, rising from her stool. "I've done my duty. You seem to be okay so I'm going to go back out there and give him a report."

Without thinking, Naomi caught her arm. "Don't go yet."

Taryn looked at her strangely. "Why not?"

"Because I'm enjoying talking to you," Naomi said truthfully, although she realized to Taryn her answer must sound lame.

Taryn frowned, but she grudgingly sat back down. Their gazes met again in the mirror. "Have we met somewhere before?"

Naomi's heart thudded against her chest. Had Taryn seen her at the school yesterday afternoon? Or through the tinted window of her grandfather's car? Or was she experiencing something else, a bond she wasn't even aware of?

Naomi swallowed. "I don't think we've ever met. I'm not from New Orleans."

"Then what are you doing here?"

"I like to come here every chance I get. I love this city."

"Yeah, it's pretty cool," Taryn agreed. "My mother's family has lived here for generations. My mother was even a Mardi Gras queen or princess or something when she was not much older than me. She got to wear a real diamond tiara and ride on one of those huge floats."

Naomi's throat tightened when Taryn spoke of her mother. "She must have looked very beautiful."

"I guess, but I don't really remember her." Taryn became absorbed in her reflection all of a sudden, as if she could conjure Aubree's image in the mirror. After a moment she said in a strange, subdued tone, "Have you ever had anything terrible happen to you? Something really tragic?"

Naomi was taken aback by the question. "I lost two children, one at birth and one ten years ago. My daughter, Sadie, disappeared without a trace from a school playground. I never knew what happened to her."

Something that might have been pity flickered in Taryn's brown eyes. "My mother died ten years ago. I guess we have something in common."

Naomi's heart gave a funny little twist as she stared at her daughter. "Yes, I guess we do."

Taryn turned to face Naomi on the stool, her gaze very direct. "Do you want to know why I can't remember my mother?"

Naomi wasn't sure that she did. "You were very young when she died."

Taryn shook her head. Her eyes were dark and piercing, very dramatic behind the layers of liner and mascara. "I've always been told that I was away with my nanny when my mother was killed, but I don't believe it. I think I was in the house that night. I think I saw the murderer, and I think it was someone I knew. That's why I blocked all those memories."

Naomi gasped slightly. Her hand reached out automatically to grasp Taryn's wrist. Surprisingly enough, the girl didn't pull away. "You shouldn't be telling me this."

The dark eyebrows lifted in surprise. "Why not?"

"You shouldn't be telling *anyone* this," Naomi said urgently.

Comprehension flickered across Taryn's face. Her gaze, if possible, darkened even more. "Because he's still out there, you mean. The killer."

Naomi said nothing, but her mouth went dry with fear. Could it be true? Could the identity of Aubree DeWitt's killer reside somewhere deep in Taryn's subconscious?

If so, she could be in terrible danger.

"Promise me you won't say anything about this to anyone else," Naomi whispered.

That seemed to snap Taryn's trance, and she pulled her hand away from Naomi's grasp, her brown gaze growing cold and resentful. "I'm not going to make you that promise."

"Taryn, please…"

"I don't even know you," she snapped. "And besides, I've got someone helping me."

"Helping you do what?"

Taryn turned back to gaze into the mirror. "I'm going to find out who killed my mother, no matter what I have to do."

BOTH NAOMI AND TARYN WERE subdued, their expressions taut, when they returned from the ladies' room. Something had happened, Alex decided, watching the almost identical expressions on their faces. Words had been exchanged, but neither of them showed any inclination toward enlightening him. They merely lapsed into silence, and the meal progressed at an agonizingly slow pace. He was relieved when Taryn and Naomi both declined dessert, and after paying the check, all three left the restaurant to linger in another uncomfortable silence on the street.

Alex glanced around. "Taryn and I can give you a lift back to your hotel."

"No, that's okay," Naomi said hastily, as if she, too, were anxious to part ways. "Thanks, but it's still early and it isn't that far."

"It'll only take us a minute—"

"No, really," she cut in. "I like to walk."

The French Quarter wasn't a place for a woman to go wandering about alone, but Alex could hardly force her to accept a ride. It *was* early, and the streets were crowded. As long as she stayed to the main areas, she'd be okay.

She headed up St. Ann, and he and Taryn continued

down Decatur to where he'd left his car. But after he'd pulled away, he kept worrying about Naomi, so much so that he very nearly turned the car around and headed back.

But that would have been a mistake. Whatever had happened between her and Taryn had obviously been distressing to both of them, and that could work to his advantage. Maybe Naomi would become disillusioned. Maybe she'd come to the conclusion that Taryn wasn't her daughter after all. Or, at the very least, that it would be too damaging to Taryn's psyche to make such a claim.

Sensing his gaze on her, Taryn turned briefly, scowled, then went back to staring out the window.

"So what did you think?" Alex asked carefully.

"About what?"

He sighed. "I don't know, Taryn. About dinner? About the weather? About Naomi Cross? I'm just trying to make conversation here."

Taryn shrugged. "Dinner was lame. The weather is hot and humid, and Naomi Cross is really weird."

"Weird?" That wouldn't have been the adjective he would have used to describe Naomi. But then, he had a feeling she tapped into very different emotions for him than she did for Taryn. "In what way?"

"I don't know, just weird. Where did you meet her anyway?"

Alex paused. "We have a mutual acquaintance." Technically not a lie, if you considered Taryn.

She gave him a sidelong stare. "Uncle Foley, right?"

Alex shot her a surprised look. "Why would you think that?"

"Because I can see them going for each other. She's

gorgeous, and Uncle Foley's really hot. Haven't you ever noticed?''

Alex scowled at the road. ''No, I can't say as I have.''

''Well, he is.'' Taryn let her head fall back against the seat and sighed. ''Too bad he's so much older than me.''

''Old enough to be your father,'' Alex pointed out.

''I know, he's ancient,'' she agreed, yawning. ''But you have to admit, Naomi is definitely his type.''

Alex wasn't about to admit any such thing. Naomi was not at all Foley's type, and the thought of them together irritated him a great deal more than it should have.

After a few moments of silence, in which Alex tried to dispel the image of Foley Boudrieux and Naomi Cross that Taryn had injected into his conscious, she said, ''Maybe I should warn you about something, Dad.''

''What?'' he asked, more crossly than he meant to.

''I have a science test tomorrow,'' she said in a rush. ''And I didn't get a chance to study before we left. So if my grade goes south this semester, don't blame me, okay? You're the one who dragged me out to dinner on a school night.''

Her grades had been going south ever since they'd moved back to New Orleans, and she'd once been a straight A student. Not for the first time, Alex wondered if he'd done the right thing in bringing her back here. She'd never been so outspoken before, never dressed so outrageously. He was afraid she'd fallen in with a bad crowd, and he wasn't sure he knew how to put a stop to it, how to get his daughter back.

"You need to keep your grades up if you're going to get into a decent college," he said sternly.

"I'm *not* going to Tulane." She folded her arms over her chest in defiance.

"Tulane happens to have an excellent premed school."

"I don't care. I don't think I want to be a doctor anymore."

"Why not?"

She turned to stare out the window. "I've been thinking I might want to go to law school instead."

That was her grandfather talking, Alex thought as a wave of anger washed over him. Joseph Bellamy had always wanted Aubree to follow in his footsteps, and when she'd dropped out of law school to get married, he'd never forgiven Alex. After Taryn was born, he'd turned his ambition on her, but in London, all Taryn had talked about was being a doctor. Now that had changed. So many things about his daughter had changed.

Alex sighed wearily as he pulled into their driveway and parked. He and Taryn didn't say another word as they let themselves in the front door, and Taryn climbed the stairs to her room.

"Taryn," he called, when she'd almost reached the top.

She stopped and glanced down at him.

"Good night, honey."

"Good night, Dad." Then, as if an afterthought, she added, "Dinner was...interesting."

He grinned. "Yeah," he said. "It was at that, wasn't it?"

THE STREETS WERE STILL CROWDED as Naomi walked back to her hotel, and even a lot of the souvenir shops remained open, selling everything from Mardi Gras masks to visors with plastic crawfish attached. Her hotel was only a short distance away, and as she neared Royal Street, she suddenly remembered the feeling two nights ago of being followed. The back of her neck prickled in fear, but tonight she wasn't afraid for herself. She was afraid for Taryn. What if she really had seen her mother's killer?

A chill swept over Naomi. Aubree DeWitt had been murdered ten years ago. Her killer was never found. *Was* he still out there somewhere? Was he someone close to Aubree's family, someone who would know if Taryn started asking the wrong questions?

Naomi didn't like this. Not one bit. She'd come to New Orleans to find her daughter, to make sure she was being taken care of. She'd been afraid that Taryn might need her. At worst, that she might be neglected. But Naomi had never once considered that ten years later, Aubree DeWitt's killer might pose a threat to Taryn.

Alex had asked her last night what her plans were concerning Taryn. If a DNA test proved that Taryn was her daughter, would she be able to walk away? The answer to his question was more clear to Naomi now than it had ever been. She would never leave New Orleans knowing her daughter could be in danger.

The phone was ringing when Naomi let herself into her hotel room. She didn't bother turning on a light. The drapes were open, and moonlight flooded through the sheer curtains into the room. She moved to the phone, and just as she reached out to pick it up, she froze.

Something was different in the room.

A subtle change…

She glanced around, her heart thudding, her breath catching in her throat. Then she realized what was wrong. The room was warm and humid, and at first, Naomi thought the maid must have shut off the air conditioner when she'd come in to turn down the bed. But a faint hum indicated the unit was working. So why was the room so warm?

Naomi's gaze lit on the French door that opened onto the balcony. It was ajar, letting in the hot night air. Had she left it open earlier?

Her throat tightened with fear. What if someone had been in her room while she was out?

Her gaze darted to the bedroom. An intruder could be hiding anywhere. In the closet, under the bed, behind the shower curtain in the bathroom.

Run! a voice inside her screamed, but Naomi forced herself to stay calm. Instinct told her that she was alone in the room, and common sense told her that she'd probably left the door open herself.

A humid breeze blew in, riffling the papers on the cherry-wood desk. Naomi knelt, picking up a picture of Sadie that had fallen to the floor.

Setting the picture aside, she moved to the French door, peering out onto the balcony before she stepped outside. Then she glanced over the edge. She was five stories up, but it was possible, she supposed, for someone to scale the wall to her balcony. Her room overlooked the street, however, so a prowler would be exposed to any passersby while climbing up to her room.

Could someone have entered her suite through the front door, and then left by way of the balcony when he heard her come in? Naomi knew that she hadn't been so careless as to leave the door to the hallway unlocked, but she also knew that even a petty thief could be inside a locked hotel room in a matter of seconds.

This is ridiculous, she told herself sternly. She was letting her imagination run away with her, just as she had the other night when she'd thought someone was following her.

Shivering, Naomi walked back inside the room and closed the door. But when she tried to lock the door, the latch seemed to catch on something. That must have been what happened, Naomi thought in relief. She had closed the door earlier, but the lock hadn't caught and the breeze had blown it ajar.

As if to prove her point, the door edged open in the breeze, and the picture of Sadie lifted off the desk and fell to the floor once again. It almost seemed symbolic somehow, Naomi thought with a shiver.

The phone had stopped ringing some time ago, but now it started again, and the strident sound caused Naomi to jump. She hesitated for a moment before walking over to the desk and lifting the receiver to her ear.

"Naomi? Are you there?"

"Yes, I'm here," she said breathlessly, recognizing Alex's deep voice.

"Are you okay? Why didn't you say anything?"

"I'm sorry. I...just got in."

"Are you sure you're okay?" he insisted. "You sound...strange."

Her gaze fell on Sadie's picture, and she clutched the receiver tighter. "I'm fine."

There was a slight hesitation, then Alex said in an odd voice, "I need to see you."

The urgency in his tone made Naomi's blood go cold. "Is it Taryn? Has something happened—"

"Taryn's fine," he cut in. "She's home, hopefully in bed. I need to talk to you."

"Tonight?"

"Yes. I'm five minutes from your hotel."

Her gaze darted to the French door. Was it possible...?

No, it couldn't be. He'd had Taryn with him when they'd left the restaurant. He wouldn't have had time to take her home and then drive back here, break into her hotel room and leave—all in the time it took her to walk back here. It wasn't possible, and she wanted to believe he wasn't capable. But the truth was, she had no idea what Alex might do if he felt desperate. Or threatened.

Naomi said nervously, "It's late, and I'm really tired."

"This won't take long." Another pause. "It's important."

His voice was edged with an undercurrent that bothered Naomi, but she found herself agreeing to meet him in spite of her reservations. "All right," she said with a sigh. "I'll meet you downstairs."

Naomi hung up, uneasiness gripping her again. Why did Alex want to see her so urgently? To get her out of her hotel room so that someone else could come back in and finish what they'd started earlier?

She had nothing of value in the suite, and she'd been up-front with Alex about everything. If he'd hired someone to break into her room, then he was wasting his time and money.

What about Joseph Bellamy?

Possible, Naomi conceded, but his actions yesterday afternoon led her to believe that he was more inclined to the direct approach. But just to be on the safe side, Naomi carried a chair over to the French door and propped it beneath the handle. Not exactly a fail-safe maneuver, but hopefully it would do until she could get someone up here tomorrow to fix the lock.

Before she left the room, Naomi took a moment to change out of the dress and heels she'd worn at dinner to black slacks, sandals and a soft pink top. Clothes that were not only more comfortable, but easier to run in, she thought wryly.

Like the night before, Alex was already on the street, waiting for her when she walked outside.

She pointed to the restaurant across the street. "Do you want to go have a drink?"

He looked tall and mysterious in the moonlight. Very handsome and very masculine. His gaze slipped over her as easily and familiar as a caress. "Could we just walk for a while?"

She nodded, and they started down the street. Though it was almost ten by now, there was still a group of tourists waiting to get into Brennan's, and Alex took her elbow to steer her around the noisy throng.

The contact sent a shiver up Naomi's spine. As they walked along in silence, she became aware of his gaze on her from time to time. Naomi wondered why he'd been so desperate to see her, because he seemed in no hurry now to unburden himself. For the moment, he appeared content to stroll along beside her, stopping occasionally to look into the window of one of the elite shops lining Royal Street.

To passersby, they must have seemed like any other couple—like lovers, Naomi thought with a quickening of her pulse—out for an intimate stroll in one of the most romantic, mysterious cities in the world.

The ambiance of the Quarter seemed to wrap around them, cocoon them. The narrow streets and overhanging balconies, trimmed with wrought-iron grillwork and lush trailing ferns, made it seem as if they were in some strange, exotic land. Behind lacy iron gates, Naomi could hear the trickle of fountains, the whisper of old secrets.

"Why did you want to see me?" she asked in a hushed voice.

They stopped in front of a shop, and Alex stared broodingly in the window, but Naomi didn't think he was admiring the wares. "You seemed upset earlier at the restaurant. I wondered why."

She shrugged. "I wasn't upset."

"Then why did you get up from the table so abruptly when I mentioned Taryn's hobby? And when you both came back from the ladies' room, I had a feeling something had happened." He turned to stare at her. Light from the street flickered over his features, making him seem at once familiar and strange. "Was Taryn rude to you?"

His question surprised her. "No. Why would you ask that?"

His expression turned grim. "Like I told you last night, she's going through a difficult time right now. She can sometimes be unpredictable."

"I'm going to find out who killed my mother, no matter what I have to do."

"She wasn't rude to me, Alex. And anyway, even if she was, I could handle it."

One dark eyebrow lifted slightly. "I wouldn't be too sure of that. You've never had to deal with a moody teenager."

"Through no fault of my own."

He said abruptly, "Naomi, I'm sorry. I didn't mean it that way."

His dark gaze made her shiver, and she turned to stare into the shop window. Inside, an array of blue gemstones glittered against midnight velvet. Naomi glanced up at the wooden shingle over the doorway. Blue Heaven.

"It's amazing some of these places stay in business," Alex murmured.

"What do you mean?"

He nodded toward the window. "This shop, for instance. Everything they sell is blue—from fabrics to feathers to blue diamonds. You would think such a specialization would limit their customers, but they've been in business for years, and owning one of their custom-made rings has become something of a status symbol in New Orleans."

"You seem to know a lot about this place," Naomi said.

The frown on his face deepened. "I should. It was one of my wife's favorite places to shop. The owner searched for two years to find a Kashmir sapphire the exact shade of Aubree's eyes. She loved that ring. She never took it off. It was the only piece of her jewelry missing after she was killed."

The mention of Aubree DeWitt's murder set Naomi's heart to pounding. Suddenly the Quarter no longer seemed quaint and romantic, but remote and dangerous, the darkened doorways and shadowy alleys providing too many hiding places for someone with sinister intent.

When Alex took Naomi's arm, a shiver tingled over her. They continued down the street, turning on St. Peter.

"Tell me about that night," she said reluctantly.

She heard the sharp intake of his breath before he

said almost angrily, "Why do you want to know about that night?"

"Because it changed my daughter's life. I think I have a right to know."

"Taryn isn't your daughter, Naomi."

She turned to gaze up at him. "You can still say that after you saw Sadie's picture?"

His face looked ravaged in the filtered light from the street. "A lot of children have similar facial features."

"It was more than that, and you know it."

"God," he said in a low, fierce tone. "I never imagined anything like this could happen. Not in my wildest dreams."

"But it has."

"Yes, and I don't exactly know what to do about it."

At the corner of Chartres and St. Peter, they stopped behind a group of tourists clustered around a woman dressed all in black, her white face glowing in the streetlight. They listened for a moment as she described in gruesome detail the route her vampire tour would take. Naomi and Abby had taken a ghost tour once, and they'd both thought it great fun. Tonight, however, the thought of spirits and vampires and other creatures of the night were not particularly appealing to Naomi. She had no desire to pay a midnight visit to St. Louis Cemetery.

Alex, silent and brooding, took her arm and steered her around the crowd. On Decatur, they waited for traffic behind a line of horse-drawn carriages, then crossed the street to the Café du Monde. They found a small table facing the street, and Alex ordered beignets and two cafés au lait.

The waiter hustled off to get their orders, returning

almost immediately with a basket of pastries and two steaming cups of coffee.

When Naomi hesitated, Alex slid the basket of beignets toward her. "Come on," he said. "We skipped dessert earlier, remember? Besides, you can't come to New Orleans without having a beignet."

Naomi took one, leaving a thick trail of powdered sugar across the table as she lifted it to her mouth. The confection was delicious but rich, and she had no appetite, so she merely nibbled. As for Alex, he still seemed tense as he sipped his coffee.

"Do you and Taryn ever talk about the night her mother died?"

Alex studied the street. "Why do you ask?"

"She told me that she has suppressed memories about that night."

Something indefinable flashed across his features. He turned with a frown. "She told you that? She's never talked to me about her mother's death. Not once."

"Why?"

"How should I know?" he asked harshly. "The better question is, why, all of a sudden, has she decided to open up to a stranger."

The answer flashed in his eyes, and Naomi almost felt sorry for him. The fact that Taryn had confided in her seemed to be yet another piece of evidence that there was a connection between them. But Alex was still in denial, and Naomi couldn't blame him. "Maybe she finds it easier to talk to someone she doesn't know," she suggested softly.

He shrugged but didn't answer.

"Was Taryn in the house the night Aubree died?" Naomi persisted.

If possible, his expression grew even more troubled. "No. Why do you ask?"

Naomi hesitated, unsure how much of her conversation with Taryn she should reveal. "It would explain the suppressed memories."

Alex shook his head. "She was away when it happened. She, her nanny and Aubree had all gone to the Bellamys' condo in Biloxi for a few days. For some reason, Aubree decided to come back early. Taryn and Louise came home the next day and found her. The police thought that the killer must have gotten inside while Aubree was upstairs sleeping. She heard a noise, and when she came down to investigate, he attacked her. She tried to get away, but when she ran out onto the terrace, he caught her. He bashed in her head with a heavy metal urn, and then he threw her body into the pool."

Naomi's stomach churned at the awful visions. "How horrible."

A shadow moved in his eyes, something dark and terrible. "The terrace was covered in blood. When Taryn and Louise got home, Taryn saw it and went outside to see what it was. She was the one who found her mother's body in the pool."

"Oh, my God."

Alex drew a ragged breath. "As you can imagine, she was very upset. Hysterical. Louise had to call a doctor in to sedate her. Taryn slept for nearly forty-eight hours straight, and when she awakened, it was as if nothing had happened. She didn't remember finding her mother's body. She didn't even remember that her mother was dead until she was told, and then she showed very little reaction. It was as if she'd put Aubree completely out of her mind."

Naomi felt almost sick with shock. That poor child, she thought, tears flooding her eyes. She wanted desperately to go to Taryn now, wrap her arms around her and hold her tight. Keep her safe. Make all the bad things in her life fade away. But no one could do that. Not even a long-lost mother.

Naomi tried to swallow past the lump in her throat. "The police didn't have any suspects?"

"Oh, they had plenty of suspects." Alex turned to stare at her across the table, and for a moment, it was as if the two of them were alone in the café. Naomi trembled at the intensity of his gaze. "And I was at the top of their list."

Chapter Nine

Alex paced back and forth across the thick carpet in Foley's office while his friend tore into a container of gourmet takeout. Foley had been out of town the day before, and this was the first opportunity Alex had had to speak with him since Naomi had sent him the picture of her daughter. He wondered if, after seeing that picture, Foley would still insist Naomi had no case.

The succulent aroma of crawfish étouffée filled the air, but rather than whetting Alex's appetite, the scent made him feel a little sick.

"Sure you don't want something to eat? Mama Tam do know her crawfish," Foley said, trying to tempt him with the name of a popular eatery on Decatur.

"I'm not hungry," Alex muttered.

"Then quit that pacing," Foley snapped. "You're getting on my nerves, and I'm trying to enjoy my lunch here."

Alex strode over to the window, staring out for a moment before he turned back to Foley "Taryn and I had dinner with Naomi Cross last night."

Foley had been in the process of taking a bite, but his fork froze in midair. "What was the point of *that?*"

Alex shrugged. "I'm not sure. She's still pressing me

for a DNA test, and I thought if she could meet Taryn, see that we're a family—"

"She'd go back to Mississippi and forget all about you?"

Alex turned back to the window. "Something like that, I guess."

"I take it things didn't quite work out that way. What happened?"

Alex pulled out the picture of Sadie Cross and the one of Taryn he kept in his wallet, and walked over to lay them on Foley's desk, side by side. "She sent me this." He tapped the picture of Sadie with his fingertip. "That's her daughter, the one who disappeared ten years ago."

Foley whistled in disbelief. "These pictures could be of the same kid. Or else—" He glanced up, meeting Alex's gaze. "They could be of identical twins."

Alex nodded, the nerves in his stomach tightening. "You want to know the irony of all this? When Naomi sent me that picture, she'd never even seen a photo of Taryn at that age. She just assumed, she *knew,* they'd look this much alike."

Foley studied the photographs for another long moment. "There are some differences. Subtle ones."

"Yes, I know," Alex said grimly. He'd studied those photos for hours on end, and he'd committed each and every deviance to memory. The pictures were of two different girls, but the differences were mostly superficial. The length of their hair. The way they smiled. The similarities far outweighed the anomalies.

"I hate to say this," Foley said, "but I'm afraid this could change everything."

"You think Naomi has a case now, don't you?" Alex started to pace again, and this time, Foley didn't try to stop him. He seemed upset, too, and Alex wondered if it was the knowledge that Naomi might now have a case, or the possibility that Taryn might not be Aubree's daughter. That Aubree might have been involved in something as dastardly as taking someone else's baby.

Foley picked up the photographs and eyed them side by side. An emotion Alex couldn't decipher flickered over his features. "I'll be honest with you, Alex. The likeness between these two girls could be enough to compel a judge to order a DNA test. And if the test turns out positive—if it proves that Taryn is, in fact, Naomi's birth daughter..."

"She could take her away from me." Alex balled his hands into fists as he kept pacing. This couldn't be happening. He couldn't *allow* it to happen. Something had to be done.

"From everything you've told me, Naomi Cross would be a formidable witness on her own behalf. Imagine her on the stand, recounting everything that's happened to her. One baby stolen at birth, the other kidnapped at the age of five. She'd have the whole damn courtroom eating out of her hand, and it would be next to impossible to go after her under cross-examination without alienating the jury."

Alex stopped pacing and came back over to sit across from Foley's desk. "So what the hell am I suppose to do? I can't lose my daughter, Foley. I *won't*."

"Just take it easy," Foley advised. "I've made some inquiries about Naomi, but now we'll start digging deep. If she's got secrets, we'll find them. We'll do whatever we have to do to discredit her."

His words left a bad taste in Alex's mouth. "There's something else that's worrying me," he said. "If Joseph really is planning to go after custody of Taryn, how will this figure into his case?"

Foley sat back in his chair. "If the DNA test disproves Naomi's claim, then it won't have any bearing one way or the other. But if she does turn out to be Taryn's birth mother, it could work to your advantage as far as Judge Bellamy is concerned."

"How do you figure?"

"It could substantially weaken his claim."

"Which is probably why he's already contacted Naomi."

"He has? What did he say?"

"She didn't say this in so many words, but I think he may have threatened her." Alex frowned at the thought. "If he thinks he can scare her off, he doesn't know her very well."

"But you do?" Foley's gaze burned into his and Alex had to glance away.

"Let's get back to the lawsuit."

"All right," Foley agreed. "Like I was saying, if a DNA test proves she's the birth mother, it could weaken Bellamy's claim, but by the same token, it would certainly enhance hers."

Alex suddenly felt more weary that he'd ever thought possible. How could he fight a two-front war? "What do you recommend I do?"

Foley put away his food. "You're not going to like my recommendation, but as your attorney, I'm duty-bound to give it to you anyway."

Alex shrugged. He was willing to consider anything short of murder, at this point. "What is it?"

"Remember when I told you that if you were married Bellamy might have a more difficult time convincing a judge to remove Taryn from your custody?"

''I remember.'' Alex had considered it a lame suggestion at the time, and he still thought so. ''But that's when we thought the biggest threat came from Joseph. Now…'' He trailed off, nodding toward the pictures on Foley's desk. ''Even if I did remarry, it wouldn't do a thing to stop Naomi.''

''Not unless you married *her*.''

''What?'' Alex couldn't have been more stunned if Foley had knocked him in the head with a two-by-four. ''You're not serious.''

Foley leaned forward, his blue eyes compelling. ''Think about it, Alex. What better way to disarm Joseph Bellamy? You'd have a wife. A stable home for Taryn. Any judge worth his salt would have to look favorably on that.''

''But it wouldn't stop Naomi,'' Alex repeated. His mind was reeling at Foley's suggestion. ''If she's the threat you seem to think she is, if she has that good of a case, why would she ever agree to something like this?''

''Because there's always a chance a judge would rule against her, and then she'd have nothing. This way, she gets Taryn no matter what. You both do. And together, you'd have a pretty formidable defense against Bellamy.''

''This is crazy.'' Alex got up, rubbing the back of his neck with the palm of his hand.

''Is it?'' Foley shrugged. ''I don't think so. Consider how it would look to a jury. A mother who was deprived of her baby at birth marries the man who raised the child. It's human drama at its most powerful. I'd put Naomi Cross on the stand and milk it for all it's worth. And this time, she'd be on your side.''

Foley was starting to make a certain amount of sense,

and that wasn't a good thing in Alex's estimation. "I must be out of my mind to even be listening to this nonsense. I barely even know this woman."

"That's why these kinds of arrangements are called marriages of convenience. They happen all the time."

"If that's supposed to convince me, it doesn't," Alex muttered.

"Just think about it," Foley advised. "When you come to a decision, let me know. I can draw up all the necessary documents. You're a wealthy man, so naturally, we'll need to protect your assets…"

But Alex was no longer listening. He'd had a sudden vision of Naomi Cross waiting for him in their marriage bed.

NAOMI WAS SURPRISED when she got a call from Alex that afternoon asking her to dinner. Like last night, there was an edge to his voice she couldn't quite define, and she wondered why he wanted to see her again so soon.

Last night he'd been worried that Taryn might have said something to upset her, and, in fact, she had. But not in the way Alex meant. Naomi couldn't get Taryn's comments about her mother's killer out of her mind. She couldn't forget Taryn's vow that she would find her mother's murderer, no matter what she had to do.

Naomi hadn't told Alex about that vow, in part because she hadn't wanted to betray Taryn's confidence, but mostly because something deep inside her warned that it might not be prudent to allow word of Taryn's search to get out. Whoever had killed Aubree had never been apprehended, and if he—or she—thought there was a chance of discovery, even ten years after the crime, Taryn could be in grave danger.

The thought of that scared Naomi half to death, and

she made her own vow to do whatever necessary to protect her daughter. No matter what.

The first thing she had to do was to find out everything she could about Aubree's murder—when it had happened, where it had happened, who was a suspect.

To that end, she drove to the library to scour the archived issues of the *Times Picayune* for articles relating to Aubree DeWitt's murder. At the Children's Rescue Network, they used the Internet extensively to coordinate their efforts with various law enforcement bodies and the national organizations for missing children. Naomi was no stranger to a computer.

Since she didn't know the exact date of Aubree's death, she entered Aubree's name into a search engine and waited for all the articles to come up.

There were dozens of hits, most of them from the society pages, but because they were listed in chronological order, she was able to scroll quickly through the pages until she found the ones she wanted.

The first article relating to Aubree's death was dated August 16.

The date stopped Naomi cold. She suddenly felt short of breath.

According to the headline, Aubree's body had been found the day before, on August 15.

A cold sweat broke out on Naomi's skin. It couldn't be true. There had to be some mistake because that day had been forever burned into her memory.

Her hands shook as she scanned the other headlines. The date leapt out at her again. Aubree DeWitt's body had been found on August 15, the same day that Sadie had disappeared.

It had to be a coincidence. Aubree had been murdered

in New Orleans, and Sadie had been taken in Eden, miles away. What possible connection—

Taryn. Taryn was the connection.

Stop it! Naomi told herself firmly. She couldn't start making wild assumptions. If she was going to help Taryn, she had to go about this in a reasonable and objective manner. A lot of things had happened on August 15 that year, and they didn't necessarily have anything to do with Sadie's disappearance. This could be nothing more than a bizarre coincidence.

But what if it wasn't?

Still trembling with shock, Naomi clicked on the first headline. The murder had made the front page, and Naomi quickly read through the lengthy article. Aubree's body had been found on August 15, but the time of death had been placed somewhere between eighteen and twenty-four hours prior to Taryn's gruesome discovery. That meant Aubree had been murdered the day before.

Naomi tried to think back to that day, the day prior to Sadie's disappearance. Had there been anything unusual? Strange cars in the neighborhood, strangers lurking about, anything? She'd been asked those questions over and over after Sadie vanished, and Naomi's answer was still the same. She hadn't noticed *anything* unusual. There had been nothing to warn her of the coming tragedy.

Naomi hadn't even known Aubree DeWitt existed back then, so what could her murder possibly have to do with Sadie's disappearance?

But could it really be a coincidence? Fifteen years ago, they gave birth at the same hospital. One of Naomi's babies had been given to Aubree to raise as her own. Then five years later, on the day that Naomi's other daughter disappeared, Aubree had been found brutally murdered. Naomi shivered, wondering in what other ways she and Aubree DeWitt had been connected.

She clicked on the next headline to bring up another article. By the second day, Aubree's murder had been relegated to page two, and by the third day, the reporter covering the story was already suggesting that the crime had left the authorities baffled, with no real suspects or concrete leads. There was evidence that the front door had been jimmied, but other than a sapphire ring, presumably taken from Aubree DeWitt's finger after her death, nothing was missing. Robbery was the obvious motive, but the detective in charge of the case, a Lieutenant James Robicheaux, hinted darkly that he thought there might be a more personal motive.

"I've promised Mrs. DeWitt's father that her killer will be found," Robicheaux was quoted. "And it's a promise I have every intention of keeping. I won't rest until Aubree DeWitt's murderer is brought to justice."

Naomi sat for a moment, trying to digest all that she'd read. Even if Aubree's murder and Sadie's disappearance were coincidental, there was still the matter of Taryn's suppressed memories that worried Naomi. What if the killer *had* been someone Aubree knew, and what if Taryn had seen him that night? She'd said she had someone helping her in her search, and Naomi couldn't help wondering who that person might be.

Jotting down James Robicheaux's name in her book, Naomi clicked off the computer and left the library with even more questions than before. She drove back to her hotel in a somber mood, and as she bathed and dressed for her dinner date with Alex that evening, a lingering premonition settled over her.

By discovering who had killed Aubree DeWitt, she might also learn who had stolen her baby fifteen years ago. She might even find out who had taken Sadie. But in uncovering the truth, she could be putting herself and Taryn in terrible danger. How much was the truth worth?

Trying to shake off her growing disquiet, Naomi studied her reflection in the full-length mirror on the closet door. She'd brought only two dresses suitable for dinner, the best of which she'd worn the night before. But she couldn't very well wear it again, so the light blue linen sheath she'd purchased from the clearance rack at Lawson's Department Store would have to do.

The dress was fine, she decided, although the hemline was a little shorter than she preferred. Frowning at her image, she remembered the photo she'd seen in the newspaper of Aubree DeWitt. Elegant, classy, confident.

"This isn't a contest," Naomi muttered. What did it matter what she wore? Or what Alex DeWitt thought of her, for that matter? Her only concern at the moment was Taryn.

She started to fasten a strand of faux pearls around her neck, then remembering the sparkle of diamonds—genuine, Naomi was certain—around Aubree's throat in the photograph, she changed her mind and tossed the beads back into her suitcase.

This time she arrived downstairs ahead of Alex. She waited in the air-conditioned lobby until she saw him crossing the street from where he'd parked, and only then did she go out to meet him.

His dark gaze settled on her appreciatively for a moment before he glanced away. He seemed nervous, Naomi thought.

"I've made reservations at Antoine's," he said. "It's a few blocks over on St. Louis. We can probably save time by walking, but if you prefer, my car's just across the street.''

''I don't mind walking.'' In Naomi's opinion, a stroll would be preferable to the close confines of his car. But as they walked along, their shoulders kept accidentally brushing, and once, Alex took her arm to steer her out of the way of a particularly noisy group of tourists in front of the Royal Street Café. Naomi almost jumped at the sudden contact.

A solicitous maître d' showed them to an intimate table for two, and Alex placed their drink orders. The cocktails arrived moments later and she sipped her drink nervously. ''Why did you want to see me tonight?''

''Let's have dinner first,'' he suggested. ''We'll talk later.''

She lifted her eyebrows at his tone. ''Should I be worried?''

His gaze on her faltered. ''I guess that depends on your perspective,'' he muttered. Then shrugging, he said, ''It's nothing to worry about. Relax and enjoy your dinner. Have you ever been to Antoine's?''

Naomi glanced around at the elegant establishment. ''No. My sister and I used to come to New Orleans sometimes, but we never ate here.'' It was far too expensive for their budget, but Naomi had a feeling Alex came here often, or at least, to places like this. He seemed quite at ease in the refined surroundings.

''Antoine's was established in 1840,'' he told her. ''Some of the dishes you'll see on the menu are the same ones that have been served here for generations.''

''It's a beautiful restaurant,'' Naomi murmured, still wondering why he'd brought her here, and why he seemed so intent on charming her. Reluctantly she let her gaze flicker over him. He looked very handsome tonight, as elegant and refined in his dark suit and silk tie as their surroundings. But as always, he wore an air of mystique that was as enticing, and possibly as lethal, as the cocktails they sipped.

Naomi shivered and tore her gaze away. She tried to relax and enjoy the meal. The food, starting with the hors d'ouevres, was delicious, the service excellent, and she wanted to savor the evening. It wasn't often that she dined out in such luxury. But she was so apprehensive she could hardly eat a bite.

Alex appeared to suffer from no such malady. He ate heartily, and all through dinner, made small talk designed, Naomi was sure, to put her at ease.

She suspected the whole evening was leading up to something momentous, and that made her even more uneasy.

"I seem to recall that you mentioned a sister," he said.

She nodded. "Abby. She recently moved away from Eden." Loneliness settled over Naomi. She and Abby had always been so close, but now her sister was embarking on a great adventure, both in her personal life and in her profession. She was leaving Naomi behind, but if anyone was entitled to happiness, it was Abby. Naomi couldn't imagine a more loyal and loving sister. "She's been accepted at the FBI Academy at Quantico."

"You must miss her," he said.

"I do. She's the only—" Naomi had almost said that her sister was the only family she had left, but that wasn't true any longer. Now she had Taryn, whether Alex wanted to admit it or not.

As if reading her mind, he fell into a thoughtful silence, and they lingered over coffee, both of them declining dessert.

"Are you sure? You haven't lived until you've experienced Antoine's Cherries Jubilee."

"Maybe next time." After their waiter disappeared, Naomi said anxiously, "Can you tell me now why you wanted to see me tonight?"

He stirred his coffee with great deliberation. When he looked up, his expression was ambiguous. "May I ask you a personal question?"

She shrugged. "You can ask."

"Where is your daughters' father?"

"He's dead."

"I'm sorry," Alex said quickly.

"Don't be sorry. At least not for me." Naomi hesitated, then said, "His name was Clay Willis. I fell in love with him our senior year in high school. He was handsome, popular, athletic. Every girl's dream, or so I thought. He persuaded me to give up my virginity one night in the back seat of his father's Oldsmobile. A month later, on graduation night, I had to tell him I was pregnant. He left town the next day and joined the army. I never saw him again. A few years later, I heard that he'd been killed in a helicopter accident."

A frown flickered across Alex's brow. What was he thinking? Naomi wondered. That hers was an old story? That she'd been young and foolish just like a million other teenage girls? Was she somehow diminished in his eyes now that he knew the sordid truth?

"What about his family?" he asked casually, but Naomi knew nothing about this evening was incidental.

"There was only his mother, and she moved back up north after Clay left town. I never heard from her again, either. So if you're worried that someone else might show up to claim parental rights, don't be.''

Alex's expression hardened. "I wish I could say the same about others.''

"Me, you mean.''

"Actually, I was referring to Joseph Bellamy. He's the reason I wanted to see you tonight.''

"I don't understand.'' Naomi took a sip of her coffee. The liquid scalded her throat, but the strong, chicory brew was also bracing.

"It's simple.'' Alex leaned slightly toward her, his gaze deeply compelling. A tremor coursed through Naomi at his nearness. "If Joseph and Gwen Bellamy are able to persuade a court to grant them sole custody of my daughter, then neither you nor I will ever see her again.''

Naomi's heart started to pound in earnest. "Are you saying…that you think I have a right to see her? Are you saying you believe she's my daughter?''

He sat back abruptly. "I'm not saying anything of the kind.''

"Then why am I here?'' Naomi asked in frustration.

A dozen emotions flashed across his face, as if he were in the throes of some deep internal conflict he hadn't yet decided how to resolve. Finally he said, "I've discussed my options at some length with my attorney. He seems to think the fact that I'm a single father, that I've taken Taryn out of the country, failed to provide a stable home life for her, might work against me in court.''

Why was he telling her this? Naomi wondered nervously. Didn't he understand that he was providing her with ammunition? Or was he that confident she posed no threat to him?

"Could you please just get to the point?" she said with an edge of resentment.

"All right." He drew a breath as his gaze met hers. "I asked you to dinner tonight because I have a proposal for you."

Naomi frowned. "What kind of proposal?"

"A marriage proposal."

The world as Naomi knew it stopped at that moment. The murmur of voices around the room faded, drowned out by the dull roaring inside her head. She couldn't have heard him correctly. The shock of learning that Aubree DeWitt had been murdered the day before Sadie disappeared ten years ago had affected her more than she realized. She was hearing things. Imagining things.

"I beg your pardon," she said in a near whisper.

"I want you to marry me."

Stunned, Naomi tried to rise, but his hand shot out and caught her wrist. "Please," he said. "Just hear me out."

She glanced around helplessly, as if expecting one of the other diners to come to her rescue. But they were all oblivious to the drama unfolding before them.

Naomi glanced at Alex across the candlelit table. "If you're not joking," she said shakily, "then you must be crazy."

He shook his head slowly. "I assure you, I'm neither. Just give me a minute to explain."

Her hand fluttered to her throat. "Maybe you'd better."

"You're not going to faint or anything like that?" he asked in sudden alarm.

She gave him an ironic glance. "I'm made of sterner stuff than that. I hardly think a marriage proposal, even my first one, would cause me to swoon."

Something flashed in Alex's eyes, but he didn't comment. He waved off the waiter who hovered nearby.

"My lawyer says that if I were to remarry, if I could prove to the court that I am providing a stable home life for Taryn that is equal to what the Bellamys could provide, then a judge would be less likely to remove her from my custody."

"And what makes you think I would go along with such a...scheme?" Naomi asked harshly. She had her own relationship with Taryn to worry about. If Alex and Joseph Bellamy bloodied each other enough in court, perhaps that could work to her advantage.

Alex seemed to understand exactly what she was thinking. "You may not have made the decision yet, but at some point, you'll want custody yourself. Or at least visitation rights." He put up a hand when she started to interrupt. "But even if a DNA test proves that Taryn is your birth daughter, you could still lose in court. A judge could refuse to take her away from the only family she's ever known. He could even decide that visitation rights would be too damaging. And then you'd be left with nothing. What I'm offering you is a chance to be with Taryn, regardless of the outcome of a DNA test or a judge's ruling. You'd be living in the same house with her. You would, in effect, be a mother to her."

The impact of his words slammed into Naomi, and she felt the breath rush up out of her lungs. She sat back in her chair, breathless, as images danced through her head. She and Taryn shopping together, laughing together, doing all the things that a mother and teenage daughter were supposed to do together. All the things that Naomi had never gotten to do with Sadie.

But now she'd found her other daughter. Now she

had a chance to be a mother again. She had a chance to hold her precious child in her arms.

Tears burned Naomi's eyes. Would it matter so terribly much if Taryn never knew who her real birth mother was?

That thought drew her up short. Was that it? Was that the real reason Alex wanted to marry her? So that she would agree to never tell Taryn the truth?

She felt herself go almost rigid with fury. "Even if I were to agree to such a ludicrous plan, I'd still want a DNA test. I'd still want to know the truth about my daughter. And someday I'd want her to know the truth about me."

Anger flashed in Alex's eyes, but he was more adept at controlling his emotions than Naomi. "I realize that," he said in a careful tone. "After we're married, I won't object to a DNA test."

Naomi was still in a state of shock. She was trembling all over. There had to be a catch. There had to be something more.

"Look," Alex said. "I know this is a shock, but when you have time to think about it, you'll realize that it's not a bad plan. This way, we both stand a good chance of keeping Taryn. And it's not as if I'm asking for a lifetime commitment."

She glanced up.

His gaze on her was steady, measuring. His voice lowered sympathetically. "I can see how that might concern you, but in three years, Taryn will be eighteen, old enough to decide for herself who she wants to live with. You and I can divorce then and go our separate ways. But in three years, you would have had ample time to form a very secure bond with her."

Yes, Naomi thought, her stomach quivering at the

prospect. She would be able to form a bond with her daughter, but she would also be able to watch over her. To protect her.

As it had since the evening before, Taryn's vow came back to haunt Naomi. *"I've made a promise to myself. I'm going to find out who killed my mother...no matter what I have to do."*

"I don't expect you to give me an answer tonight. Take some time to think about it," he said.

Naomi's gaze lifted. "I don't need time. I can give you my answer right now."

Chapter Ten

The next few days passed in a blur for Naomi. Once she gave Alex her answer, he immediately set about taking care of all the details. He arranged for a marriage license and contacted a judge who agreed to conduct the ceremony in his chambers on Friday of the following week. They met with Alex's attorney, Foley Boudrieux, to iron out all the legal considerations. If he and Alex had thought she would balk at signing a prenuptial agreement, they must have been greatly surprised. Naomi cared nothing about Alex's money. Taryn was her only concern.

However, Alex insisted on setting up a checking account for her, but Naomi knew she wouldn't touch the money except for necessities. She had a little nest egg put away, mostly money she'd inherited from an insurance policy after her mother died. It wasn't much, and hiring a private detective to locate Taryn had cut into it severely, but she still had enough left to give her a sense of independence. Relying solely on Alex for support seemed a little too much to Naomi like she'd been bought and paid for.

At Foley's suggestion, she and Alex began spending a great deal of time together, for appearance' sake. They had dinner with each other almost every night, and Alex always took her to one of the city's famous restaurants—Commander's Palace, Galatoire's, Court of Two Sisters—where they were sure to be seen together.

One night, he even invited her to his home, and Naomi, following his directions, had been enchanted as she'd driven through the Garden District. She and Abby had toured the area once aboard a streetcar, and she'd been duly impressed by the large homes and the oak-lined streets. But the knowledge that she would be living in one of those houses soon with her daughter made Naomi look at the neighborhood in a whole new light.

The house on Octavia Street was everything Naomi had imagined it to be and more. Live oaks dripping with Spanish moss stood sentinel along a narrow driveway, while huge azalea bushes, which would be breathtaking in the spring, crowded thickly against the front of the house. The inside was all high ceilings, polished oak floors, and through floor-to-ceiling windows in the living room, Naomi saw the sparkle of a swimming pool in back.

Alex had already told Taryn about their marriage plans, and although her manner was aloof and faintly resentful, she managed to be polite if not enthusiastic when Naomi asked her to be her maid of honor.

"I'm not sure I can get out of school," she said with a shrug.

"Oh, I think we can arrange that," Alex said, with a great deal more enthusiasm than Naomi was sure he felt.

Taryn had simply shrugged again, and muttered, "Whatever," as if she had no strong feelings about the marriage one way or the other. It was almost as if she didn't want Alex to think that she cared what he did.

The tension between Alex and Taryn was almost tangible at times, and Naomi hoped their coming marriage wouldn't make things worse. She wanted a chance to talk to Taryn alone, try to get a feel for the girl's true emotions, but after dinner, Taryn went straight up to her room.

Just as puzzling as Taryn's lack of emotion was Louise Wheeler's overt animosity. She'd opened the door for Naomi, sour faced and disapproving, and all through dinner, as she'd served the meal, Naomi felt the woman's gaze on her. When she looked up, Louise's eyes would dart away, but there was no question that she did not approve of the hasty wedding plans. Maybe she was worried she would soon be out of a job, Naomi thought.

When the evening drew to its conclusion, Alex walked her to her car. "That wasn't so bad was it?"

"No, it was fine."

He smiled slightly. "I'd say it was better than fine. Taryn was civil at dinner, and these days, I count that as a success."

"All girls go through a difficult stage," Naomi said. "And I'm sure she must have been shocked when you told her we were getting married."

"I would have thought so." He gazed off into the darkness. "But you saw the way she acted tonight. It's like she doesn't even care."

"Maybe she just doesn't want to show how much she does care. For your sake. Maybe she's afraid if she told you how she really feels, you'd be obligated to back out of the marriage."

"That's a nice thought, but she's hardly been concerned about my feelings for quite some time," he said with a resigned sigh.

"Are you sure we're doing the right thing?" Naomi asked softly. "I'm worried about her."

He gave her a quick, anxious glance. "We're doing this for her, remember?"

"But we're also doing it for ourselves. Are we being selfish?"

"Selfish would be if you tried to take her away from her home, from the only father she's ever known. Selfish would be if I refused to let her get to know the woman who may have given birth to her. If I tried to keep the two of you apart. We're making the best of a very difficult situation, Naomi."

"I know. But it just seems…"

He tilted his head, staring down at her. "What?"

She shrugged. "I don't know. I don't have any answers. I don't know if what we're doing is right. I just know that I'd give anything to spend time with my daughter. I'd do anything to protect her."

"Even marry me?" There was a smile in his voice, and Naomi's heart gave a funny little trip. "You don't have to answer that."

Naomi swallowed. "We both know why we're doing this."

"Yes." There was a note of regret in his voice. "Will I see you tomorrow night?"

"No, I'm driving back to Eden for the weekend," she said. "I have a lot to do before next Friday."

"Naomi…"

"Yes?"

He said nothing, merely gazed into her eyes. Naomi's pulse quickened, and her mouth went dry with nerves. Alex moved slightly toward her, his face shadowed and mysterious. He put a hand up to her cheek, and she closed her eyes.

''I know this isn't going to be a conventional marriage, but we can make it work,'' he murmured.

She didn't trust herself to speak. The touch of his hand on her face sent a tremor of desire coursing through her. It had been so long since a man had touched her as if...he wanted her.

Everything stilled inside her as he lowered his head and brushed his lips against hers. It was a soft kiss, gentle and sweet and almost tentative. She would not have thought Alex DeWitt capable of such tenderness, but if she'd learned anything about him in the past few days, it was that he was a man full of surprises.

The kiss was over in seconds, much too soon for Naomi, but the feel of his mouth lingered on her lips. She drove away, hardly daring to breathe for fear the magic of that moment would be lost forever.

Perhaps she hadn't given enough consideration to what being married to Alex DeWitt would entail, she thought. Living in the same house with him day in and day out—not to mention the nights. She was attracted to him, had been from that first day in his office. How would she handle those feelings when they were alone together as man and wife?

The question wasn't one she could shove to the back of her mind, and she pondered it at length as she drove home to Eden the next day. But packing up her clothes, paying bills, attending to the million and one details that had to be addressed before she could return to New Orleans soon took her mind off everything else.

She spent Friday afternoon handling personal business matters—transferring her meager checking and savings accounts to a New Orleans bank, arranging to have the utilities disconnected at her home. Eventually she might decide to lease the house, but she wouldn't sell it outright because in three years, when Taryn went off to college and Naomi's marriage to Alex dissolved, she'd need a place to come home to.

But she didn't want to think about that right now, either.

She spent Friday going through boxes of pictures, and she grew weepy as she reflected on how many people she'd lost in her life. Sadie. Her mother. Grandmother Eulalia. And though Abby was still alive, she was in Virginia starting a new life for herself. Naomi felt very alone at that moment, and she had to remind herself that she, too, was embarking on a new life, one that would bring her closer to her daughter. She had every reason to be grateful, and not a single one to feel so melancholy.

But it was in this fragile state of mind on Saturday that she met with her co-director, Mary Ellison, of the Children's Rescue Network. Naomi had begun organizing the Network six months after Sadie had disappeared. She'd had no funds, no experience, nothing really except her own dogged determination, her driving need to make sense of her tragedy.

When Mary had shown up on her doorstep, offering not only her assistance but also her expertise in working for years with other such organizations, Naomi had been thrilled. Mary's own son had been kidnapped several years before that by her ex-husband, who'd taken him out of the country. Like Naomi, she'd dedicated her life to searching, not just for her own son, but for other missing children.

She and Naomi had traveled all over Mississippi, speaking at schools and various civic organizations, and they never missed an opportunity to be interviewed on television or in the print media because publicity generated donations to the foundation. They kept their overhead to a minimum, maintained contact with national organizations for missing and exploited children, the FBI, the Mississippi Highway Patrol, and various other statewide law enforcement bodies. They'd compiled a huge database of names and phone numbers so that literally within minutes of a child's disappearance in Mississippi, they could activate a massive volunteer effort in the search.

Thanks in large part to Mary's organizational skills, the Children's Rescue Network operated like a fine-tuned engine, and Naomi couldn't help but feel that she was throwing a monkey wrench in all their hard work and planning.

But Mary didn't see it that way. Her dark eyes filled with tears when she heard Naomi's story, and she pulled her into her plump arms. "All these years, I've prayed we would find your little Sadie, safe and unharmed, but that wasn't meant to be. But to learn you have another child, to find her after all this time—it's a miracle, that's what it is."

Naomi nodded, her throat tight. "I know."

Mary held her at arms' length, her expression stern as she searched Naomi's face. "You go be with her, and you don't look back. I'll take care of things here. The Children's Rescue Network is my mission now. You just take that girl of yours in your arms and you don't ever let her go, you hear me?"

"Yes," Naomi whispered. "I hear you."

"And you be happy. If anyone deserves a little happiness, God knows it you."

Naomi prayed that she was right.

Driving back to New Orleans on Sunday afternoon, she stopped in Jackson to meet with Michael Donnelly, the private detective who'd located Taryn. Normally his office was closed on Sunday, but she'd called him from Eden on Friday, and he'd agreed to see her.

His office was located in a large nondescript building just off the freeway, and he was waiting in the lobby to let her in when she arrived. They made only perfunctory conversation as they rode the elevator to the ninth floor, but once they were settled in his office, Naomi told him everything that had happened since she'd seen him at the beginning of the previous week.

When she finished, his expression showed little of what he was thinking, but Naomi knew he was shocked. She still found it astonishing herself that she had agreed to marry a man she'd known for less than a week.

"Are you sure you know what you're doing, Miss Cross? Marrying this man seems a little drastic."

"I know it must sound that way," Naomi agreed. "But it makes sense to both of us. Alex is worried that Joseph Bellamy is going to sue for custody of Taryn, and given his connections in New Orleans, he could win. Alex's lawyer seems to think he'll stand a better chance in court if he can show that he's providing the same stable environment for his daughter that the Bellamys are offering."

"And that's where you come in," Donnelly said skeptically. When Naomi nodded, he said, "Don't you think the court will see through this ruse? The two of you have known each other less than a week."

"We've talked about that. That's why we spent so much time together last week, and we'll see even more of each other when I return to New Orleans. It may look suspicious, but whirlwind romances do happen."

"But this isn't a romance."

For a moment, Naomi felt the tingle of Alex's kiss

on her lips, could imagine the dark passion in his eyes as he bent toward her, and then she blinked, dispelling the image.

"Even if the marriage helps him retain custody of his daughter, what do you get out of it?" Donnelly persisted.

"That's easy. I get to be with my daughter. And Alex has also agreed to a DNA test."

A frown played at Donnelly's brow. "Why not hold off on the marriage until after the test? If you can prove you are Taryn's birth mother, then you'll have grounds to go after custody yourself."

"I thought about that," Naomi said with a sigh. "But there's no guarantee I would be awarded custody. The court might decide it would be too damaging to remove Taryn from the only family she's ever known. And besides, how could I do that to her? Alex is her father in every way that counts. Even though they're going through a difficult time right now, I know she loves him. I don't want to take her away from him."

"Yes, but there's no guarantee that the court won't grant custody to the grandparents anyway, in spite of this sham marriage. Or maybe even because of it."

Naomi smiled sadly. "If there's one thing I've learned over the years, it's that there are no guarantees in life. If I marry Alex DeWitt, then I'll get to be with my daughter. That's all I want to think about right now. I'll deal with the rest as it happens."

"Some people would say that you're making a hasty, ill-advised decision," Donnelly said.

Naomi lifted her chin. "I'm sure that's true. But I'd be willing to bet those same people have never lost a child. Marrying a man I hardly know seems almost inconsequential to me if it means I can spend even one precious moment with my daughter.''

Donnelly took off his glasses and rubbed the bridge of his nose. ''I can see there's no talking you out of this.''

''No, there isn't,'' Naomi agreed. ''But my upcoming marriage really isn't the reason I wanted to see you.'' She paused, unsure how she wanted to approach him. ''When I hired you to find Taryn, I didn't tell you much about my other daughter's disappearance, did I?''

''No, not really.''

''Nor did you spend much time investigating Aubree DeWitt's murder.''

He slipped on his glasses and gazed at her for a long moment. ''I'm not sure where you're going with this, Miss Cross, but I feel I need to defend myself here. You didn't hire me to look into Sadie's disappearance, nor Aubree DeWitt's murder. You asked me to find out who else had given birth the same night you did at Eden Memorial Hospital, and to learn the whereabouts of said person and her child. I did that.''

''Yes, I know,'' she said quickly. ''You misunderstand me. I'm not criticizing your investigation. Far from it. You did exactly what I asked you to do, and you did it very well. But now...something else has come up.''

His features relaxed a little. ''Go on.''

She moistened her lips, suddenly nervous. What if he thought she was completely off her rocker? What if he refused to help her? Naomi didn't know who else to turn to. ''Aubree DeWitt's body was found on the exact same day my daughter Sadie was kidnapped. I'm not convinced the timing was a coincidence.''

Donnelly stood abruptly and came around the desk

to perch on the edge, gazing down at her. His eyes were very blue and very intense behind his glasses. "Let me get this straight. You think Aubree DeWitt's murder and Sadie's disappearance are somehow connected?"

Naomi stared down at her hands. "I don't know, but I think it's possible that *everything* is connected, and it all began that night fifteen years ago when my baby was swapped for Aubree DeWitt's. Supposing that five years later, she somehow found out that she hadn't given birth to Taryn. Supposing she confronted the person who arranged the swap. Supposing she threatened to expose this person. Kidnapping is a federal offense. Faced with a serious prison sentence, he could have panicked and killed Aubree."

"You've given this a great deal of thought, I see."

Naomi nodded. "I think about little else. But I still can't figure out where Sadie's kidnapping fits in."

"Can't you?"

Something in his voice made the hair at the back of Naomi's neck stand on end.

Donnelly stood abruptly and went around to sit behind his desk again, as if he needed to put some distance between them. He folded his hands on the desk very deliberately as his gaze met hers. "If all that you say is true, if Aubree was killed because she threatened to expose the truth about Taryn's birth, then the killer would have known there was another person who could have revealed the truth as well. Not because of what she knew, but because of how she looked. Taryn's identical twin."

A cold, dark dread seeped into Naomi's soul. Ever since the remains had been found in Grover County, she'd been trying to brace herself for the inevitable. Sadie was dead. She wasn't ever coming back. But this scenario as to why she might have been taken filled Naomi with grief. *My baby,* she wept silently. *My poor Sadie.*

"This is only speculation," Donnelly said gently. He shoved a box of tissues toward Naomi, and she plucked one. "Aubree DeWitt's murder may have had absolutely nothing to do with your daughter's disappearance. Or even the incident at the hospital fifteen years ago. The motive for her murder might well have been nothing more unusual than robbery, as the police suspected."

"I understand that." Naomi took a moment to dab at her eyes and regain her composure. "But I can't shake the feeling that it *is* connected. If I find out who killed Aubree DeWitt, I'll also know who swapped my baby for hers fifteen years ago. And maybe even who took Sadie and why." Tears threatened again, and she drew a ragged breath. "I want to hire you to find out the truth, Mr. Donnelly. I want you to investigate Aubree DeWitt's murder for me."

"Miss Cross—"

"I know what you're going to say," she cut in. "That after ten years, the trail will be cold." Naomi leaned forward, her tone almost desperate. "That may be true, but you also know things the police didn't know back then. You know that my baby was taken from the hospital fifteen years ago and given to Aubree as her own. You know that my other daughter was kidnapped from a school playground five years later, on the same day Aubree's body was discovered. The police didn't know any of that at the time, and if I went to them now, I'm not sure they'd even listen to me. Why would they want to open up a ten-year-old murder when they have a dozen new ones every day to solve?"

"You make a good point," Donnelly conceded.

"Then you'll help me? I'd be willing to keep you on the job for as long as my money holds out. Same agreement we had last time."

He hesitated. "I tell you what I'll do. I'll make some phone calls, do some research, maybe try to get a look at the police file. If I think we're on to something, I'll call you and we'll decide how to proceed from there. Fair enough?"

Naomi nodded in relief and rose. "Again, I don't know how to thank you, Mr. Donnelly."

"I'm not certain I'm doing you any favors," he said gruffly. "When I told you your daughter was in New Orleans, I never dreamed you would go down there and get yourself engaged to Alex DeWitt."

Naomi smiled. "No. But you knew I'd do anything to be with her."

"That was what worried me so much. I'm still concerned about you."

"Don't be. I'm going into this with my eyes wide-open. I'll be fine." She shook his hand, then turned to leave.

When she was at the door, he called her name, and she paused. "Yes?"

"Assuming Aubree *was* killed because she found out about Taryn's birth, has it occurred to you yet that the person who would have benefited the most by keeping this secret from being revealed is the same person who profited most from Aubree's death?"

Naomi shook her head. "You're wrong about Alex. He didn't kill his wife."

"How can you be so sure?"

"Because I've seen him with Taryn," Naomi said softly. "I know how much he loves her. No matter how he might have felt about Aubree, he would never have harmed his own child's mother.''

''You sound pretty certain of that.''

Somehow she was.

A FEW HOURS LATER Naomi pulled her Jeep into the parking garage of the Spencer Hotel. She was facing the street, and she sat for a moment, soaking up the sights and sounds of the Big Easy.

This is it, she thought with a quiver of excitement in the pit of her stomach. *New Orleans is going to be my home.*

There was no turning back now.

AFTER NAOMI UNPACKED, she showered, donned her pajamas and then settled in for a cozy night of television. She didn't really expect to hear from Alex until the next day, but when the phone rang, she knew instinctively it was he. Consequently, her heart was already pounding when she picked up the phone.

''So you're back,'' he said in her ear. Had she noticed before how intimate and darkly sexy his voice sounded over the phone?

She wound the cord around her finger. ''I just got in a little while ago.''

''Get everything taken care of?''

She thought about her meeting with Michael Donnelly. ''Pretty much.''

Alex hesitated, and when he spoke again, Naomi thought his voice sounded even more intimate. ''I would ask you to dinner, but you're probably tired from your trip.''

''I am pretty bushed,'' Naomi admitted, although her fatigue had miraculously diminished at the sound of his voice. With very little persuasion, she knew she would have gotten up, dressed and gone out to meet him.

"Maybe I should just say good-night then."

Naomi closed her eyes. "Good night."

But instead of hanging up, he said softly, "Naomi?"

She squeezed the phone cord. "Yes?"

"I'm glad you're back."

"I am, too." And as she hung up the phone, she realized it was true. She was glad to be back. Come what may, her future was irrevocably tied to Alex DeWitt's, and the emotion she felt most strongly at the moment was excitement, not trepidation.

SOMETHING AWAKENED HER.

Naomi had no idea how long she'd been asleep, but as she opened her eyes, she knew instantly that something was wrong. She lay on her side, facing the windows, but the drapes were closed, shutting out all but a sliver of light. The room was almost unbearably warm, and she could smell smoke. Cigarette smoke.

Fear shot through her veins, turning her blood to ice. But before she could even scream, he was on her, clapping a hand over her mouth as he straddled her. Naomi fought him for all she was worth, but he was strong and he'd caught her completely by surprise. Pinning her arms to her sides with his knees, he leaned toward her. Naomi felt the cold, sharp sting of a knife blade press against her throat, and she went completely still.

"That's better, *chère*. We gonna have us a little fun tonight, no."

His breath was hot and fetid against her face. He smelled of cigarette smoke, booze and, oddly enough, brine. A wave of nausea rolled over Naomi as his hand replaced the knife at her throat, and he ran the blade caressingly down the front of her pajama top, then sliced open the buttons.

She tried to scream, tried to struggle away from him, but the knife was immediately back at her throat. "We can do this fast or we can have our fun, *machère*. Me, I like 'em with some fight."

The thought of his mouth on hers made her gag. And there would be so much worse to follow.

She couldn't let this happen. She couldn't!

As he shifted his weight, her right hand came free. Naomi flailed out wildly, grabbing the first thing she came into contact with. Her hand closed around the ceramic base of a bedside lamp, and she brought it up to smash against his temple. He grabbed her wrist, deflecting the blow, and then he jerked the lamp from her hand and flung it across the room where it shattered against the wall.

She squeezed her eyes shut, trying to beat back the panic and horror. If she had any chance at all of survival, she had to somehow keep her wits about her. And there were certain things she had to notice—his age, his size, any distinguishing marks—so that she could keep him from doing this to other women.

But it was so dark inside the room, Naomi could see nothing more than a silhouette hovering over her. He was large, though. She could tell that from the way he towered over her, the press of his weight against her. As he moved down to kiss her, the splinter of light between the drapes fell across his arm, and Naomi saw the tattoo.

A shudder of horror ripped through her. She knew him. Oh, God, she knew who he was!

Gasping for breath, sobbing out loud, Naomi finally

managed to free her other hand and her legs, and she jammed one knee into his groin as hard as she could.

Far from subduing him, the act merely infuriated him. Grunting with pain and rage, he came after her again, but he no longer had the element of surprise, although his size and strength were a definite advantage. But Naomi had fear on her side, and an innate will to survive. She thought of Taryn, had a terrible vision of this animal going after her next, and Naomi fought him even harder.

Swinging her hand up, she plunged her thumb into his left eye socket, digging in as hard as she could. He roared in agony, and fell back, cursing her violently. The knife dropped to the floor with a thud as he clamped both hands over his eye. Blood seeped between his fingers.

Beyond fear now, Naomi slid off the bed and scrambled toward the door. But he caught her, grabbing her legs, dragging her to the floor, and then, in a split second, he was on her again. Both hands closed around her throat, squeezing, squeezing, closing off all her air. Naomi clawed at those hands, tried to buck him off her body, but he was almost crazed now. His hands pressed down harder on her windpipe.

Naomi felt herself weakening, losing consciousness. With one last effort, she flung her hands out, searching along the floor. Cold, sharp steel bit into her flesh, but she was beyond registering pain. She barely had the energy to raise the knife and drive it into the man's throat.

Blood spurted from the wound, splattering Naomi, but at first, the man didn't react. It was as if he were

too intent on squeezing the life from his victim to realize that he'd been mortally wounded himself.

Finally, blood bubbling from his mouth, he fell to the
floor, and the sound of his death throes was something
Naomi knew she would not soon forget.

Chapter Eleven

An hour later, Naomi sat huddled in a blanket in the night manager's office while he paced back and forth behind his desk. Donald Bessant had been very solicitous ever since he'd escorted Naomi downstairs, but it was obvious he had other concerns on his mind at the moment.

"Mr. Spencer will be very upset when he hears about this unfortunate incident," he worried, wringing his hands as he paced. "I gave him my personal guarantee that we would look after your every need, and now this! I can't imagine how that man got into your suite."

"The lock on the French door was damaged." Naomi's voice came out in a croak. Her throat was still very raw from where the man had tried to choke the life out of her. She pulled the blanket more tightly around her in an effort to keep her teeth from chattering. "Someone came up to fix it a few days ago, but it must not have been repaired properly. The police think he must have climbed up the balconies below mine, and because the lock was faulty, it didn't take much for him to get inside." What the police also now suspected was that the man may have been stalking Naomi for days, staking out her hotel room, and that he may have been the one to damage the lock in the first place.

"Oh, dear me," Mr. Bessant murmured.

Naomi almost felt sorry for the poor man. He was meticulous and delicate in both his demeanor and dress, and something as messy as a murder in his hotel, on his watch, was enough to give him apoplexy for weeks.

He managed to give Naomi his most sympathetic grimace as he ran a nervous finger along his thin, neatly trimmed mustache. "You must have been so terrified, Miss Cross. I can't begin to imagine! But how lucky that you were able to fight him off. And how brave!"

Naomi shuddered. She knew she was lucky to have survived the attack, but at the moment, she didn't feel very brave. She didn't feel anything except a lingering horror.

"Please rest assured that we'll do everything in our power to help you through this trying time," Mr. Bessant was saying. "If you choose to continue your stay with us, and I certainly hope that you will, another suite will be provided for you at once, and every precaution will be taken to insure your safety."

As he prattled on, Naomi tried to return to the numbness she'd experienced right after the attack. But reality was finally sinking in, and she felt herself slipping into shock. She'd killed a man tonight. How did one cope with something like that?

But she'd been through far worse, Naomi reminded herself. She'd lived through what she'd thought was her baby's death, and she'd survived Sadie's disappearance. Somehow she'd get through this as well.

Besides, if she hadn't killed that man, he would have killed her. What if he'd gone after Taryn? Naomi's stomach churned violently, just thinking about what could have happened.

The phone rang on Mr. Bessant's desk and he picked it up with a neurotic jerk of his hand. He listened for a moment, murmured something into the receiver, then hung up.

"There's a detective waiting outside to see you. I'm afraid I can't put him off."

Naomi nodded. She'd already given her statement to the uniformed officers who'd first arrived at the scene, but she knew there would be more questions, more interviews. The next few days were not going to be easy.

Mr. Bessant went to the door and beckoned to someone standing just outside. When the detective entered the office, the elegant night manager took his leave with ill-disguised relief. Naomi was someone else's problem now.

The detective was in his late forties, with a heavy, muscular build, a weak jawline, and crystalline blue eyes that were startling against his olive complexion. His light, enigmatic gaze moved over Naomi, then flicked around the room, as if in that split second he could take in dozens of details.

She wondered fleetingly what he thought of her appearance. Disheveled hair, bloody clothes, bruises at her throat. It was probably just business as usual for him.

He held out his wallet identification and shield. "I'm Lieutenant Robicheaux, NOPD." His voice was low and raspy, edged with a latent violence that seemed perfect for a cop. "I'll try to be as brief as I can, but I'll need to ask you a few questions.

Naomi stared at him in shock. "*James* Robicheaux?"

His blue eyes expressed a mild curiosity. "Why, yes. Have we met?"

"No, but...I read about you recently in the newspaper."

"You don't say." He walked around Mr. Bessant's desk and sat down. Tossing his pen and notebook on the surface, he glanced at Naomi. "Which case?"

She hesitated, pulling the blanket even more tightly around her. "Aubree DeWitt's murder."

His dark eyebrows arched in surprise. "You must be behind in your reading. That murder happened ten years ago. But then, I guess I can understand why you'd be curious." When Naomi didn't respond, he said, "You're about to become the second Mrs. DeWitt, I hear."

"How did you—"

He gave her a slight smile. "Alex DeWitt hasn't made a move in this town since he's been back that I haven't known about."

Naomi's heart thudded against her chest. There was something about James Robicheaux that made her very nervous. "What do you mean? Are you having him followed?" Was he having *her* followed?

Again that smile. Naomi didn't like it much. "Let's just say, I've got friends around town who keep their eyes and ears open for me. Besides, a marriage license is a matter of public record. You weren't trying to keep the nuptials a secret, were you?"

"No, of course not."

"It does seem sudden, though," he went on, as if she hadn't spoken. "You haven't been in New Orleans all that long, have you, Miss Cross? Let's see..." He consulted his notebook. "You checked into the Spencer last Tuesday. This is Sunday. So by my calculation, you and DeWitt have known each other less than a week." His smile sent a shiver up Naomi's spine. "That's what I call love at first sight."

"You're assuming we didn't know each other before I came to New Orleans."

The black eyebrows peaked again. "Did you?"

"No," she conceded. "But sometimes you meet a person, and you feel as if you've known them forever. Haven't you ever experienced that, Lieutenant Robicheaux?"

"As a matter of fact I have." His gaze was very intent. Naomi found the lightness of his eyes oddly disturbing. "For instance, you and I have just met, and I feel I know quite a bit about you already."

Naomi swallowed painfully. "You do?"

"I know you're from a little town in Mississippi called Eden. I know you founded an organization called the Children's Rescue Network, which helps locate missing and exploited children all over Mississippi. I know that your own daughter disappeared ten years ago and was never found. I know that until very recently you believed another child, a baby, had died shortly after her birth." He leaned across the desk as his gaze on her deepened. "I know why you came to New Orleans, Miss Cross."

Naomi started to tremble again, and she pulled the blanket around her, gripping it with both hands. But the warmth didn't help because her chill came from within. "How do you know all this? Am I under surveillance as well?"

"Obviously not, or what you went through tonight would never have happened. I told you before, Alex DeWitt doesn't make a move I don't know about. When you started showing up around town in his company, I had you checked out."

"Why?"

"Why?" His gaze deepened. "Because his wife's murder has never been solved, that's why."

Naomi's pulse quickened with apprehension. "Are you saying Alex is still a suspect? He wasn't even in the country when his wife was murdered. The investigation proved that."

He regarded her coolly across the expanse of the desk. "Have you never heard of murder for hire, Miss Cross?"

Naomi's blood went suddenly cold. Had someone hired that man to kill her?

The detective said grimly, "Make no mistake, Alex DeWitt is still very much a suspect in his wife's murder. Everyone who had any connection whatsoever to Aubree DeWitt is still a suspect."

"And just how long a list might that be, Lieutenant?"

He gave her an enigmatic smile, but the look in his eyes was anything but amused. "Enough about ancient history," he said brusquely. "Let's talk about what happened to you tonight. I want to hear, in your own words, how a man who must have outweighed you by at least a hundred pounds somehow got between you and a switchblade."

IT WASN'T UNUSUAL for Alex to arrive at the Ventura Oil Building in the Central Business District before daylight. Sometimes he would have already put in an hour or so at his desk by the time dawn broke, and then he'd set aside his work long enough to stand at the long windows in his office and watch the sun rise over the cityscape. New Orleans had a split personality, he'd always thought. Lazy and insolent by day, dark and dangerous at night. But always mysterious. Always beguiling.

He was native to the city, but the world he lived in now was a far cry from where he'd grown up in Gentilly. His mother had been a schoolteacher, his father an electrician. Good, decent, salt-of-the-earth people who'd led honest, ordinary lives with none of the turmoil and intrigue that seemed to encompass his.

Sometimes when Alex stood at this window looking out over the city, he was amazed by the twists and turns his life had taken, all the strange and foreign places he'd visited over the years, the roads he'd traveled and the ones he hadn't. The mistakes he'd made.

There'd been plenty of those, he thought, drawing a weary hand across his eyes. And yet when all was said and done, he'd ended up back at the very place where his troubles had started. New Orleans was like that. You could leave the city, but the city never left you. No matter how far you traveled, something lingered, something haunted, something kept calling you back. It was like a first love. After enough time passed, the bad memories gave way to melancholy.

He couldn't say he was sorry he and Taryn had returned to New Orleans, but their lives had certainly been less complicated in London. Still, the problems, he now knew, had been there all along. The lingering threat from Joseph Bellamy. Taryn's unresolved feelings about her mother's death. It was all there, waiting to bubble over in time. The catalyst had been his transfer back to New Orleans, but regardless of where they lived, the problems eventually would have to be faced.

And Alex had a feeling there was nowhere in the world he could have taken Taryn that Naomi wouldn't have somehow found them. She was that determined.

Was their coming marriage a mistake? Undoubtedly. But with threats aimed at him from all sides—from Bellamy and from Naomi—Alex simply didn't know what else to do. At least if he and Naomi were together, she wouldn't try to take Taryn away from him.

And, to be honest, he wasn't exactly dreading being married to her. She was an interesting, fascinating woman, and he'd be lying if he didn't admit he was attracted to her. Who wouldn't be? She was the most gorgeous woman he'd ever known and by far the least pretentious. The combination was powerful in itself, but throw in the sadness in her eyes, that melancholy smile, and it'd take more than a mere mortal man to resist her.

No, it certainly wasn't going to be a hardship being married to Naomi. The difficulty would be in keeping his hands off her if she insisted on a marriage-in-name-only arrangement.

They hadn't even spoken of that. They'd talked about everything *but* that. Legal and financial concerns. Taryn.

But the marriage bed was a subject they'd both avoided. Just how, exactly, was he going to handle the wedding night? Play it cool and let her make the first move?

But what if she didn't? What if they both waited for the other to initiate intimacy until the moment had long since passed?

Maybe it would be best if they *did* discuss it beforehand, Alex decided. Or better yet, maybe he ought to plan a little honeymoon. That would make the marriage appear more legitimate.

Unfortunately, it was too short notice to be away from work for more than a day or two, and besides, it might also seem a little presumptuous on his part.

Maybe the best thing to do was just to let nature take its course.

"Not thinking about jumping, are you?"

Startled, Alex spun from the window. The outer office where his secretary worked was dark, and for a moment, all he could see was a shadow standing in the doorway. Then the man moved into the room, and a sour taste rose in Alex's throat. "What the hell are you doing here?"

"It's been a while, eh, Alex?"

"What do you want, Lieutenant? Or is it Captain now? Did you finally earn that promotion you were so hell-bent on getting at my expense?"

Robicheaux laughed. "No, I'm still just plugging away in the trenches." He came into the office and sat down without waiting for an invitation. His dark suit was rumpled and smelled a bit fishy, as if he'd just come from the docks. "I'm a homicide dick at heart anyway, but you—" He gave an appreciative whistle as he glanced around the spacious office. "You've come up in the world, I see."

"What do you want?" Alex walked back over to his desk and sat down, scowling at Robicheaux. He didn't like the man, and wasn't about to pretend that he did. James Robicheaux had been the lead investigator on Aubree's murder case, and Alex had always had a nasty suspicion that he was on Joseph Bellamy's payroll. That was why he'd gone after Alex so hard even though he had an airtight alibi. When Robicheaux couldn't pin anything on him, he'd leaked some ugly innuendos to the press. He was the one who'd gotten the rumors started that Alex had inherited a lot of money from Aubree's estate.

Ha! Alex thought. What he'd inherited from Aubree's

estate was a massive debt load. By the time he'd paid everything off, his own savings had been almost completely wiped out. He'd had to start all over when he'd gone back to London with Taryn, and everything he owned today, he'd gotten by the sweat of his own brow.

But Joseph Bellamy and James Robicheaux had planted the seed of doubt in people's minds, and there'd been little Alex could do to dispel it. It seemed that there was still very little he could do.

If James Robicheaux was sniffing around again, it could mean only one thing. Joseph Bellamy had sent him.

Robicheaux smiled, as if reading Alex's mind. "Ten years is a long time to stay away, Alex, but I didn't come here to take a stroll down memory lane with you. I want to talk to you about Naomi Cross. I'm wondering if you have any idea who might want to kill her."

A shock wave rolled over Alex. "What the hell are you talking about?"

Robicheaux's brows shot up. "You don't know? I'm surprised she didn't call you, being as how you two are so close and all."

"Just tell me, damn it."

"A man broke into her hotel room sometime after midnight and tried to kill her."

Alex stood abruptly. "My God. Is she all right? Where is she?"

"She's still at the Spencer, and she's fine. Just a little shaken up."

Anger flooded over Alex, along with a protective instinct more fierce than he could ever have imagined. "And the man who tried to kill her? You apprehended him?"

"Not exactly."

He leaned across the desk, temper blazing. "Then why the hell aren't you out there trying to find him? He could come after Naomi again—"

"That man ain't coming after nobody," Robicheaux said with a dry chuckle. "Miss Cross stabbed and killed him with his own knife."

Alex sat back down again. He felt stunned, blind-sided. He pulled a hand through his hair. "Are you sure she's all right?"

Robicheaux gave him a sly look. "Why, Alex, if I didn't know better, I'd say you genuinely care about this woman. But then, the two of you *are* getting married, I hear."

Alex didn't bother to ask how he knew. He'd learned a long time ago that Robicheaux had eyes and ears all over the city. "I want to see Naomi."

"Maybe she doesn't want to see you."

"Did she say that?" Alex demanded.

"No. But I can't help wondering why she didn't call you."

Alex's jaw tightened at the innuendo. "You're out of your mind if you think I had anything to do with this."

Robicheaux spread his hands. "I haven't accused you of anything, have I? I just want to ask you a few simple questions. Then you can go see Miss Cross. Assuming of course, that she'll see you."

Alex fought back his anger as he glared at Robicheaux. "What do you want to know?"

The detective flipped open his notebook. "Does the name Ray Beauchamp ring a bell?"

"No."

Robicheaux glanced up. "You said that pretty quickly. Don't even need to think about it?"

"I don't know any Ray Beauchamp," Alex snapped. "Is he the man who attacked Naomi?"

Robicheaux nodded. "Nasty character, Ray. Into a lot of nefarious activities from what I've been able to gather. Even did some jail time a few years ago. But what I find most interesting about the man is the fact that he worked for Ventura Oil. Out on one of the offshore drilling rigs. Sure you don't know him?"

"Ventura employs thousands of people. I can't be expected to know them all."

"You used to work on one of those rigs yourself during summer when you were in high school and college. Isn't that right? Thought your paths might have crossed back then."

"That was twenty years ago," Alex said impatiently. He was anxious to go find Naomi, see for himself that she was okay. "If our paths crossed, I doubt I'd remember him."

"Oh, I don't think you'd forget Ray. Like I said, he was a pretty nasty guy. Got real mean when he drank. Had a snake tattoo on his arm, a great big one. You couldn't miss it."

"Half the men who work those rigs have tattoos. I'm telling you, I don't know this guy."

"I'll have to take your word for that, I guess." Robicheaux made a production of putting his pen and notebook away. He strode across the room, but at the door, he glanced back. "If you have any plans on leaving the country, going back to England, say, I'd put 'em on hold, if I were you."

NAOMI HAD DISCARDED her clothing as soon as she'd locked the door of her new suite behind Mr. Bessant, who had by then been accompanied by the day manager. Both men had bent over backward to see to her every need, but all Naomi had really wanted was to be left alone so that she could claw her way out of her bloody pajamas.

Stripped, she'd stood under a hot shower for as long as she'd had the energy to remain on her feet. She hadn't been allowed into her old room to get her clothes or any of her belongings, but thankfully, a thick terry-cloth robe had been furnished by the hotel, and Naomi belted it around her after she'd dried off, grateful to be wearing something clean. Untainted.

But now that she'd showered, there was nothing left to do. The day stretched endlessly before her, and she suddenly felt more alone than she had in years. She thought about calling Alex, but it was still early, and she didn't want to wake up the whole household. She especially didn't want to alarm Taryn.

She wanted to call Abby, but Naomi knew her sister too well. She'd be on the first plane to New Orleans regardless of how it would affect her training at Quantico or her future with the FBI. Naomi couldn't let her do that, and besides, just talking to Abby would chip away at the fragile veneer of courage she'd managed to maintain.

The courage, however, was only an illusion, which shattered the moment someone knocked on her door. Naomi jumped, her heart catapulting to her throat. Calm down, she told herself firmly. It was probably just one of the hotel managers coming to check on her again, hoping, no doubt, to ward off a lawsuit.

They had nothing to fear from her. Naomi wished she could put the attack behind her and never think of it again, but that wasn't going to happen anytime soon. Maybe not ever.

She glanced through the peephole, and her heart pounded even harder. Alex stood outside.

Naomi quickly unlocked the door and pulled it back. His dark gaze raked over her.

"I just heard. Why the hell didn't you call me?" His gaze lit on the bruises at her throat, and his expression hardened. "You are hurt."

"No, I'm fine," Naomi said hoarsely. "Really." She stood back so that he could enter, and then closed the door behind him. "I was going to call you, but I didn't want to alarm Taryn, and—" she broke off, her eyes filling with tears."

"I'm sorry, Naomi. God—"

It was amazing to Naomi how natural it seemed that he would take her into his arms, that he would hold her so tightly she could hardly breathe, and that she would press her cheek against his shoulder, feeling warm and cozy and protected.

"I can't believe this happened." He stroked her hair. "Are you sure you're okay? Have you seen a doctor?"

Naomi pulled back a little. "My throat's still a little sore, but I'm fine."

He drew her over to the couch and they both sat down. "Can you tell me what happened?"

Naomi shuddered. "When I woke up, he was in my room. He attacked me. I think he was going to rape me and then—"

Anger flashed in Alex's eyes. "How did he get inside?"

Naomi told him about the faulty lock, and the police's theory that the man had been stalking her.

"Wait a minute," Alex said. "You saw this man following you? Why didn't you report it to the police? Or tell me?"

Naomi shrugged. "Because I saw him once in a restaurant. There's no crime in that. I was never sure he actually followed me. It was just a feeling I had. You can't call the police because of a feeling."

"No, but you could have told me."

"And what could you have done?"

He scowled. "I get your point. There was nothing I could have done to help you."

"There was nothing anyone could have done."

He got up suddenly and began to pace. When he turned, his expression was more grim than Naomi had ever seen it. "Do you think this was just a random attack? Do you think he singled you out because of the way you look? Because I could buy that. I mean, look at you." His gaze flickered over her. "But I can't help worrying about the timing. You've been in New Orleans less than a week, and you're almost killed."

"New Orleans is a dangerous city," she said.

He resumed his pacing. "I realize that."

Something Lieutenant Robicheaux had said came back to Naomi. *"Have you never heard of a murder for hire?"* And suddenly she knew what Alex was thinking. She rose. "Are you afraid someone sent him here to attack me? Someone paid him to kill me?"

Alex shrugged. "I don't want to believe that."

"Who?" she asked hoarsely. "Who would want me dead?"

"Think about it, Naomi. You show up in New Orleans, claiming to be Taryn's birth mother. Claiming you have a right to her. You tell me. Who would be the number one suspect?"

She gasped. "You?"

"You can bet if things had worked out differently,

Robicheaux would have had a lot more questions for me this morning than he did.''

Naomi's hand fluttered to her throat. ''But who, other than you, would want me dead—'' She stopped short. ''Joseph Bellamy?''

''He could get rid of us both in one fell swoop. With you murdered and me in prison, he and Gwen would be given custody of Taryn.''

''But he'd be taking an awful risk,'' Naomi protested. ''His reputation, his name.''

''Maybe. But with James Robicheaux on his payroll, he may have figured he had all his bases covered.''

''Robicheaux?'' Naomi asked in shock. There had been something about the man she hadn't liked, but she hadn't figured him for a dirty cop.

''I wondered why he came after me the way he did when Aubree died,'' Alex said. ''I thought for a while it was because he had a thing for her. A lot of men did. But then I figured out one day that his zeal wasn't personal. It was bought and paid for by Joseph.''

''How did you manage to get Taryn out of the country so quickly? Didn't they try to stop you?''

He shrugged. ''They had no evidence against me. No reason to hold me. And Taryn was my daughter. I was her legal guardian. I had every right to take her back home with me.''

''I'm not questioning your decision,'' Naomi said softly. ''I was just wondering.'' She paused for a moment. ''There's something you should know about Aubree's murder. Something I found out that I haven't told you. Her body was found on the same day my daughter Sadie disappeared.''

His scowl turned to confusion. ''What are you saying, Naomi?''

''Just that given what happened fifteen years ago in that hospital in Eden, I find it hard to believe that the timing of your wife's murder and my daughter's disappearance could be a coincidence. How could it be?''

He gazed at her in astonishment. ''How could it *not* be? What possible connection could there be between those two events? Why would someone kill Aubree, and then drive to an obscure town in Mississippi to kidnap your daughter? It doesn't make sense.''

''I didn't think so, either, at first, but then...'' Naomi trailed off and glanced away. ''I've talked to a private investigator about this. The same one who helped me locate Taryn. I've asked him to look into Aubree's murder—''

He grabbed her arm. ''My God, why? Why would you do that?''

She blinked at his sudden anger. ''*Why?* Because I think there's a connection between Sadie's disappearance and Aubree's murder, that's why. I want to find out what it is.''

''Naomi.'' His grip on her tightened. ''I can understand why you'd want so desperately to find out what happened to your daughter. I can't even begin to imagine what the past ten years has been like for you. But you're grasping at straws again. I'll admit the timing seems suspect, but it has to be a coincidence.''

''No, it doesn't.'' She pulled away and stared up at him. ''What if Aubree was killed because she found out Taryn wasn't her child? What if she threatened to expose the person who swapped our babies? The person panicked and killed her.''

''And Sadie?''

''She was taken because she looked exactly like

Taryn. If anyone saw her, they'd know Taryn wasn't Aubree's daughter.''

It had sounded so much more logical in Michael Donnelly's office. Now it sounded like what it was—the desperate ravings of a desperate woman.

"Naomi," Alex said softly. "Suggesting someone might be frightened enough to kill Aubree in cold blood to save his own skin is one thing. But to harm an innocent child—'' He broke off when he saw the look on her face. "How long have you thought this?"

"I found out about the date last week, and then I talked to a private detective over the weekend."

"Would you mind if I talked to him, too?"

She frowned. "Why?"

"Because Aubree was my wife. She was my daughter's mother. If someone's going to be prying into her background, I think I have a right to be involved."

"Because Aubree was my wife." Was he still in love with her? Naomi wondered. In spite of the bitterness with which he spoke of her, could he still harbor deep feelings for her? Naomi drew a breath. "His name is Michael Donnelly. He has an office in Jackson, Mississippi. I have his number in my old suite, but I can't go in there right now because…" She trailed off as images flooded through her. The blood-soaked carpet. The splattered walls.

Naomi put trembling fingertips to her lips. Something in her face must have showed her horror, because Alex was beside her in a flash. He put his arms around her and drew her close. "It's okay. Shush. It's okay."

The rumble of his voice, the slow, steady beat of his heart brought fresh tears to her eyes. It had been so long since anyone had held her, since anyone had soothed her this way.

She drew back and stared up at him. His hand moved up to gently caress the bruises at her throat. ''I could kill him for that.''

Naomi shivered. ''I already did,'' she whispered, and then when she started to tremble again he pulled her back into his arms.

''I'm glad you killed him. If anything had happened to you—''

She felt his lips in her hair, and when she tilted her head back to gaze up at him, he trailed kisses down her face until he found her mouth.

This kiss was not a gentle brush of his lips against hers as their first had been. No, this was a real kiss. A deep, passionate, heart-pounding, soul-shattering, major-league kiss, and without hesitation, Naomi opened her mouth to his. She surrendered to his seduction with nothing so much as a whimper.

And when he walked her backward to the couch, when he pressed her back against the cushions, she did whimper then, but not in protest. She cupped her hand around the back of his neck and pulled him to her, kissing him as deeply and as passionately, although with perhaps less finesse, as he'd kissed her.

''Are you sure?'' he whispered raggedly into her ear.

''Yes, yes,'' she breathed.

His hand moved up to slide inside the lapels of her robe, and Naomi instantly froze. She could feel the cold edge of steel against her skin and she shuddered.

Alex instantly drew back. ''What's wrong.''

''I'm sorry.'' She reached up and pulled her robe tightly together. ''It's just…everything that happened…''

His gaze lit on her bruised throat, and he understood. ''I know. It's too soon.''

"It's just—"

"Naomi." He sat up, taking her hands and pulling her up with him. "You don't have to explain. I understand. Maybe everything considered, we should postpone the wedding."

"I don't want to do that. There's no reason to change our plans. I think it's more important than ever that we're together."

"Why do you say that?"

She drew a long breath. "Because there's something else I haven't told you. Taryn wants to find out who killed her mother. She says she has someone helping her, and I'm worried who it might be. I'm worried what happened to me...might happen to her."

Chapter Twelve

The next afternoon, Alex took a chopper out to one of Ventura's offshore drilling rigs, ostensibly to try and lay the groundwork for negotiations that would hopefully ward off a strike that had been threatening for weeks. But his real reason lay buried in the company's personnel files he'd had his secretary scour all morning.

The day was hot and clear, with unlimited visibility and sunlight glimmering on the whitecaps. The helicopter skimmed over the water, heading due south, toward a black dot on the horizon. As it neared the drilling platform, Alex stared out the window. It never failed to amaze him, the lengths humans would go to for energy. The Gulf waters were relatively mild most of the time, but Alex had seen the aftermath of a drilling rig that had been torn apart by a sudden squall in the North Sea. The crews barely had time to evacuate before the platform had collapsed into the sea.

He could see men down there now, going about their duties. Some of them glanced up as the chopper circled, and then the pilot vectored in on the landing platform.

The moment they touched down, Alex removed his headset and climbed out. Leaning forward, he hurried from beneath the rotating blades as a man came out to meet him.

"Mr. DeWitt?" The man extended his hand. "Larry Crawford."

Alex shook hands with him. "Ray Beauchamp worked on your crew?"

"Yeah. Come on inside. I've got what you wanted to see."

Alex followed the man down a narrow, noisy passageway. The platform was huge and well anchored, but Alex could feel the pull of the sea, the slight sway beneath his feet when he tried to stand still. When he'd worked on a similar rig twenty years ago, he'd been one of the lucky few who'd adapted quickly, but there'd been plenty who hadn't. Seasickness was common, and the hours were grueling and stressful. They'd worked in shifts, twenty-four, seven for three weeks straight, and then a week off. Some of the men never came back after that first stint. But the money had been good, and Alex had been able to save enough to put himself through college.

Crawford's office was small and messy, and he made a swipe at some papers on his desk as he sat down. "Have a seat."

Alex remained standing. "You've got Ray Beauchamp's personal effects?"

Crawford bent down, picked up a cardboard box from the floor, then dropped it on his desk with a thud. "This is it. Everything that was in his locker."

"Have the police contacted you?"

Crawford rubbed a hand along his chin where gray bristles were starting to show. "I hadn't talked to anybody until your secretary called this morning. That's the first I'd heard about Ray."

"Was he due back yesterday morning?"

"Yeah, he'd been off for a week. You never knew if he was going to turn back up or not. I wasn't especially surprised when he didn't."

"If he was that unreliable, why'd you keep him on?"

Crawford rubbed his chin again. "Because, as you can see, the accommodations out here aren't exactly what you'd call commodious. Some people can't take it. We have fellows coming and going all the time. That's why, when you get somebody like Ray, you're willing to put up with some crap just to keep him on. Say what you will about him, but he was the best damn welder I ever saw."

Alex rifled through the box of Ray Beauchamp's personal effects. There wasn't much. A paperback novel, a couple of *Penthouse* magazines, some odds and ends of clothing.

"According to his personnel file, he'd only been working for Ventura a few months," he said.

"That's right. But he had prior experience. That's why I hired him on. He'd worked these rigs for years."

Alex glanced up. "Did you know him before he came to work for Ventura?"

"Yeah, we both used to work for Exxon, years and years ago."

"Did you know anything about his personal life, his family? Anything like that?"

Crawford shrugged. "Not really. He stayed pretty much to himself. There was one time, though, we ended up on the same rotation. We were off the same week. When we got back to town, he took me to some seedy bar down in the Quarter for a few drinks. He got to talking after a couple. He told me this story about his old man. The guy was a New Orleans cop a long time ago, and he up and went crazy one night, chopped up Ray's mama with a butcher knife, right there in front of Ray and his sisters. He would have killed them, too, Ray said, if his older sister hadn't gotten them out of the house. Turned out, the old man had killed a whole bunch of other people before that. Some kind of damn serial killer, I guess. He got sent up, but they didn't keep 'em on death row like they do now. Fried 'em pretty quick back then. Ray said he and his sisters watched the old man get the juice. After that, the two girls changed their names, because of what their old man did. But Ray…'' Crawford shook his head. ''He acted like he was kinda proud of it.''

''He tell you anything else?''

Crawford shrugged. ''No. And to tell you the truth, I never knew whether to believe him or not. He told it dead serious, but like I said, he'd had a couple of drinks. Any more than a couple, and Ray got real mean.''

''Do you know if his sisters are still alive?''

''Ray said one of them was still living in New Orleans, but like I said, that was years ago. I don't know if she's still there or not. I didn't associate with him much after that night. He quit his job a few weeks later, and I never saw him again until he turned up here.''

''You're sure this is everything that was in his locker?'' Alex asked, closing the flaps on the box.

Crawford hesitated. ''Look, I know you've got a lot of clout with Ventura, and if you say this is none of my business, that's the end of it as far as I'm concerned. But I can't help wondering what your interest is in Ray Beauchamp, why you came all the way out here to look at a few puny possessions. You figure Ventura might have some liability where that woman he attacked is concerned?''

"That woman he attacked is my fiancée," Alex said.

Crawford looked astonished. "You don't say. Nobody told me anything about that." He sat back and whistled. "Man, she must be one helluva woman, is all I can say, if she got the better of ol' Ray Beauchamp."

"She is," Alex said, and realized he meant it.

Crawford looked suddenly nervous. "All right, there is something else. Something I didn't put in that box. But I don't want you to think I kept it for myself. I was afraid if I put it in with all that other junk, it might just walk off, if you get my drift. And I kinda had in mind to try and find Ray's sisters when I got the time. Give it to one of them."

"What is it?"

Crawford unlocked his desk drawer, pulled out a plastic bag and handed it to Alex. "I don't know much about jewelry, but it looks pretty real to me. Where do you figure a guy like Ray Beauchamp got something like that?"

Alex unzipped the bag and let the ring slide into his palm. Light from a window behind Crawford's desk sparkled off the diamonds that surrounded an exotic blue gemstone. A Kashmir sapphire, the exact shade of Aubree's eyes.

On Friday morning, Naomi stood before the full-length mirror in the bedroom of her suite and critiqued her appearance. Did she look like a bride? she wondered nervously. She certainly felt like one. The butterflies in her stomach had been going wild ever since she'd awakened at five o'clock that morning.

She'd shopped for hours the day before, finally coming across a boutique on Royal Street that carried a collection of the most feminine, romantic dresses she'd ever seen. After hours of deliberation, she'd finally settled on a two-piece ivory silk brocade, simple in design but exquisitely cut. It fit like a dream, and as Naomi stared at herself in the mirror, she wondered what Alex would think. Would he like it? Would he think her beautiful?

As beautiful as Aubree?

Stop it! she chided herself. This wasn't even a real wedding. What did it really matter what Alex thought? The only reason they were getting married was because of Taryn.

Then why did it feel like a real wedding? A little voice persisted. Why was she spending so much time fussing with her appearance? Why was she so apprehensive about...tonight?

What would he expect of her?

Naomi grew even more nervous thinking about it. She'd only been with one man in her entire life, and that had been years ago, when she was just a teenager. And Clay Willis had hardly been a man of the world. He hadn't taught her a thing about the fine art of seduction, but merely how cramped and uncomfortable lovemaking could be in the back seat of a car.

Would she be able to please Alex? Did she even want to try?

What if he didn't expect anything of her? What if he really wanted a marriage in name only?

No, no, that kiss proved otherwise, didn't it?

Oh, she was making herself crazy, and she had to stop thinking about it before she changed her mind about the whole thing.

A knock sounded on the door, and Naomi started. She hadn't slept well all week, not since the attack, and she told herself, as she went to answer the door, that it was perfectly natural she'd be jittery. Someone had tried to murder her, and now days later, she was getting married to a man she'd known just over a week. She'd be concerned about herself if she wasn't on edge.

Glancing through the peephole, she saw a man wearing the maroon blazer with the monogrammed *S* on the breast pocket, which signified the Spencer staff. She drew back the door, and the man smiled as he offered her a package.

"This just came for you, Miss Cross."

When she took the box, he didn't wait for a tip. "Have a nice day," he said cheerfully.

Naomi carried the package into her suite and sat down on the sofa to open it. It was beautifully wrapped in delicate silver tissue paper trimmed with a silver-and-white bow. With trembling fingers, she tore it open, and then when she saw the blue velvet box inside, she grew even more excited.

Opening the hinged lid, she breathed a silent "Oh!" as she stared down at the single strand of pearls. They reminded her of moonbeams, lustrous and delicate. And the diamond stations that went all the way around glittered like starlight.

The card inside said simply, "Alex," and without quite knowing why, Naomi burst into tears, completely ruining her makeup.

"WILL YOU STOP that infernal pacing?" Foley demanded. "One would think you're a real bridegroom with honest-to-goodness prenuptial jitters."

"I *am* a real bridegroom," Alex snapped. "And since this was your idea, I'd think you'd be a little more understanding."

"Oh, I feel sorry for you, buddy. I really do." Foley clapped him on the shoulder. "Having to be married to a woman who looks like Naomi Cross—jeez. You must be really dreading the wedding night."

"Oh, shut up," Alex muttered, but in truth, he'd been thinking of little else all morning. Not that he *was* dreading his wedding night with Naomi. Far from it. He just didn't want to appear too eager. He didn't want to make her nervous or frighten her. She'd been through a terrible ordeal, and she needed patience and understanding. He just didn't feel all that patient at the moment.

And, of course, the fact that he hadn't told her about Aubree's ring being in Ray Beauchamp's possession was also weighing on him. He'd thought about going to the police with the information, but Alex didn't trust James Robicheaux. Somehow he knew that Robicheaux would find a way to turn the tables and implicate Alex. After all, Ray Beauchamp worked for Ventura.

So instead, Alex had gotten in touch with Naomi's private detective. Whether it had been the right thing to do or not, he had no idea.

He turned to Foley. "What time is it?"

"Two minutes later than the last time you asked me. Relax. She'll be here."

"She's late, isn't she?"

"Only a couple of minutes.

What if she wasn't coming? What if she'd changed her mind?

Alex's gaze drifted across the room to where Taryn sat quietly reading a book. He hadn't been certain she'd actually come today even though she'd reluctantly agreed to be Naomi's maid of honor. She'd been strangely subdued all week. Rather than reacting with shock and indignation about Alex's sudden decision to marry, she'd continued to show nothing but indifference. When he'd tried to talk to her about it, she'd just shrugged and said philosophically, "You're a grown man. You can do whatever you want."

"But I don't want to make you unhappy."

"I'm not unhappy. I have my own life."

And that was exactly what worried Alex. What was going on inside that head of hers? Was she really trying to find out who'd killed her mother? Could she really be in danger, as Naomi seemed to think?

A shiver of dread coursed through him. If anything happened to Taryn…if anything happened to Naomi…

He had to find some answers, and fast.

Foley tapped him on the shoulder and he turned. Naomi had just come into the outer office of the judge's chambers, and the moment Alex spotted her, his heart stopped.

Beside him, Foley muttered under his breath, "Lord have mercy—"

But Alex tuned him out. He tuned everything out as he walked over to Naomi. They might have been the only two people in the room. "I was worried there for a minute you'd changed your mind."

"No, I just…" She touched the pearls at her throat. "Thank you for my gift. They're beautiful."

"You do them justice," he said, then cleared his throat. An awkwardness came over them both, and suddenly Alex didn't have a clue what to say to her.

Naomi saw Taryn, and her eyes, as always, lit in pleasure. "She came."

Alex didn't say anything, but his throat tightened as he watched Naomi glide across the room and sit down beside his daughter. They had the same dark hair, the same brown eyes. He'd never noticed before how much they resembled each other. Like mother and daughter.

And in that moment, he knew. A fist of pain closed over his heart.

TARYN GLANCED UP when Naomi sat down beside her. She didn't smile, but her gaze was neither hostile nor friendly. She looked a bit…confused.

"I'm glad you came today," Naomi told her.

Taryn tossed back her dark hair. "I told you I would."

"I know. But under the circumstances, I would have understood if you'd changed your mind."

Taryn merely shrugged, but Naomi couldn't help wondering if the short, black dress Taryn had chosen to wear was her own subtle way of conveying her displeasure.

"Taryn, there's something I want to say to you," Naomi began tentatively.

The dark eyes, so like Sadie's, turned on her. "Let me guess. You aren't going to try to take my mother's place, but you hope eventually we can become good friends."

Naomi smiled ruefully. "One would almost think you'd been through this before."

"No. But what else is there to say?"

Naomi got the message loud and clear. Taryn wasn't going to protest this marriage, but she wasn't going to welcome Naomi with open arms, either. It wasn't going to be easy, but maybe in time…what? They'd become friends? Naomi wanted more than that. So much more.

"I have something for you." She opened her handbag and withdrew a tiny, gold-wrapped package.

Taryn looked surprised. "What is it?"

"Open it and see."

She took the package, but her gaze remained skeptical. "You didn't have to buy me a present."

"It's customary for the bride to give something to her maid of honor. Go on." Naomi nodded to the package. "Open it."

Taryn reluctantly tore away the paper and opened the lid of the jeweler's box. Inside, nestled against black velvet, was a tiny butterfly charm suspended from a delicate gold chain that sparkled brilliantly when Taryn lifted it. The tiny wings were encrusted with gemstones no bigger than the head of a pin.

Naomi had found it yesterday while she'd been shopping for earrings to match her dress. The moment she'd seen the pendant, she'd wanted it desperately for Taryn. She'd forgotten all about the earrings.

"It's beautiful." Taryn's dark eyes shimmered with what might have been tears, but she quickly glanced away.

"Shall I fasten it for you?"

"It doesn't exactly match what I'm wearing," she muttered, but she handed the chain to Naomi and pulled aside her hair.

Naomi's fingers trembled as she struggled with the tiny clasp, and she thought to herself that she would do anything, *anything,* to have more moments like this.

And then it was time to go inside, and before Naomi could even begin to have second thoughts, the ceremony was over. She and Alex exchanged their vows, and when she looked down as he slipped a ring onto her finger, she saw the sparkle of yet more diamonds. A girl could get used to this, she thought dizzily.

When it was her turn to slip the ring she'd bought for Alex on his finger, she was relieved that it slid over his knuckle without effort. Almost as if it was meant to be. He bent to kiss her, a brief closing ritual, nothing more, but Naomi's lips parted automatically, and she heard him catch his breath.

For just a moment, the kiss deepened. His arms tightened around her, and Naomi closed her eyes, relishing the moment. She could feel his heart beating against hers, and an image flashed through her mind. The two of them together, tonight, in an even more intimate embrace.

When he released her, their gazes clung, and Naomi could have sworn she saw her own fantasy reflected in the depths of his eyes.

HE TOOK HER TO LUNCH at the Palm Court Restaurant on Chartres. Taryn had begged off the celebration, insisting that she had a math test that afternoon she couldn't miss. Alex had been on the verge of insisting that she come with them, but Foley had stepped in and offered to drive her to school. "You two lovebirds want to be alone anyway," he said with a wink.

So Naomi and Alex had headed off to the restaurant alone, and once they were ensconced in a cozy alcove that looked out on the restaurant's famous fountain, he ordered champagne. Naomi sipped hers slowly as she studied the menu, trying like crazy to avoid eye contact with Alex. She felt like a teenager again. She felt the way she had after her first time with Clay Willis, when they'd hurriedly dressed and then hadn't known what to say to each other for the rest of the night.

"Naomi."

A shiver slipped up her spine at the way Alex said her name. He wasn't Clay Willis. Far from it. "Yes?"

"You're not eating your lunch."

"I suppose I'm a little nervous," she admitted.

"No need to be nervous now. The deed's done."

Not quite, she thought. "Marriage is a big step, Alex. No matter the reason."

He smiled suddenly, surprising Naomi. "You know, I believe that's the first time you've called me by my first name."

Naomi blushed. "I couldn't very well keep calling you Mr. DeWitt, could I?"

"No, I suppose not." He glanced at her barely touched plate. "Do you want me to order you something else?"

"No, the food is delicious. The restaurant is beautiful. Everything is perfect. Thank you for going to so much trouble."

"This was your first wedding," he said. "I know it's probably not the way you imagined it would be, but...I wanted to make it special for you."

Naomi's eyes glistened with sudden tears. "It is. And the fact that Taryn came—"

When she broke off, Alex's gaze on her deepened. "You love her very much, don't you?"

"Yes."

"Even without the DNA test."

"I don't need any test to prove she's my daughter."

Alex drew a long breath. "Naomi—"

Their waiter came by then to present the check, and Naomi never knew what Alex had meant to say. She excused herself to freshen up, and once in the ladies' room, she sat down at the mirror and stared at her pale reflection. The same reflection that had stared back at her this morning, only that woman had been Naomi Cross. Now she was Mrs. Alex DeWitt.

Naomi began to tremble uncontrollably.

When the door opened, she hastily pulled a tube of lipstick from her bag and pretended to freshen up.

Instead of going to one of the stalls, the woman came over and sat down beside Naomi. Their gazes met briefly in the mirror before she pulled out her own lipstick and began to expertly reapply it.

She was an older woman, late fifties, but still very attractive, with blond hair and vivid blue eyes. She wore a navy suit and the most exquisite gold jewelry Naomi had ever seen.

"You don't know who I am, do you?" she asked.

Naomi glanced at her in surprise. "No. Should I?"

"I'm Gwen Bellamy. I saw you come in with Alex, and I couldn't resist having a word with you."

Naomi remembered the threat Joseph Bellamy had made the other day, and she stared at the woman in trepidation.

"You look like a deer caught in the headlights," Gwen said with an airy laugh. "Don't look so frightened. I don't bite."

Good to know, Naomi thought.

"It might surprise you to learn that I'm on your side in all this."

"How do you even know who I am?" Naomi asked in confusion.

Gwen made a production of fluffing her blond hair. "Don't be ridiculous. My husband has had you thoroughly checked out, and when he becomes preoccupied with a woman as young and as lovely as you, you can bet I have her checked out as well."

"Mrs. Bellamy—"

"Gwen."

Naomi shrugged helplessly. "What do you want?"

The pleasant expression disappeared from Gwen Bellamy's attractive face, replaced in an instant by a look of cold calculation. "Taryn has been telling Joseph every move you and Alex make. He knows that the two of you have plotted this quickie marriage because you think that together you'll be able to thwart his efforts to get custody. But you won't stop him. Not that way."

Naomi stared at her in shock. "What do you mean?"

Gwen Bellamy turned on the stool and faced Naomi, her expression hard and brittle beneath the expertly applied cosmetics. "I'm going to let you in on a little secret. I despised Aubree. I hated everything about her. She was just a little girl when Joseph and I married, but even then she was a manipulative, selfish little witch who tried to destroy anything and everyone who crossed her path. She maligned me to Joseph every chance she got, and he always took her side over mine. I was glad when she grew up. Glad when she moved out and took Louise with her. I couldn't stand either one them. They were always plotting behind my back, always figuring new ways to torment me. I thought things would get better after they left." Her mouth tightened, showing her age. "But Joseph couldn't let her go."

"What are you saying?" Naomi asked almost fearfully.

Gwen's gaze met hers, then flickered away. "He adored her. He would have given her the world on a silver platter, but she cared nothing for him. She used him like she used everyone else, and that only made him cling all the harder to the glorified image he had of her. To the dreams he had for her. The only thing Aubree ever cared about was her daughter." She paused, her eyes going very dark and very cold. "That's why I want you to take that away from her."

Naomi gasped. "Aubree is dead, Mrs. Bellamy."

She swung around to the mirror, staring at her own reflection. "Not to Joseph. He sees her in Taryn. He'll never be free of her while Taryn is still alive."

Naomi's blood went cold.

Gwen Bellamy's hand crept to her throat. "If Taryn is your daughter, then claim her legally. Do it now. It's the only way to stop Joseph. Get her out of New Orleans, do you understand? Alex should never have brought her back here. It was bound to stir memories—"

"What memories?" When the woman remained silent, Naomi said, "Memories of the night Aubree was murdered?"

Gwen's gaze met hers in the mirror. "If Taryn is your daughter, then you have to get her out of New Orleans. The sooner the better. And if she really is Aubree's daughter—" the blue eyes closed briefly "—then God help her."

THE HOUSE ON OCTAVIA STREET was silent when Naomi and Alex arrived after lunch. "I've given Louise the weekend off so we have the place to ourselves," he explained as he tossed his keys into a crystal bowl that sat on a carved oak table in the foyer.

Naomi cleared her throat. "What about Taryn? Won't she be home from school soon?"

"She's spending tonight and tomorrow night with a friend."

"Do you think that wise?" Naomi asked in alarm. After her conversation with Gwen Bellamy, she didn't want to let Taryn out of her sight.

"Taryn's supposed to be grounded, but I decided to make an exception just this once. I thought it might be easier if you and I had some time to...get used to things.

I know the girl's parents. She'll be okay. Besides. You can't keep a teenager locked in her room, Naomi.''

He was probably right, and Naomi appreciated his thoughtfulness, but she couldn't get Gwen's warning out of her head. She went into the living room and stood gazing around at the room, her home now. When Alex came up beside her, she was acutely aware of his presence.

He was very tall and very masculine, and he made her want things she'd long ago given up wanting.

Naomi wished suddenly that they were a normal bride and groom, with not just the evening to look forward to, but the rest of their lives. Their marriage, however, was far from normal, and the events that had led up to it were even more extraordinary.

''What kind of relationship did Aubree have with her father?'' she asked quietly.

Beside her, Alex stiffened. ''Why do you ask?''

She turned to face him. ''I saw Gwen Bellamy in the ladies' room at the restaurant today.''

''So that's what's bothering you. I knew it was something. What did she say to you?''

Naomi tucked her hair behind her ears. ''She said that if Taryn really is my daughter, I should get her out of New Orleans. The sooner the better. And I think she has a point.''

Alex's brow furrowed. ''Taryn is legally my daughter. You can't just waltz off with her.''

''I realize that. But I'm becoming more and more convinced that the reason she has suppressed memories is because she saw something the night Aubree died. I think coming back to New Orleans has triggered something for her. You said she's undergone a drastic change. Maybe that's why. Maybe it's the reason she's become so obsessed with finding Aubree's killer. But if she starts asking the wrong questions…if she starts to remember…''

Alex took her arms. ''You're forgetting something, Naomi. Taryn wasn't in the house that night. She and Louise didn't come back from the beach until the next day.''

''So Louise says.''

''Why would she lie?''

Naomi shrugged. ''I don't know. But there's something…odd about that woman.''

''You can't accuse someone of murder because they're odd,'' Alex said grimly.

''I'm not accusing her of murder,'' Naomi defended. ''From what you've told me, she and Aubree were very close. But maybe she's protecting someone.''

''Who?''

Naomi moistened her lips. ''Someone she felt as much loyalty to as she did to Aubree.''

He gazed down at her in astonishment. ''You mean Joseph? He was crazy about Aubree. He would never have hurt her.''

''People do a lot of sick things in the name of love,'' she said softly. ''He put Aubree on a pedestal. He had this golden image of her. What if she did something…what if he found out something that destroyed that image? That threatened to destroy everything he cared about?''

''But *murder?*'' Alex's hands dropped from her arms. He looked suddenly stunned.

''Maybe that's why he tried so hard to pin it on you.''

A look of rage flashed across Alex's features. He turned and strode from the room. After a moment, Naomi hurried to follow him. He was standing in his study, phone to his ear as he paced back and forth. ''No, no, that's okay. I don't need to speak with her. I just wanted to make sure she's okay.'' He listened for a moment, then said, ''Look, I'd appreciate it if you'd keep a close eye on Taryn. I know the girls were talking about going to a movie or something, but maybe they could just rent some videos. I'll explain everything when I see you on Sunday.''

He hung up and glanced at Naomi. ''Taryn's fine. I don't think we need to worry about her tonight. I know this family. I trust them. They'll take good care of her.''

Naomi wanted to believe him, but she was still worried. ''Everything's connected,'' she said. ''The hospital in Eden. Aubree's murder. Sadie's disappearance. I know they're all connected, and that's why someone sent Ray Beauchamp to kill me.''

Alex came around his desk to stand in front of her. ''I don't know how they could be,'' he said grimly, ''but I'm afraid you may be right.''

ALEX showed Naomi around the house that afternoon. It was a lovely home, full of beautiful furnishings and interesting objects of art that Alex and Taryn had collected in their travels overseas. But Naomi couldn't relax and enjoy the tour. Nor could she appreciate the anticipation of sharing such a comfortable home with Alex and Taryn. None of them would have any peace until they found out the truth about Taryn's birth and Aubree's death.

Except for Louise's quarters, which were off the kitchen in the back, the other bedrooms were upstairs. The master suite was at the far end of the hall, secluded from the others by an archway that led to a private corridor. The suite was large and airy, done mostly in

bold autumn shades of gold, brown and hunter-green.
A masculine room that made Naomi shiver in awareness.

Her suitcases were on the bed. Alex had had someone
from the hotel deliver them earlier, along with her Jeep.

"You probably want to get unpacked and changed,"
he said, backing toward the door. "I'll give you some
privacy."

Naomi nodded, trying to keep her gaze from drifting
to the king-size bed.

"You can rest for a while if you want," he said.
"We're not on a timetable. We can go out to dinner
whenever you want."

"All right."

Alone to unpack, Naomi felt oddly self-conscious,
putting her things in dresser drawers that had been
cleared out especially for her, and a closet that had been
rearranged to accommodate her meager wardrobe.

Alex's presence was everywhere—his shaving sup-
plies in the bathroom, his cologne on the dresser. Manly
things that did very feminine things to her insides.

Once everything was put away, Naomi glanced
around, unsure what to do next. She could go downstairs and find Alex, but he had seemed in a hurry to
leave her, as if he needed some time to himself. Maybe
that was what they both needed—time to adjust.

Removing her wedding outfit, Naomi hung the skirt
and top in the closet, then turned back the bed and
crawled between the sheets in her slip. She suddenly
felt very tired, and a nap might help refresh her, might
ease her trepidation for the coming night.

But her dreams were far from restful. As if watching
from a distance, she saw Aubree's body floating in a
bloodred swimming pool. Taryn stood on the side,

screaming that someone had killed her mother. Naomi wanted to go to her, but she couldn't move. Not even when a menacing shadow appeared behind Taryn.

Run! Taryn, run! she wanted to scream, but no sound came out. Naomi could only watch in terror as the shadow moved closer. She thought for a moment it was Ray Beauchamp, but it wasn't. It was—

"Naomi! Wake up!"

She opened her eyes with an effort. When she saw a shadow leaning over her, she gasped and tried to move away.

"It's me. It's Alex," he said soothingly. "You were having a nightmare."

She struggled to sit up. "How long have I been asleep?" she asked groggily.

"A few hours."

"A few hours!" No wonder the room was so dim. She glanced toward the window, saw that darkness had fallen outside.

"What time is it?"

"After nine."

She'd been asleep for five hours! She ran a hand across her eyes. "I'm sorry. Is it too late to go to dinner?"

"Not in New Orleans. Do you feel like getting out?"

Not really, she thought. The bed felt so warm and cozy and safe. Outside, in the darkness, evil lurked.

"Taryn—" she said in alarm.

"I just talked to Taryn. She's fine."

Naomi lay back against the pillows. "I had a dream about her. I dreamed she was in danger."

"Taryn's safe and sound. It's you I'm worried about. You're the one who was almost killed," he reminded her grimly.

Naomi sighed. "I know."

"Tell you what," he said, patting her arm. "You stay put. I'll fix something downstairs and bring it up to you."

"You don't have to wait on me," she protested. "I'm not used to that."

"I know," he said. "That's why I want to do it."

He started to get up, but Naomi caught his arm. "Alex?"

"Yes?"

"We did the right thing, didn't we? For Taryn?"

He sighed. "I don't know, Naomi. All I know is that I'd do anything for my daughter. If a DNA test proves that you gave birth to her, I don't want to lose her. I don't want you to take her away from me."

Naomi's eyes flooded with tears. "I wouldn't do that."

"No," he said. "I don't believe you would. Not unless you thought it in her best interest. But this way, we can both be with her, for as long as she'll let us." He lifted his hand and pushed back her hair very gently.

Naomi shivered as he trailed his fingers down the side of her face. "It won't be so bad," he whispered.

At the moment, Naomi didn't think it was bad at all. She was feeling quite...good.

He leaned over her, his gaze deep and intense in the shadows. "I'm very attracted to you, Naomi."

She didn't know what to say to that, so she moistened her lips and tried to forget the fact that she wore only a silk slip beneath the covers.

His fingers glided over her throat, where only faint remnants of the bruises remained. He traced the outline of lace where her slip dipped between her breasts, and

Naomi's heart threatened to pound its way out of her chest.

Very deliberately, he took the edge of the cover and pushed it away, exposing her, and his gaze moved greedily over the slip, her bare legs. He drew his breath in sharply.

"God, you're beautiful," he murmured. "I think I've wanted you from the first moment you walked into my office."

A little over a week ago, but it seemed like a lifetime. So much had happened. Naomi felt as if she'd been waiting for this moment forever.

She put her hands up to his shoulders and drew her to him. Their mouths touched, and Naomi trembled. He knew just how to kiss her. He knew how to awaken needs inside her that she hadn't even known existed. He was certainly no clumsy teenager, and this wasn't the back seat of a car. And yet there remained a forbidden aspect to their lovemaking that thrilled Naomi to her core.

He tugged the straps of her slip down her arms, and then slid the silky fabric over her hips, along her legs. The other bits of silk followed, until she wore nothing but moonlight. When he stood to remove his own clothing, she reached down and drew the sheet over her.

He lay down beside her. "Don't cover up. Let me look at you."

"I'm shy."

"Why would a woman who looks like you be shy about her body?"

Her gaze met his in the darkness. "I'm inexperienced. I've only been with one other man."

He looked surprised. "The boy who got you pregnant? I say boy, because I certainly wouldn't call him a man," he said scornfully. Then he gave her a reproachful look. "That was a long time ago, Naomi. A long time to be celibate."

"I've...had other things on my mind."

His voice grew sober. "I know." He reached under the cover to take her hand and then lifted their entwined fingers to his lips. "You're an extraordinary woman, Naomi."

"No, I'm not. I'm a survivor, that's all."

"Any man would be lucky to have you as the mother of his children."

Naomi was deeply moved. A tear coursed down her cheek, and he thumbed it away. "Hey," he said softly. "I didn't mean to make you cry. This is not a night for sadness."

"I'm not sad," she sniffed. "I'm just emotional. There's a difference."

"Then let's get more emotional, shall we?"

She smiled shyly. "I thought you'd never ask."

They were lying side by side, and he drew their bodies together, until they were touching so intimately Naomi could hardly breathe. But this wasn't like the other times she'd known. The few times. There was no fumbling. No hurrying. Alex took his time with her, arousing her body in ways she'd never even imagined.

He stroked her, whispered to her, kissed her long and deep until she grew hot and shivery all over. A strange tension began to build inside her, and she clutched Alex's shoulders as he moved over her. And then they were moving together, the tension growing tighter and tighter...

She whispered his name on a heated plea.

''Let it happen,'' he murmured.

And it did, a glorious release that lifted Naomi from her everyday world and dropped her, for one brief instant, into paradise.

Chapter Thirteen

Taryn came back on Sunday afternoon. She'd gone straight upstairs to her room when Alex had first brought her home, but later Naomi saw her walking across the backyard toward a greenhouse.

Since Alex was working in his study, Naomi thought it might be a good opportunity to try to get to know Taryn a little better. She was anxious to spend some time alone with her.

Located just beyond the pool, the greenhouse was a massive structure with a pointed roof made of heavy glass panels that could be opened and closed by a system of pulleys and cranks. Stepping inside was like walking into some remote, tropical jungle.

Plants and flowers grew in profusion, but what caught Naomi's attention, what held her enthralled, was the profusion of orange-and-black monarchs that swarmed the clay pots of heliotrope, snapdragons and lantana. Wire mesh cages suspended from the ceiling housed the more exotic varieties of butterflies.

She saw Taryn at the back and, hoping she wouldn't mind the intrusion, Naomi started toward her. Taryn's attention was rapt as she stared into one of the cages, and as Naomi approached, she saw the source of the girl's fascination—an adult butterfly crawling from a newly split chrysalis.

Taryn glanced up, acknowledging Naomi's presence. Naomi smiled. "I hope you don't mind. I wanted to see your butterflies." She turned, gesturing with her hand. "This is incredible. I've never seen anything like it. You've done all this by yourself?"

Pride flashed in Taryn's dark eyes, before she tossed her dark hair and shrugged. "The greenhouse was already here when we moved in, but Dad had some renovations done for me."

"How did you ever learn to raise butterflies?" Naomi asked in awe. "I know enough to plant butterfly bushes and trumpet vines in my backyard to keep them coming back year after year, but this!" She lifted her arms as a half-dozen or so monarchs landed on her bright yellow shirt.

"They like yellow," Taryn said. "And red. Are you really interested in learning about butterflies?" she asked skeptically.

"Absolutely."

"Most people just plant nectar sources in their backyard, if they want to attract butterflies, like your trumpet vines, but you also need host plants where females can lay their eggs and the caterpillars later can feed."

"What do caterpillars eat?"

"Milkweed attracts monarchs and swallowtails. Others, like the Elfin and painted ladies, like clover, parsley, Queen Anne's lace." She named a few more, then held out her hand and a tiny blue butterfly landed in her palm. "Butterflies taste with their feet. I bet you didn't know that. And they drink nectar through a strawlike structure called a proboscis." She blew gently on the tiny creature, and its wings lifted into the air.

Naomi was mesmerized. "When did you become interested in growing butterflies?"

"I don't know. I've just always loved them."

"Look, Mama, they came back. Just like you said they would. Aren't they beautiful?"

Naomi's eyes filled with sudden tears and she glanced away. But Taryn didn't seem to notice as she busied herself with one of the cages.

"May I ask you something, Taryn?"

"About butterflies?"

"No. I want to talk to you about our conversation at the restaurant last week,"

Taryn glanced up, her gaze shuttered. "You mean the night you told me that you and my dad were just acquaintances? That there was nothing going on between you? Oh, don't worry," she hastened to add. "I don't care that you married my dad. I really don't. It'll keep him out of my hair."

"So you can do what?"

Taryn turned back to the cage. "Whatever I want."

"Like finding your mother's killer?"

She whirled, her gaze accusing. "I bet you couldn't wait to tell him about that, could you?"

"It wasn't like that," Naomi said. "I didn't want to break your confidence, but I thought it was something he should know about."

Taryn gave Naomi a defiant look. "It doesn't matter. He can't make me stop."

"What do you mean?" When Taryn didn't answer, Naomi said anxiously, "You mentioned you had someone helping you. Will you tell me who it is?"

Taryn hesitated. "If I tell you, you'll just report back to my dad."

"Would that be so bad?"

She shrugged. "He's not going to stop me, and neither are you."

Alarmed, Naomi took Taryn's arm. "Why don't you let me help you?"

She brushed off Naomi's hand. "How can you help me? You didn't even know my mother."

"I never met her, but I feel we're...connected."

"Because of my father?"

Because of you, Naomi wanted to tell her. "I know of a private investigator," she said. "I think he can help us."

"How could he help?" Taryn said scornfully. "Don't you get it? The evidence isn't out there." She spread her arms, waving toward the glass walls of the greenhouse. "The evidence is in here." She tapped her finger against her temple. "All I have to do is find the key."

"The key to what?" Naomi asked helplessly.

"My suppressed memories. I know a woman in the Quarter who can help me unlock them using hypnosis."

"Hypnosis?" Naomi started to put her hand on Taryn's arm again, but then thought better of it. "Hypnosis can be dangerous unless you're dealing with a trained professional. A therapist. It's not something you should be messing around with."

"I'm not messing around. This isn't a game," Taryn said angrily. "Besides, she's already put me under several times. I'm a very responsive subject, she says. She's even given me a posthypnotic suggestion so that each time it will get easier and easier to induce a trance."

"Did...you remember anything?" Naomi asked almost fearfully.

She shook her head. "Not yet. She says I won't remember until I'm ready. I can't force it. But I think I'm getting close.''

THAT EVENING Alex, Naomi and Taryn sat down to their first meal together as a family. Naomi was so nervous she could hardly sit still. She'd cooked a simple dinner of meat loaf, mashed potatoes and homemade biscuits, and she'd set the table in the kitchen, rather than the dining room, hoping the more casual atmosphere would help calm tensions.

But the moment all three sat down, an awkwardness settled over the table. Naomi and Alex tried to keep the conversation flowing, but Taryn picked sullenly at her food. She said nothing throughout the meal, and when Naomi caught her eye from time to time, Taryn would flash her a defiant look, as if she were daring her to tell Alex about the hypnosis.

The dinner was so strained that Naomi was almost relieved when the phone rang. Alex must have felt the same way because he jumped up to answer it before anyone else could.

''This is Alex DeWitt.'' He listened for a moment, then said in a tense voice, ''Where are you?'' Another silence. ''I can be there in twenty minutes.''

He hung up and walked back over to the table. ''Sorry. Something's come up. I have to leave for a while.''

Naomi stared up at him in consternation. ''What's wrong?''

He shrugged, but there was something in his eyes she didn't like. ''Nothing's wrong. I'll be back as soon as I can.''

Taryn slanted him a sly look. ''What happened? Ventura stock plunge a few points and everyone at headquarters is threatening to jump?''

He tweaked her nose. "Don't be so cavalier. Ventura stock is going to put you through college."

"I told you I'm not going to college."

"I thought you'd decided to go to law school," he reminded her.

"I think I might like to be a cop." Her gaze met Naomi's. "Or a hypnotist."

Alex rolled his eyes as he turned to leave. Naomi followed him out to his car. "Alex, what's really going on? I can tell something's wrong."

He opened the car door but stood for a moment, gazing down at her. "Nothing's wrong. There's just something I have to take care of."

"Something I should know about?"

He hesitated. "I'll tell you all about it when I get back."

Thunder rumbled in the distance, and Naomi shivered. "It's going to storm."

Alex searched the sky. "I should be back before it hits. Just stay inside and keep an eye on Taryn for me, will you? Make sure she doesn't try to sneak out."

"Do you think she might?"

"I don't think so. I came down pretty hard on her the last time she went someplace without my knowing. But just the same…"

Naomi wrapped her arms around her middle as the thunder boomed closer. "I'll take care of her. But Alex…" She caught his arm. "Hurry back, okay?" She was suddenly very apprehensive about her and Taryn being alone in the house with darkness and a storm approaching.

"I'll probably be back within the hour." He bent and

brushed his lips against hers. "By bedtime for sure," he murmured.

MICHAEL DONNELLY WAS WAITING for Alex in the lobby of the Place d'Armes Hotel on Royal Street. The two men had never met, but Alex recognized him immediately, and Donnelly seemed to know him.

They shook hands, then went into the bar for a drink. The place was almost deserted. Rain splattered against the windows, and Alex could see lightning flashes over the city. He thought about Naomi and Taryn home alone, and suddenly he couldn't wait to get back to them.

"You've got some information on Ray Beauchamp?"

The man opened his briefcase and pulled out some papers. "I didn't have a lot to go on except for that story you said someone had told you about his father being a New Orleans cop who was executed for several murders. So I spent some time down in the morgue at the *Times-Picayune*. Turns out that story was true. He was executed back in 1960. And your source was right about the kids, too. Two girls and a boy. I don't know who arranged it, but somehow they were allowed to witness the execution. Something went wrong. His clothing caught on fire. It was a really bad scene, and the kids were pretty traumatized, as you can imagine. The oldest girl was around eighteen, the other girl ten, and Ray was eight."

How in the hell were kids that age allowed to witness an execution? Alex wondered. Either a lot of palms had been greased, or else someone was just plain sick. "Were you able to track down the sisters?"

"Not exactly."

Something in his tone made Alex glance up sharply. "What does that mean?"

"I wasn't able to track them down, but I found out what their names were back then. The older one's name was Willa Beauchamp."

"Willa," Alex repeated softly. The name tugged at a memory. And then he had it. Naomi had mentioned her on the first night Alex had gone to see her at her hotel, when she'd told him how she'd come to believe that Taryn was her child. The woman who had disclosed the information about the baby swapping had worked at Eden Memorial Hospital fifteen years ago.

"I see you recognize the name, too," Donnelly said.

"The nurse from the hospital in Eden was named Willa."

Donnelly nodded. "Willa Banks. She was also responsible for one of the recent kidnappings in Eden."

"You think it's the same woman?"

The detective's expression turned grim. "That's why I called you. I don't think there's any doubt about it."

"And the other sister? Do you know her name?" Alex asked anxiously.

"I've got it right here. Her name was—"

A clap of thunder exploded overhead, shaking the rafters in the bar and eliciting startled squeals from a couple of women who sat near the window. They both scurried away from the glass.

Donnelly shoved the paper across the table toward Alex, and he stared down at the name.

Oh, my God.

TARYN WENT STRAIGHT UP to her room after Alex left, and Naomi lingered downstairs just long enough to clean up the kitchen and start the dishwasher. She gazed out the kitchen window, watching the storm clouds move in from the Gulf. A particularly loud clap of thunder rattled the window and Naomi jumped.

It wasn't even eight o'clock yet, but darkness had fallen early because of the storm. With nothing to do but watch the lightning, Naomi went upstairs to the master suite and tried to settle down to watch a weather report on TV. *This is not good,* she thought. This reminded her of that night fifteen years ago when she'd been home alone and had gone into labor. She felt the same sense of unease building that she had that night.

Walking over to the window, Naomi glanced up at the black, roiling clouds, punctuated by jagged streaks of lightning. A narrow balcony ran the length of the house, and several sets of French doors opened onto it. Naomi started to step outside, but then thought better of it. Instead, she checked to make sure the latch was secure.

She was so on edge that when the phone rang, she gave a startled little gasp. Then she hurried across the room to answer it.

"Naomi?"

"Alex?"

"Listen to me, Naomi, and just do as I say. You and Taryn have to get out of the house."

Naomi's heart started to pound. "What? Why? What's wrong?"

"Just do it! Get Taryn out of that house!"

"Alex—" Naomi broke off as her breath caught in her throat.

"What?" he demanded. "What's wrong?"

"I thought I saw someone on the balcony outside the bedroom."

Alex swore. "Listen carefully, Naomi. Go into

Taryn's room and lock the door. Don't let her leave, and don't let anyone inside. I mean anyone! Do you understand?''

Naomi didn't bother to answer. She hung up and whirled toward the door. Racing down the hallway, she rapped once on Taryn's door, then opened it and stepped inside. "Taryn, we have to—"

In a flash of lightning, Naomi saw that Taryn's bed was empty. She was gone!

Chapter Fourteen

Lightning strobed again, and then Naomi saw her. Taryn was curled in a corner, knees drawn up, arms wrapped around her legs. Naomi was beside her in a flash.

"Taryn? What's wrong? Are you afraid of the storm? Listen, honey. We have to—"

"I want my mama." The voice was tiny, shrill, like a little girl's.

Naomi's heart stopped. "What?"

"Please. I want my mama. I'm scared." Taryn knuckled her eyes as if she'd been crying.

"Taryn—" Naomi didn't know what to say. Without thinking, she reached a hand and pushed back Taryn's hair. "It's all right. It's all right," she crooned.

Taryn's eyes were closed, and for a moment, Naomi wondered if she was dreaming or sleepwalking. But as she studied Taryn's expression in the flashes of lightning, a chill seeped through her. There was danger all around them, danger in this house. But the look on Taryn's face stole Naomi's breath. She couldn't move.

"Taryn? Can you hear me?"

No response, but her eyes moved rapidly beneath her lids, as if she were in a very deep sleep.

"I want my mama." The voice was very soft, very high.

The chill inside Naomi deepened. She didn't think Taryn was sleepwalking, but her behavior was very strange, almost dreamlike. Could something, the storm perhaps, have triggered the posthypnotic suggestion she'd mentioned earlier? Was she in some kind of hypnotic trance?

If so, how do I bring her out of it? Naomi wondered desperately.

She touched Taryn's arm. "Let me help you up. We may have to go—"

Taryn drew away frantically. "No, please don't! Don't make me go! Mama said not to! Don't go anywhere with a stranger!"

Naomi went very still and then her heart slammed into her chest, beating double time. She said very softly, "Where are you?"

"Hiding."

"Hiding where?"

"My secret place. No one can find me here." Taryn looked momentarily confused. "How did you find me?"

Naomi's heart was pounding so hard she couldn't answer. But she didn't have to. Taryn wasn't talking to her.

When Taryn spoke again, her voice was deeper, older. Stern. "Come on! I'll take you to your mama, but we have to hurry. She needs you. She sent me to get you! Now, come on before it's too late!"

A whimper, then the little girl spoke again. "Mama's hurt?"

Her voice deepened. "Not if we hurry. Now, come on!"

Naomi put her hand to her mouth.

Taryn grew very still, sniffling.

"Where are you now?" Naomi finally managed to ask.

Taryn's head lifted, as if she were looking around. "In a car."

The older voice said, "Keep down! Don't let anyone see you! If the bad man sees you, he'll follow us. He'll find your mama and hurt her. You don't want that, do you? Then stay down!"

Naomi's pulse thundered in her ears. "Who's in the car with you?"

"A stranger. Mama's going to be so mad at me." The child started to cry.

Naomi fought back her own tears. She squeezed her eyes closed. "No, she won't. She'll understand. She will."

That seemed to calm Taryn. She fell silent again.

After a moment, Naomi said, "Where are you now?"

"In a house. I can hear the ocean. Mama took me to the beach once. I liked it then, but I don't like it now. Mama's not here. I'm cold and hungry and I'm scared. I want my mama."

"What is the stranger doing?"

"She's cutting my hair." Taryn's expression changed rapidly. Her voice deepened. "Hold still, now. Don't move a muscle. I don't want to slip and cut off your ear. 'Course, that's not half as painful as what the bad man will do to us if he finds us. That's why we have to change the way you look, and why we can't use your real name. You have to do exactly as I say."

Naomi moistened her lips. "Where are you now?"

A pause. Taryn's eyes moved rapidly. "Another house. It's big. Pretty. But I don't like it here, either."

Her voice changed, deepened, grew coaxing. "Your mama's here somewhere. I know she is. We just have to find her. I know. Maybe she went outside. Why don't you go look for her out there?"

"It's dark—" the little girl whispered.

"You're not afraid of the dark, are you? A big girl like you? Go on. I'll turn on the light for you."

Silence.

"What do you see?" Naomi prompted.

Confusion flickered over Taryn's features. "I see a big swimming pool. Mustn't go over there. Mama says never to go near water without her." Another pause. "I don't like it out here. There something red and sticky all over the ground, like someone's spilled Kool-Aid—" She broke off. Her chest heaved, and she started to breath very rapidly.

"What is it?" Naomi asked in a whisper.

"Someone's in the pool—" Her face went rigid with fear, and she tried to cover her eyes. "Mama! Mama!"

Naomi caught both her hands, tried to draw her into her arms, but the child fought her. "No! No! No!"

"It's okay, baby. It's okay," Naomi said desperately. "I'm not going to hurt you."

The older voice grew agitated. "Stop that! You hear me? Stop that! He killed your mama, Sadie. Do you understand? That's your mama in that pool. Come here and look. Look! That's what the bad man did to her. See all that blood? He'll do the same to you if you don't stop that screaming!"

Oh, God, Naomi thought. Oh, God, oh, God, oh God.

"Listen to me! You've got to remember everything I told you. Your name is Taryn from now on. You have to remember that. Your mama's dead, but I'm still here, and I'm going to protect you. I won't let the bad man hurt you. I'm here and I'm never going to leave you."

Naomi closed her eyes briefly. The scenes in her head were so vivid it was like watching a movie. A terrible, terrible movie. "Where are you now?" she asked in a whisper.

"Floating."

That tiny, frightened voice broke Naomi's heart. She swallowed. "Floating?"

"She wants me to sleep, but I'm floating instead."

"What do you see?"

"I see me sleeping...except it's not really me." She looked puzzled. "It's the girl she wants me to be. It's Taryn. But I'm still here, too. I've found a place to hide where she can't find me. Where no one can find me."

"Where?"

She touched a fingertip to her temple. "In here."

A clap of thunder caused them both to jump, and Taryn glanced up, blinking, as if she'd suddenly just awakened.

And then as lightning flashed, they both saw the woman at the window. Saw her lift the knife and start hacking at the French doors.

Naomi grabbed Taryn's hand. "Run!" She jerked the girl to her feet and shoved her toward the door. Taryn fumbled with the lock, then drew the door open, glancing back.

"Go!" Naomi screamed. She turned back just as Louise swung a patio chair through the window. The glass shattered, and she reached inside to turn the latch.

Naomi jerked up a lamp and threw it across the room. She missed, but Louise had to stop and duck. That was what Naomi wanted. To buy enough time for Taryn to get to safety.

She grabbed up Taryn's desk chair and used it as a shield as Louise lunged toward her. When the woman was close enough, Naomi thrust the chair between them, ramming into Louise with all her might. The momentum carried them back through the shattered French doors onto the balcony. The rain had slickened the surface, and Louise lost her footing. She fell into the railing, and Naomi heard the crack of splintering wood. Then the railing gave way, and Louise toppled backward.

Gasping, half-sobbing, Naomi glanced over the railing. She couldn't see Louise's body below. It was possible the thick foliage beneath the balcony had broken her fall.

And then Naomi saw something that froze her blood. In a flicker of lightning, she saw Taryn running toward the greenhouse.

Oh, God, Naomi thought. Louise would see her in there!

Naomi whirled and bolted inside. Within seconds, she was racing downstairs, then out the back door. Outside, the storm had unleashed a torrent of rain and broken tree limbs. Wiping rain from her face, Naomi rushed toward the greenhouse. Inside, she stood dripping, frantically looking around.

"Taryn?" she called softly.

No answer. Or at least, Naomi couldn't hear her over the sound of rain against the glass and the boom of thunder outside.

She finally found her in the back, crouched beneath a worktable, knees drawn up, arms around her legs. Naomi knelt and touched her arm. "Are you okay?"

Taryn lifted her terrified gaze. "She's found me."

"I know. We have to get out of here—"

A draft of wind stole inside, and Naomi put her fingertip to her lips. Then she turned and moved silently away from Taryn.

"I had to do it!" Louise called out. "Don't you understand? Just come out and talk to me. Let me explain. Taryn? Where are you, honey?"

Naomi eased her way toward the front of the greenhouse, using the hanging cages for cover.

"There was nothing else I could do!" Louise said desperately. "I didn't mean for it to happen. It was just a terrible accident, but no one was going to believe me. They would have sent me to prison…they would have killed me. Strapped me in a chair and sent so much electricity into my body, I would have caught on fire."

Naomi used the sound of Louise's voice to guide her toward the woman.

"Maybe if I just explain…maybe if I just tell you what happened, you'll understand. Taryn? Are you listening? We came back early from the beach that day. Oh, not you. The other Taryn. The real Taryn. I told the police it was Aubree who came back early, but it was us. Aubree wanted to stay another night at the beach because she had someone coming to see her. I didn't know, but I suspected it was Foley Boudreaux. I guess something went wrong. They must have had a fight because Aubree decided to come back that night, too.

"When she got home, Taryn…the other Taryn…had already been in bed for hours. She'd been cranky all afternoon, and I was worn out, so I'd given her a little dose of the medicine I kept on hand to settle her down. After that, she went right to sleep. I took some, too, just to settle my nerves. And I had a drink. Just one, or maybe two. But no more than that. What was the harm? Taryn was asleep upstairs. Nobody else was around. I was always careful to never drink when anyone was around. Except for Taryn, of course, and she didn't know. I guess I dozed off, because the next thing I knew, Aubree was shaking me awake. 'Where's Taryn?' she yelled. I never saw her so mad.

"'She's in bed,' I say. 'Been asleep for hours.'"

"'No, she isn't. I just looked in on her. She's not anywhere upstairs. Get up and help me look for her!'"

LOUISE TRIED TO SHAKE OFF *the lingering effects of her drug-induced lethargy, but she must have taken more than she meant to. She couldn't seem to think.*

Aubree stared down at her angrily. "What's the matter with you? Have you been drinking?"

"No, I—"

"You've taken something. Your eyes look strange. Louise, I swear, if anything has happened to Taryn while you lay passed out—" She broke off as she strode to the French doors that opened onto the patio and the pool beyond. Her back went stiff, and a low groan erupted from her lips. "No! Oh, God, no! Taryn! Taryn!"

She ripped open the door and rushed onto the patio. Louise followed slowly behind her. "What is it—"

Without even taking off her clothing, Aubree dove into the pool. It was only then that Louise saw what was floating on the bottom. Taryn...

Aubree lifted the child from the pool and lay her on the deck. "Call 911!" she screamed. Frantically, she started CPR, but Louise, watching from above, knew it was hopeless. The child was dead. Had been for hours. There was no bringing her back.

Aubree finally realized it, too. She glanced up and saw Louise standing exactly where she'd been moments before. "You did this!" she screamed. "You did this to her! You let this happen!"

Louise took a step back. "No. It was an accident—"

"You killed her! You killed her!" Aubree was beyond thinking, beyond rationalization. Louise could see that. Grief had left her half-crazed. She needed someone to blame, and she was blaming Louise.

Fear rose inside Louise. Everyone would blame her. Aubree's father. The police—

Oh, God, the police—

She would go to jail. They'd strap her in that chair! Her clothes would catch on fire and then her hair...

Aubree rose and, like a wounded tiger, lunged at Louise. She stumbled backward, landing against a wrought-iron table. Her back exploded with pain, and when Aubree came at her again, Louise reacted instinctively. Her hand closed around a heavy urn planter on the table, and she swung it with all her might.

"THERE WAS BLOOD EVERYWHERE," Louise said. She sounded very distressed. "I never saw so much blood. I knew she was dead, and I just stared down at her and all I could think was that she was the only person who'd ever been kind to me. The only person, other than her father, who had ever taken me in.

"But then I knew I had to think of myself. Aubree was gone. Taryn was gone. I couldn't bring them back. I had to save myself. I had to figure out what to do.

"Then I remembered all the people who didn't like Aubree. I figured, without Taryn's body, they'd think a jilted lover had killed Aubree. Or a robber. It didn't matter, so long as I covered my tracks.

"I called my brother, Ray, to come help me. The first thing he did was take Aubree's sapphire ring off her finger, but I didn't care. I just wanted him to tell me what to do. 'We got to get rid of the kid,' he said. So we wrapped Taryn's body in a blanket and put her in my car. I had in mind just to bury her somewhere, but Ray said, 'No, idiot, that won't work. She'll still be missing, and you're the last one who saw her. You'll still get blamed.'

"Then I remembered the other girl. The other twin, and I knew what I had to do. While Ray took care of Taryn, I went to get the other one."

If her daughter's life hadn't been in danger, Naomi would have gone after Louise right then. She would have attacked her just as Aubree had. She would have killed the woman for what she had done to both her daughters. Taryn and Sadie.

"You want to know how I knew where to find you, Sadie?" Louise paused. "You've been wondering about that, too, haven't you, Naomi? You see, I'm the one who talked Willa into giving one of your babies to Aubree. I was with her that night. We were driving to Memphis when she went into labor. I knew we could never make it that far, but she wouldn't hear of us turning back. She said she didn't want to be in town when Alex got home. She wanted to make him worry about her. Make him suffer. 'It's just false labor, anyway. I'm not due for another couple of weeks,' she said. But her contractions started coming so fast, and I thought of Willa. She was a nurse. She could help us.

"Then we got caught in those storms. I thought we were both going to die, but somehow we made it to the hospital. The place was in such an uproar, no one paid any attention to me. I just let myself fade into the woodwork. Then when Willa told me Aubree's baby was dying, I said, 'No, no, that's not fair.' Aubree had been too good to me. And I knew with a baby around, she'd need me. She wouldn't turn me out.

"Willa said, 'Yes, it is a shame. Especially when the

other one has two healthy babies that she can't take care of.'

"So we did it. We made the swap, and the first thing we did was make sure the twins were separated, so no one would figure out what we'd done. Willa arranged for Taryn to be sent to a Memphis hospital. The other one went to County hospital with you, Naomi. It all worked so well.

"But it ate at Willa. She became obsessed with you, Naomi. Followed you around everywhere, only you never knew it. I was always afraid she was going to go off the deep end and confess. When she died and I read about all that mess with the other little girl in the paper, I knew it was only a matter of time before you'd come here looking for your daughter. Only you thought it was the baby that was stolen from the hospital. You didn't know it was Sadie."

Naomi could see her now. The woman was standing in the middle of the greenhouse, gazing around, the knife clutched in her hand.

A clap of thunder rattled the glass panels, and sparks flew outside as lightning struck a nearby tree. The sound was like a gunshot, and then a tree branch fell against the roof of the greenhouse. The glass panels cracked against the weight, and Louise looked up. Her eyes widened.

The glass was giving beneath the weight of the tree limb. As if in slow motion, the panel shattered, and heavy glass shards rained downward.

Naomi was paralyzed for a moment, and then she felt herself knocked backward. She thought at first Louise had attacked her, but then she saw that it was Alex. He was lying on top of her, covering her body with his.

"We've got to get out of here," he said. "The limb loosened the braces. The whole roof could collapse."

Naomi clutched at his arms as he pulled her up. "Taryn is still in here. She's in the back—"

"Get outside," he said grimly. "Go! I'll find her."

"Alex—"

"Go!"

"Louise—"

But Louise wasn't going to hurt anyone anymore. She had been directly under the path of the falling glass, and Naomi had to turn her head.

She heard the other panels cracking, giving way. They wouldn't hold much longer.

And then she saw Alex, carrying Taryn. He hurried toward the door as the cracking grew louder. A panel dislodged behind them and crashed to the floor.

"Hurry!" Naomi screamed. She opened the door and waited until Alex and Taryn had rushed through. Then she ran after them.

Alex set Taryn down gently and they all turned as the panels crashed downward one by one, a waterfall of shimmering glass.

Naomi put her hand to her throat. So close, she thought. So close...

Beside her, Taryn gave a little cry. "I remember now. I remember what happened. I'm not Taryn. My name is Sadie. My name is Sadie!" And then she collapsed sobbing in Naomi's arms.

Naomi held her close, held her as she had wanted to hold her for ten long years. "Sadie," she whispered. "My Sadie Belle. It's going to be okay. I love you, Sadie. I love you so, so much."

And then she saw Alex's face. Saw the emotions flash across his features. Shock. Disbelief. Fear. And a terrible, terrible sadness.

Without a word, he turned and walked back to the house alone.

Chapter Fifteen

A week later, the remains that had been found in Grover County were positively identified as matching DNA with samples taken from Sadie's.

They laid Taryn to rest in a crypt next to Aubree's. Naomi had first thought she wanted to return her child to Eden, but she'd never gotten the chance to know her daughter. Never held her in her arms, never rocked her through a long, sleepless night or nursed her through childhood illnesses. Aubree DeWitt had done that for Taryn. She'd been the only mother Taryn had ever known, and she'd loved her. It comforted Naomi to know that they were together.

Yesterday, they'd driven to Eden, and Naomi had shown Alex where his and Aubree's baby had been laid to rest.

This morning, they'd had a memorial service for Taryn. Abby and Sam Burke had flown in from Virginia. Mary Ellison had driven down from Eden. Joseph Bellamy had come in alone, sat in the back and left alone.

The past several days had been fraught with so much emotion, and Naomi was exhausted, but she was also at peace. She knew what had happened now and why, and she would always grieve for the baby she never knew, for the child whose life had been cut short, for the years she'd missed in both her daughter's lives. But Sadie was home. After ten years, Sadie was finally home.

It wasn't going to be easy, she knew. Sadie would need therapy. She would need all the help and support Naomi could give her, but somehow they'd get through this. Somehow Sadie would be able to live a normal, happy life. Naomi would do anything to make that happen.

Beside her, Alex wiped a hand across his eyes as he gazed at the marble angel atop Taryn's crypt. "I never knew her," he said in a soft, haunted voice. "I wasn't there for her. If I hadn't gone to London, maybe none of this would have happened."

"And if I'd gotten to school sooner to pick up Sadie, Louise wouldn't have had the chance to take her. There's enough blame to go around for all of us, Alex, but I think what we have to do now is find a way to forgive ourselves, so that we can move on. For her." She nodded toward Sadie.

He turned to her suddenly. "Please don't take her away from me. I've been her father for the past ten years, and I love her. More than life itself. I don't know what I'd do if I lost her." He paused, gazing down at Naomi. "I know you have every right to take her back to Eden. Every legal right and maybe every moral right, but...I don't want you to go."

"It doesn't matter where we live," Naomi said softly. "She thinks of you as her father, even now that she remembers what happened. You *are* her father, in every way that counts. I would never cut you out of her life, even if—'' She broke off, glancing at Sadie. ''I'm very worried about her.''

''She's your daughter, Naomi. She has your strength. And she has you now. She'll get through this.''

''I know she will,'' Naomi said almost fiercely. ''But she's going to need us both.''

''What about you?'' he asked softly.

Naomi's heart started to pound. ''What do you mean?''

''I don't want a divorce, Naomi. And not just because of Ta—Sadie. I can't imagine my life without you.''

''But we've known each other such a short time,'' she said, hardly daring to believe that he was voicing everything she felt in her own heart.

''Time is relative, and we've been through so much. You're the most extraordinary woman I've ever known, and I don't want to lose you.''

''I don't want to lose you, either,'' she said breathlessly.

''We can make this work. We can have a good marriage, and we can have a happy family.''

''Because of our daughter?'' Naomi whispered.

''Yes. And because I've fallen in love with you.''

She swayed toward him, and he put his arms around her, drawing her close. Naomi lay her head on his shoulder. ''I love you, too,'' she whispered.

''Then let's go home.'' He stroked her hair. ''Let's take our daughter home.''

They both turned to Sadie then, but she hardly seemed aware of their presence, much less of the soul-shattering declaration they'd just made to each other. She was staring at a tiny blue butterfly that fluttered around a bouquet of roses she'd laid at the angel's feet.

Lifting her arms, she unfastened the tiny gold butterfly from around her neck and slipped it over the statue.

Then she put her hand down to the flowers, and for just an instant, the blue butterfly lit in her palm before it spread its wings and flew away.

COMING SOON...

AN EXCITING
OPPORTUNITY TO SAVE
ON THE PURCHASE OF
HARLEQUIN AND
SILHOUETTE BOOKS!

*DETAILS TO FOLLOW
IN OCTOBER 2001!*

YOU WON'T WANT TO MISS IT!

PHQ401

HARLEQUIN®
Makes any time special®

Silhouette®
Where love comes alive™

Harlequin truly does
make any time special. . . .
This year we are celebrating
weddings in style!

A
Walk
Down
the Aisle
WEDDING CELEBRATION

To help us celebrate, we want you to tell us how wearing the Harlequin wedding gown will make your wedding day special. As the grand prize, Harlequin will offer one lucky bride the chance to **"Walk Down the Aisle" in the Harlequin wedding gown!**

There's more...

For her honeymoon, she and her groom will spend five nights at the **Hyatt Regency Maui.** As part of this five-night honeymoon at the hotel renowned for its romantic attractions, the couple will enjoy a candlelit dinner for two in Swan Court, a sunset sail on the hotel's catamaran, and duet spa treatments.

A HYATT RESORT AND SPA

the Magic Isles™
Maui • Molokai • Lanai

To enter, please write, in, 250 words or less, how wearing the Harlequin wedding gown will make your wedding day special. The entry will be judged based on its emotionally compelling nature, its originality and creativity, and its sincerity. This contest is open to Canadian and U.S. residents only and to those who are 18 years of age and older. There is no purchase necessary to enter. Void where prohibited. See further contest rules attached. Please send your entry to:

Walk Down the Aisle Contest

In Canada
P.O. Box 637
Fort Erie, Ontario
L2A 5X3

In U.S.A.
P.O. Box 9076
3010 Walden Ave.
Buffalo, NY 14269-9076

You can also enter by visiting www.eHarlequin.com
Win the Harlequin wedding gown and the vacation of a lifetime!
The deadline for entries is October 1, 2001.

HARLEQUIN®
Makes any time special ®

PHWDACONT1

HARLEQUIN WALK DOWN THE AISLE TO MAUI CONTEST 1197
OFFICIAL RULES
NO PURCHASE NECESSARY TO ENTER

1. To enter, follow directions published in the offer to which you are responding. Contest begins April 2, 2001, and ends on October 1, 2001. Method of entry may vary. Mailed entries must be postmarked by October 1, 2001, and received by October 8, 2001.

2. Contest entry may be, at times, presented via the Internet, but will be restricted solely to residents of certain geographic areas that are disclosed on the Web site. To enter via the Internet, if permissible, access the Harlequin Web site (www.eHarlequin.com) and follow the directions displayed online. Online entries must be received by 11:59 p.m. E.S.T. on October 1, 2001.

   In lieu of submitting an entry online, enter by mail by hand-printing (or typing) on an 8½" x 11" plain piece of paper, your name, address (including zip code), Contest number/name and in 250 words or fewer, why winning a Harlequin wedding dress would make your wedding day special. Mail via first-class mail to: Harlequin Walk Down the Aisle Contest 1197, (in the U.S.) P.O. Box 9076, 3010 Walden Avenue, Buffalo, NY 14269-9076, (in Canada) P.O. Box 637, Fort Erie, Ontario L2A 5X3, Canada.

   Limit one entry per person, household address and e-mail address. Online and/or mailed entries received from persons residing in geographic areas in which Internet entry is not permissible will be disqualified.

3. Contests will be judged by a panel of members of the Harlequin editorial, marketing and public relations staff based on the following criteria:

   - Originality and Creativity—50%
   - Emotionally Compelling—25%
   - Sincerity—25%

   In the event of a tie, duplicate prizes will be awarded. Decisions of the judges are final.

4. All entries become the property of Torstar Corp. and will not be returned. No responsibility is assumed for lost, late, illegible, incomplete, inaccurate, nondelivered or misdirected mail or misdirected e-mail, for technical, hardware or software failures of any kind, lost or unavailable network connections, or failed, incomplete, garbled or delayed computer transmission or any human error which may occur in the receipt or processing of the entries in this Contest.

5. Contest open only to residents of the U.S. (except Puerto Rico) and Canada, who are 18 years of age or older, and is void wherever prohibited by law; all applicable laws and regulations apply. Any litigation within the Province of Quebec respecting the conduct or organization of a publicity contest may be submitted to the Régie des alcools, des courses et des jeux for a ruling. Any litigation respecting the awarding of a prize may be submitted to the Régie des alcools, des courses et des jeux only for the purpose of helping the parties reach a settlement. Employees and immediate family members of Torstar Corp. and D. L. Blair, Inc., their affiliates, subsidiaries and all other agencies, entities and persons connected with the use, marketing or conduct of this Contest are not eligible to enter. Taxes on prizes are the sole responsibility of winners. Acceptance of any prize offered constitutes permission to use winner's name, photograph or other likeness for the purposes of advertising, trade and promotion on behalf of Torstar Corp., its affiliates and subsidiaries without further compensation to the winner, unless prohibited by law.

6. Winners will be determined no later than November 15, 2001, and will be notified by mail. Winners will be required to sign and return an Affidavit of Eligibility form within 15 days after winner notification. Noncompliance within that time period may result in disqualification and an alternative winner may be selected. Winners of trip must execute a Release of Liability prior to ticketing and must possess required travel documents (e.g. passport, photo ID) where applicable. Trip must be completed by November 2002. No substitution of prize permitted by winner. Torstar Corp. and D. L. Blair, Inc., their parents, affiliates, and subsidiaries are not responsible for errors in printing or electronic presentation of Contest, entries and/or game pieces. In the event of printing or other errors which may result in unintended prize values or duplication of prizes, all affected game pieces or entries shall be null and void. If for any reason the Internet portion of the Contest is not capable of running as planned, including infection by computer virus, bugs, tampering, unauthorized intervention, fraud, technical failures, or any other causes beyond the control of Torstar Corp. which corrupt or affect the administration, secrecy, fairness, integrity or proper conduct of the Contest, Torstar Corp. reserves the right, at its sole discretion, to disqualify any individual who tampers with the entry process and to cancel, terminate, modify or suspend the Contest or the Internet portion thereof. In the event of a dispute regarding an online entry, the entry will be deemed submitted by the authorized holder of the e-mail account submitted at the time of entry. Authorized account holder is defined as the natural person who is assigned to an e-mail address by an Internet access provider, online service provider or other organization that is responsible for arranging e-mail address for the domain associated with the submitted e-mail address. **Purchase or acceptance of a product offer does not improve your chances of winning.**

7. Prizes: (1) Grand Prize—A Harlequin wedding dress (approximate retail value: $3,500) and a 5-night/6-day honeymoon trip to Maui, HI, including round-trip air transportation provided by Maui Visitors Bureau from Los Angeles International Airport (winner is responsible for transportation to and from Los Angeles International Airport) and a Harlequin Romance Package, including hotel accomodations (double occupancy) at the Hyatt Regency Maui Resort and Spa, dinner for (2) two at Swan Court, a sunset sail on Kiele V and a spa treatment for the winner (approximate retail value: $4,000); (5) Five runner-up prizes of a $1000 gift certificate to selected retail outlets to be determined by Sponsor (retail value $1000 ea.). Prizes consist of only those items listed as part of the prize. Limit one prize per person. All prizes are valued in U.S. currency.

8. For a list of winners (available after December 17, 2001) send a self-addressed, stamped envelope to: Harlequin Walk Down the Aisle Contest 1197 Winners, P.O. Box 4200 Blair, NE 68009-4200 or you may access the www.eHarlequin.com Web site through January 15, 2002.

Contest sponsored by Torstar Corp., P.O. Box 9042, Buffalo, NY 14269-9042, U.S.A.

PHWDACONT2

TRUEBLOOD, TEXAS

In October 2001 look for

A FATHER'S VOW

by Tina Leonard

Lost

One twin. Ben Mulholland
desperately needs a bone marrow
donor to save his little girl, Lucy.
The brother Ben never knew he
had is her best, maybe only, chance.
If he can just track him down…

Found

The miracle of hope. Caroline St. Clair
has loved Ben forever and she'll do
whatever it takes to ensure he doesn't lose his precious
daughter. In the process, old wounds are healed and flames
of passion reignited. But the future is far from secure.

Finders Keepers: bringing families together

HARLEQUIN®
Makes any time special ®

HARLEQUIN®
INTRIGUE®

43 Light St.

has been *the* address for outstanding romantic suspense for more than a decade! Now REBECCA YORK* blasts the hinges off the front door with a new trilogy—
MINE TO KEEP.

Look for these great stories on the corner of heart-stopping romance and breathtaking suspense!

THE MAN FROM TEXAS
August 2001

NEVER ALONE
October 2001

LASSITER'S LAW
December 2001

COME ON OVER...
WE'LL KEEP THE LIGHTS ON.

Available at your favorite retail outlet.

*Ruth Glick writing as Rebecca York

HARLEQUIN®
Makes any time special ®

Visit us at www.eHarlequin.com

HILIGHTST